Caroline

J. Bock

Caroline

ISBN: 9798655746152

jbockwrites.com

For Lalyn, who taught me how to embrace chaos.

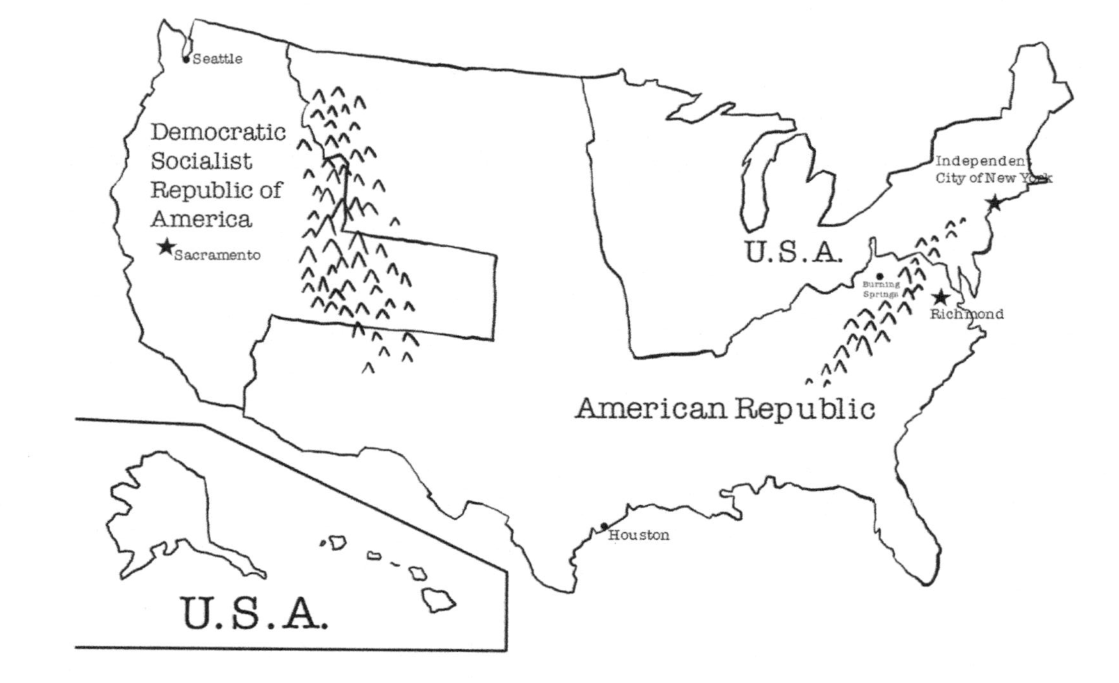
Seattle
Democratic
Socialist
Republic of
America
Sacramento
U.S.A.
Independent
City of New York
Burning
Springs
Richmond
American Republic
Houston
U.S.A.

<one>

"I have no idea how it broke this time," I say knowing exactly how I broke the damn thing. Playing dumb is my best shot at saving some scrip.

"Look here." Kayla shows me my watch's cracked face as if I hadn't been obsessing over it the entire walk down here. "See? What happened, Levi, is that you cracked it on something and *then* dunked it into whatever flavor of sludge you were working in at the time".

She takes it back behind the counter and looks at it through the magnifier she has strapped to her head. She spins a knob on the right-hand side of the watch face to release the fluid. It drips onto the counter between us.

Kayla shakes it dry and opens up the back revealing a blackened, shorted-out circuit board. "It's totally fried." She puts the watch onto the counter and scratches the back of her head. "I'm sure this isn't what you wanted to hear, but this is going to cost you. You're going to need a new holo emitter, a graphics card, and probably, even a new motherboard. Gina's going to be pissed."

My boss, Gina, is already getting pissy about me not wearing my watch as often as the employee manual says I should. Well, she's getting pissy that her boss is getting pissy about me not wearing my watch as often as I should.

"Do you think the company will cover the cost?" I ask.

"I doubt it. I can try to write it up as incidental damage due to work environment, but this is like the third time in what? Five months? If Financial Management rejects the request, then it's up to Gina to appeal it for you. So, ultimately, you'll have to deal with her eventually. Or we skip all that if you have the scrip."

"Please try to expense it first. I'll take the hit if they say no. I can afford to fix it, but that'll be *all* I can afford this month."

"Sorry, I know these things aren't cheap," Kayla softens her tone and sighs through her nose. "I'll do what I can, but for now, I'll get you a loaner."

"Thanks."

She disappears into the back room behind the counter for a minute and returns with a new-to-me, but older model of watch. "Give me a minute to sync it to your corporate accounts and wallet. But, for the love of God, don't break this one. Just wear it around your neck like the rest of guys at the 'shed."

"Kayla, I'm not a dog."

"Oh save it, Levi." Her tone is now not so soft. "Everyone who comes here with a watch problem complains about the same things. And you know what? Whether we like it or not, yes, they track our location. Yes, it feels like a dog collar, and yes, people think its invasive. And yes, the whole idea pisses me off, too, but it's also part of the job that I get paid to do. So, please just deal with it, okay?"

"Yes, ma'am." I look up to the ceiling. She turns her attention to computer beside her. I let her clack on the keyboard for a few moments before confronting the unexpected silence between us. "So... are you going to the all-hands meeting tonight?"

"It's mandatory, ain't it?" she answers with a smirk, but she doesn't look up.

"Just like everything else."

"Oookay. All done." She puts the loaner on the counter and taps the screen. The holoprojector kicks on and my ID card complete with my goofy company picture hovers in the air.

"Ha! That looks like an old one," Kayla laughs.

"Yup. That photo is six years old and long before I realized the importance of getting a hair a cut," I say. Kayla turns off the projection and hands me the new watch. I strap it to my wrist. "Thanks. We all done?"

"You're all set."

"Great. Seeya at the meeting." I head for the door.

"Hey, Levi!" Kayla says after me. "The long hair was cute. You should bring that back."

"I... really?"

"No. Not really. See you."

"Seeya." I leave the IT Lab with a rush in my stomach the same as I just jumped from the roof. That was a signal. I think.

Outside the IT building, I start the trek back to work passing the other Energy Alliance employees milling about the company town. It seems the summer sun brought entire company out, away from their computers. Except for Kayla, of course.

I start the ascent up the trail and tap the wooden sign at the trailhead that leads back up the mountain. The OLED screen underneath the permanently etched in Energy Alliance logo blinks out the company town's population. Today, it reads "2,052", a far cry fewer than the five thousand it read a few years ago. As the gas dries up, so do the jobs.

I think I've got a couple years left to keep my job, though. It's not as easily automated away as others' and I've got seniority. It's is in my job title. I'm the "Senior Hydraulic Engineer", and I have barely done any work at all today. That's good. If I'm not working that much, that means everything's running smoothly.

Most of my days are spent staring at screens ensuring the automated control systems do their jobs, normally done from the top of the mountain at an area of the campus we call the 'shed (short for watershed), but really I can do that anywhere from my watch.

I step to the side of the trail to an overlook of a view of The Base. It seemed busier when I was next to the IT Building, but really there are only a few people out. There are some at the restaurant across the street, a few more outside the conference center. Down at the end, some are moving around the hospital, but that's it. The town will be busier closer to the time for the all-hands meeting, I reckon. And afterward the bar will get busy; I hope. Maybe I'll ask Kayla out for a drink tonight.

I breathe in the dust and fire up my new watch's

holoprojector. Light emits from the front face loading the Energy Alliance Hydraulic Monitoring System (or HMS) dashboard into the air. A map of the entire campus's plumbing operations reads green. I follow the main gas line that runs up the mountain with my finger, noting the pressure levels in my head. Everything is functioning as intended. I switch over to the Vehicle Monitoring System.

I take note of two rigs currently in use drilling out plugs at the well pad on the other side of the mountain. A flow-back crew is scheduled to come in after to check how viable this spot will be. If it's like the rest of the mountain, we'll be fine. A notification tells me I have a direct message. It's Micah, a roustabout that works at the well pad across from the one I'm staring at on the hologram.

His team is ready to pump produced water out of that well, and Micah wants to use three water bottles (automated tanker trucks) to transport the produced water to the 'shed. We call them "water bottles" because, well, they hold water. I tap over to his official job request and digitally sign off on it.

Satisfied with my minimal amount of productivity, I shut off my watch's holoprojector and continue my hike up the mountain. I pause when I get up to the well pad just above town. All brush has been cleared giving the once forested mountains unnatural dusty brown faces. You can see well pads from any point on campus. It's unsettling to see at first, but the brush clearing has a purpose. It allows the automated drilling rigs to move freely. We have dozens of well pads under our supervision and the Energy Alliance has hundreds across West Virginia: all of them bald, dusty and the same. Only up top, near The Watershed, a few trees and bushes remain. They give the old mountain a funny green toupee.

A few giant drilling rigs have returned home to sit idle, waiting to be sent back out. Another has moved to the other side of the path noisily drilling a hole thousands of feet deep below the Earth. Several operators stand around a terminal not far from the rig. I walk past them getting some funny looks.

"Odd seeing you down here, Mr. Pickering." A man says. I have no idea who he is. I think his name's "Mike". Not positive.

"Yeah, I decided to double-check the entrance valve in person," I say without breaking my stride, giving "Mike" a perfectly plausible albeit half-true reason as to why I'm here. I absolutely am not going to say that I'm really just procrastinating talking to Gina about breaking a stupidly expensive piece of equipment that I don't want to pay for.

I walk over to the pipeline to feign an inspection. I know it's fine. I trust the computer readouts, but I like to admire my work. I designed our entire campus's plumbing operations and was a part of the small team that got it built. I fondly remember installing all of these massive pipes that climb the mountain in neat, organized lines. Everywhere they run, they dwarf everything around them: humans, power stations, the small trailers we use as office buildings and company homes sprinkled across the campus.

The pipelines are our campus's arteries. One carries fracking water from the 'shed down to the station at the well pad. Another carries water in the opposite direction. It starts at our primary water source, the Little Kanawha River, and up the base to the 'shed. Specifically, it goes to the water treatment facility caring the water that's to be mixed with additives for hydraulic fracturing also known as "fracking"– the process in which rigs use the water to bore deep holes into the ground where natural gas is believed to be.

Fracking and wastewater management is just one section of our campus's plumbing operation. The smaller pipelines carry potable water down to The Base. That water is also treated at The Watershed. The second-largest metallic pipeline, the one about a foot in diameter, carries human wastewater from the near side of the base back up to the top of the mountain. The one bigger than that, the one a foot and half in diameter, carries the natural gas out of the campus to whoever needs it. To my understanding, the Chinese buy most of it. Although, the Energy Alliance does not let us forget that our gas operations are integral to keeping the heat and lights on for the entire country.

I could stare at and talk about these pipes all day, but I can feel the other guys' eyes watching me stare blankly up the mountain. I dust my hands off, *another job well done*, and walk back to the trail. My watch buzzes. An urgent message from Gina:

"Get your ass up here!!!!"

Four exclamation marks is a little excessive, but like a good boy, I respond with an "OMW" and double-time it the rest of the way up the mountain.

Once there, I'm greeted by the smells of the football field-sized pools of water mixed with chemicals, sediment, algae, and human waste that top this once beautiful mountain. I remember when the air was cleaner.

The young scientist, Dr. Tobias Boyd, is standing knee-deep in a bright green algae-covered pond. That pond is also the foulest smelling impoundment up here, and that's because it's filled with poop. As usual, Tobias's face is buried in a tablet. A plastic clip squeezes his nostrils shut. He notices me come up the trail and waves me over.

Tobias isn't my boss, but I wish he were. There's little doubt he's done the most good here in the shortest amount of time. He's only been here for a little over two years, but he's managed to turn our wastewater into a resource. For his Ph. D. dissertation, he genetically engineered a new type of algae that's resistant to temperature change. The Energy Alliance hired Tobias to grow his algae for biofuel that's used in the rigs, water bottles and generators in the advent of a power outage.

"Hey, man. How's the slime?" I ask.

"Hungry." He sounds annoyed. "But, I think you might be able to help me with that. But, later though. Gina came by. She's looking for you. Seemed pissed," he says without looking up from his tablet.

"I know she is. I'll find her in a minute." Or ten. I'm definitely not in a hurry now. "What do you think I can help with?" I ask searching for a *legitimate* reason to delay my meeting.

"So, like I said, the algae are hungry. Less people at The Base means less food. And nutrient-starved algae do not make good biofuel."

Tobias's algae literally eat shit. A lot of it, too. One of the main sewer lines drains directly into this man-made pond providing the algae its main food source. The population of our campus has been steadily decreasing for the last few years, so the algae had to undergo a pretty strict diet.

"Well, I'll do what I can but I'm just one man." I pretend to undo my belt.

"Funny. I never get enough poo jokes," he says with no appreciation for my wit. "Is it possible to reroute the secondary sewage line into this impoundment? With the population decrease, I think this one can handle both lines."

I turn on my watch and navigate to the map of the 'shed to look at the water levels of Tobias's impoundment. "Yeah, you're right about its capacity, but rerouting the line is a major project." I switch the view to show the entire campus and zoom in the opposite side of campus. "The secondary line serves the people that live at the base and carries the waste out of town. We'd have to bridge the secondary line into the primary and maybe even install a bigger pump."

"I was afraid that, but what you're saying makes sense. I didn't have much hope for the idea anyway, but I thought I'd ask."

"Hey, don't give up, yet. There might be a way, but for now I can't think of it making sense financially. Figure some numbers on how much fuel you can project to produce with the potential increase in um, algae food, and I'll see if I can come up with a cheap solution to alter the sewer lines. If the return is there, you might get it to happen."

This is Tobias's first job out of school and he's still a bit green when it comes to thinking of his projects in terms of profit. He was smart to identify the unused resources in the wastewater and brilliant in the bioscience of growing the algae, but he could be falling into the pet-project-trap. I may be a bit hypocritical in that thought. I'll stay on this mountain as long as I can, but when my work runs out here, I have no plans. I'll either be onto a new campus or out on my ass. Dad helped get me this job, but I don't know if he'll be able to help me again.

"Thanks, Levi. I'll get you my estimates as soon as I can." Tobias returns to his tablet, tapping at it with renewed purpose.

"Yep. I'll start drawing and keep you updated."

I look over to the small shack we use as an office where I assume Gina's waiting for me, and the small rush I got from the idea of starting a new project fades. I look back at Tobias. That kid's smart and for sure going places. If we work well together, he might take me with him. *Actually*, I think it to be an even better idea that he go somewhere with me.

"Hey, why don't you come with me to see Gina? We'll go ahead and run your idea by her now before I put any real time into doing the initial designs and cost estimations."

"Nice try. Gina was pissed when she talked to me. Like scary-Gina pissed. I don't know what you did, but I don't want to be anywhere near that meeting."

"I don't blame you."

This is my battle and mine alone. But I need to formulate a strategy. I think I can play this one of two ways: be apologetic. Say it will never happen again; grovel real hard, *or* I can come in angry. Match Gina's level. I'll speak out against corporate tyranny. Why should we *have to* wear the watches anyway? Sure, it's a useful tool in the field but I don't need to wear it *all the time*. It's obvious why they want us to, it's so management can a constant stream of our bio and location data. And why should they care about that if we're getting our jobs done? The productivity and quality of our work should be enough to judge us as employees. It's bad enough that we're only paid in company scrip that we can only spend at Energy Alliance owned businesses, but they don't own *us*. We're human beings. And now they want me to *pay* for that tyranny? It's not acceptable. I might even write to corporate or get a petition together. Surely, Gina will see the injustice.

Having already won the argument before it started, I march over and open the door to the small control center to find Gina sitting at a monitor looking concerned. She turns to me, narrowing her eyes and shooting fire into mine. She can see through me. She sees every embarrassing thing I've ever done. I feel twenty years younger.

"Where the hell have you been!? I've been trying to call you and I couldn't locate your GPS signal on the-- oh, God *damn it*, Levi! You broke your watch again, didn't you?"

"Gina, I'm sorry I broke another one. It's just so hard to wear the damn things when I'm unclogging filters." I pause. "Wait, you didn't know?" I remember Tobias's warning. She was supposed to be mad already, but she *just* realized I broke my watch. She's not that mad at *me*.

"No, I didn't know. I've been busy. We've got bigger problems."

"What's going on?" I walk over to the monitor. She pulls up a weather radar map of North America.

"There is a derecho coming. Corporate says we have to shut *everything* down." She looks up from the monitor, eyes wide and gestures out away from the computer. "*Everything*, Levi. In two days."

A derecho is a mean rain and windstorm that comes in waves. They come on fast and usually without much warning. We're lucky to have any time at all.

"How bad do they say it's going to get?" I ask.

"They can't be sure, but it's bad enough for corporate to act. Non-essential staff and all family members are to be evacuated from every mining campus across central Appalachia. Ground transportation will be coming tomorrow to evacuate our campus." She looks back at me and swivels her chair away from the monitor. "I expect their entire plan will be laid out at the all-hands meeting, tonight." Gina sighs deeply. She taps her feet quickly on the floor.

"What aren't you telling me?" I look her in the eyes. She's making me nervous. Nothing shakes Gina.

"After this storm, they might not resume operations here, Levi. This could be it." She turns back to the computer and pulls up list in place of the weather map. She reads it out loud. "We need to shut off all pipelines and operations starting with gas production. Then sewage and potable water pipelines are to be shut down tomorrow..." Gina reads the checklist projected in front of her out loud. I stop listening.

<two>

Unemployment is bad. Very bad. This doesn't make sense. I pull up a chair next to Gina and sit down hard. I run both my hands through my hair and let out a held breath.

"A storm? This is what they're going to close it over?"

"They say that if we don't shut everything down, the potential wind damage could destroy equipment, buildings and even the pipelines. That could lead to a gas and or a wastewater spill. Energy Alliance doesn't want to pay the state for an environmental disaster. If it came to that, with us being this close to the river, the effects could be felt as far as Parkersburg." Gina slumps forward, matching my own dejected posture. "We were just another year or so from closing anyway. I guess corporate thinks rebuilding won't be cost-effective. Do you remember what these derechos are like?" she asks.

"I was in college when the last one came through, but we just rode it out in the dorms It was nothing major. I was too young to remember the one in 2012."

"There's no telling exactly how strong this one will be until it's here, but these storms are like hurricanes. Winds can surge over a hundred miles an hour. So, we need to get everything done quickly and take shelter in the conference building at The Base. Our trailers will be moved out with non-essential personnel during the evacuation. I expect most of the mechanical shutdown to be automatic. You should have plenty of time to secure your belongings."

"Wait, they're taking my trailer too? Can't I just like, tie it down and board it up?" I ask.

"It's not *your* trailer."

"C'mon, you know what I mean."

"I do, but we're just renters. Corporate doesn't want to risk them getting damaged," she says. I lean back in my chair.

"Damn, Gina. Losing my job and my house? What else are they taking?"

"I know this sucks. This place has been home to me, too." I rest my hands on my head and we make eye contact for a long while. We're thinking of our homes, of course, but there are more than two thousand others. This is too big. I look at Gina's feet. They've stopped shaking.

"Hey, focus," she says "There are a lot of logistics to figure out and not a lot of time to do it."

I exhale and sit back up. "Ah, yeah. Ok. You're right that the control system will be able to automate most of the shutdown. I'll just need to log in, double-check for any routines that need to be updated and set the timer. I expect the larger logistical problem will be the evacuation, and we have to take care of wastewater impoundments. We can tarp them, but they'll flood if we get a lot of rain. We'll need every water bottle available to carry out wastewater. Tobias will be devastated for his algae."

Gina turns back to the monitor and pulls up the VMS and clicks on the logistics tab. "That's a problem. Looks like we'll only be able to use two."

"What? Why? If it rains hard enough with the pumps down, the sewage impoundment will flood straight down the mountain."

Gina pulls up the map of the watershed and zooms in on Tobias's wastewater impoundment as I did earlier. "I assume corporate looked at the diminished levels in the sewage pool and decided it wouldn't be an issue." she reasoned.

"Still sounds like a dumb risk to me."

"Me, too. But it's corporate's call. We'll tarp it the wastewater and you can use the two water bottles we have to deplete the impaired water impoundment. But don't empty it."

"Why not empty it? Aren't we just packing up after the storm anyway?" I ask.

"Well, maybe not." She smiles. "In the advent that the storm predictions are overblown, our little skeleton crew will use the trucks and one rig they're leaving us to finish drilling at the pad just above The Base. I don't want to give you too much hope, but we may not be done here, yet."

Despite her advice, I let my hopes soar. I'll secure this whole damn campus myself if it buys me another few months' work.

"So, I'm not being evacuated?" I ask.

"Nope. Neither am I. And we need to pick the others. Other departments will be doing the same."

Shit. I don't want to choose who gets laid off *or* who has to face down the storm. I think through our staff directory.

"Let's start with the job tomorrow. How many guys do you need to secure The Watershed? Include a number to pump out wastewater, too."

I pause for some mental math. "I think twelve for everything. They can work in teams of four and we can supervise." I let my legs bounce a little to burn off some nervous energy. "I need at least three to stay behind after the storm including a hydro tech. After clean up, engineers and roustabouts will have to wear different hats if we're going to get this place operating to a level anywhere near normal. I'd like four, but I can make it happen with three."

"Who do you want to keep behind?" Gina soldiered on pulling up the staff directory on her monitor.

Worst-case scenario– the impoundments and watersheds are destroyed. We'll need muscle and a backhoe operator to rebuild. I don't want to break up anyone with families that will be evacuating. The staff directory in my head gets a little shorter.

"I think Zeke and Micah should stay. Zeke's a workhorse and Micah can operate excavation equipment as good as anybody." I say. Gina pulls up Micah's staff profile and reads it over.

"Good," she confirms.

"We're also going to need someone who can help me with patchwork and a possible redesign if need be. Hear me out, but I think Tobias could do it. He's not a hydraulic engineer, but that—" Gina put her hand up to stop me.

"You're not getting Tobias. He's being evacuated first thing in the morning. Corporate sees him and his biofuel projects as a potential savior in the event of a long-term power outage. He might come back to this site to reboot his work, but he's not staying through the storm."

"You mean he's not expendable like the rest of us," I say.

"Hah! You might be right." Gina finally relaxes. She shrugs. "How about Silas? He's no dummy and he doesn't have family at The Base."

"Silas *is* a dummy, but he'll do," I say. Gina smirks and shakes her head. Silas has been with us since the beginning. He's also as close as to a best friend I've got in this place, so I'll be glad to have him, but I honestly think Tobias would be more useful.

"Okay, then." Gina stood up. "I'll go break the news to everyone. Do you want a ride down to the conference center later?"

"Yes, please. Give me an hour to look over the automated shutdown procedures? I'll set the timer to shut off the gas extraction at midnight tonight."

"Sure." Gina leaves the control center and me to my work.

I slide my chair over to face the monitor. I notice the map of the storm Gina left minimized on the screen. We're not the only ones getting hit. It's coming across Indiana and will pick up strength into Ohio. It could be a monster by the time it gets to West Virginia. The old United States government will help Ohio and Indiana, but not us. The Energy

Alliance will secure its assets but the people of West Virginia may be on their own. The new American Republic government hasn't had to deal with a major natural disaster, yet. I don't think people can expect much outside help. Hell, the American Republic government hasn't even seen snow, yet.

I switch to the HMS and log in. Everything still reads green and operating at optimal efficiency. I'm afraid this might be the last time I see the readout like this. I've seen it so many times like this now, but at one time I had to obsess over every detail to get it to look as perfect as it does today. I laugh in the empty room. There were so many problems in the beginning.

It truly is fitting that Silas will be with me to rebuild after the storm. He's always been trailing behind me breaking down my designs of whatever I wanted to build to make me rethink and rebuild it over and over. Silas is our Quality Assurance Engineer. It was a frustrating process for both of us, but it got the perfect results this screen is showing me. Silas works in water filtration, now, but I'm sure he could pick up his old job again in no time.

He'll hate it.

I navigate through the HMS submenus to the gas pipeline controls. I spend the rest of the hour meticulously going over every procedure and triple check the date and time for the shutoff timer. Yes, 12:00 AM on June 14, 2032. I enter in my passcode and confirm.

"That's it," I say to no one. I log out, slap the desk three times and walk out of our tiny control center. The evening sun greets me harshly.

The Watershed is mostly deserted. I assume

everyone went back to their trailers to start packing or are already hiking down to the all-hands meeting.

I head over to Gina's trailer As I raise my hand to knock on her door, it swings open.

"Levi!"

A man the size of the trailer itself shouts down at me. I jump back; trying not to be too shook. He steps towards me and I back-peddle down the stoop of Gina's porch. He closes the door hard behind him.

"Hey, Zeke," I say. "You scared the hell out of me." Zeke Evans is built like a big black brick shithouse.

He wouldn't hurt me, though. I don't think.

"Sorry! Gina told me you're coming," he says. "I've got to thank ya for putting me on the team. T'be honest, I didn't think you thought me to be very useful."

"Uh, sure. Not sure why you'd think that, though. You were actually the first person I thought of." Zeke's a roustabout, and his work ethic is legit. People think he's dumb, but that ain't right. He's just from Boone County and has an accent. He knows *how* to work. Does a lot more than just what he's told.

"Who knows'll what storm is going to do to this place, but at least I'll still be workin'," he says, "Not all of us have daddies to just hand us our next job."

It's true my dad helped me this job, but I am qualified. And my dad can't just give me a new position. But his influence isn't useless, either. You got to take what opportunities you're given, I think. I'd bet Zeke would do the same if he could, but he can't.

Zeke comes from a family of coal miners. He's

proudly told me that, several times. His grandfather was a coal miner and so was his grandfather's grandfather, but Zeke's father was not a coal miner. He was an alcoholic that sometimes painted houses.

"You could always be a painter," I say

Zeke lowers his head to look me dead in the eye. Then, he slaps me on the back hard and laughs harder.

"Seriously, though. I'm glad you want to stick around. I was thinking you might want to leave with everyone else."

"And go where?" He shrugs. "Don't worry. We'll rebuild this place no matter how jacked up it gets." I appreciate his confidence. I'll try to share it.

The trailer door closes. Gina comes outside and steps around Zeke. The size difference between the two people in front of me is laughable. I don't often see them standing next to each other. The top of Gina's head is about the same height as Zeke's belt. And she probably only weighs about as much as one his legs. I stare at them vacantly.

"Wait, what were you doing in Gina's trailer, Zeke?" I ask.

"He was helping me pack." Gina says.

"I was helping Gina with a lot of things," Zeke says through a grin.

"Oh." I squint.

Gina raises her eyebrows and walks passed us to her side-by-side. "Are you ready to go?" she asks.

"Yep, I'll ride in the back," Zeke says. "Too cramped up front for me." He steps up into the bed of the tiny truck. I get into the cab with Gina and try to shut off my imagination.

"Did you get to talk to everyone?" I ask.

"No." She starts the car with the keys, overriding the onboard AI. "But news will spread. I talked to Micah and Silas, of course. Micah was fine, but Silas wasn't happy."

"I didn't think he would be. He'll do his job, though."

The drive down only takes a few minutes. People from all over the base are swarming the conference building. Zeke hops off the back, bouncing the cab.

The three of us head to the conference center's main entrance. We spot Kayla by the door about to go inside. She notices us, too and waves. I wave back. Gina also waves and walks around me toward Kayla. Oh. Right. Zeke and I follow them inside.

"Hey, lady. Are they keeping you, here, too?" Gina asks Kayla.

"Oh God, yes. Me and a few other people from IT are to get the network back up after the storm. Corporate has to keep that data flowing."

I try to shoehorn into the conversation. "Guess we're going to be in this mess, together."

Kayla looks back at me without breaking her stride and forces a smile "I guess so." She turns back to Gina. "You weren't too hard on him, were you?"

"Not yet." Gina gives me a quick side-eye.

We walk through the main hall equipped passing many meeting rooms to arrive at a massive auditorium capable of seating six thousand. All-hands meetings are held here.

Corporate calls them "meetings", but they're more like sermons.

The sermons do little to renew my faith, but I am very grateful for the daily bread. Gina leads our group to a pew where the rest of the crew from the 'shed are already seated. I plop down next to Tobias. Zeke plops down next to me, and Kayla and Gina sit at the end. Silas is seated in the pew behind us with his arms crossed.

"Can you believe all this shit?" he asks me.

I lean my head back but don't turn all the way around. "Sorry, man. I tried to get you out of it."

"I know you did. Gina told me it was her decision."

"Suck it up, Silas," Gina quickly turns around, lifts the corners of her mouth at us and faces forward again.

"Hey, I'm just pissed at the situation. What if the storm is as bad as they say and we can't rebuild anything?"

"We'll have to figure it out as we go, I guess. We'll be all right," I say and look at Tobias. He's whiter than usual. I guess he's heard the news, already, too. "You all right?"

"Mm. Got a lot to think about," he says.

Silas uncrosses his arms and leans forward. "Yeah, lot of good shit to think about. He's leaving."

"I heard," I say.

"Corporate contacted me directly not long after I talked to you. I'm going to Houston."

"Woah, I didn't know that. Sounds like a promotion! Good for you, man. We should celebrate." I try to turn the mood. Tobias stares blankly at me for a moment.

"C'mon. C'mon. There's no better time. It's our last chance," Silas says.

Tobias looks up and rubs his eyes underneath the lenses of his glasses. "You're right. Last chance." He pulls his hands from his eyes. "Okay. How about a bonfire after the meeting? Behind my trailer." He looks back to me. "We haven't told anyone yet because my results have been less than perfect, *but* I've figured there are lots of uses for the old equipment at the water distillery *and* the grocer has had a pretty good deal on apples, lately."

"Ha!" I let my surprise come out loud. A few turn their heads. I put up a hand to apologize.

"I'll bring up my grill and some meat." Zeke peers around me, having eavesdropped on us. I turn to him and then back to Tobias and shrug. Zeke beams a big stupid smile back at Tobias and nods.

"Sounds good, Zeke. I've got hamburger if you'll play grill master." Tobias obliges and looks down the aisle. "Invite Gina and Kayla, too."

"We should also invite Micah. He'll be staying behind with the rest of us. He should get a night off before things get crazy."

"No problem," says Tobias. "I feel for you guys. I really do. If it weren't an opportunity for advancement, I'd stay behind with you and help out."

"I'll try to save your slime. Come back when you can and get our biofuel production back in order, will ya?" I say.

"I'm not sure what they'll have me doing, but I promise I'll try," he says.

I check my watch. The meeting will start soon, but the auditorium is virtually empty. I've been to dozens of these all-hands meetings and it used to be as crowded as a basketball game. Now, less than a third of the auditorium's seating is filled. Most of us are all bunched together in front of the main stage. There are more empty rows than filled stretching up to the back of the exit doors. The lights dim. The murmurs of the crowd fade. It's time for church.

<three>

The projector at the back of the room lights up the darkened auditorium. Orchestral music featuring a rapid melody of violins backdrops an equally rapidly moving shot over the Appalachian Mountains on the screen above the stage. The mountains are densely forested with the green canopy of summer. The camera slows with the music and zooms down into the canopy to emerge through the trees, eye level with a well pad.

The red Energy Alliance logo fades onto the screen, and the music fades away. "The Energy Alliance board of directors welcomes you to this all-hands meeting." From behind me, I hear Silas doing his best impression of the narrator. At this point, we all have this intro memorized. His impression is pretty good.

We are shown a brief slideshow of peoples' faces that I've only ever seen on this presentation. The faces are credited by names that I never bothered to remember. Both Silas and the narrator continue.

"Before we get started with today's agenda, we'd

like to show you just how your important work benefits your communities and your country."

"And China!" someone shouts. It gets a few laughs.

The screen turns black and fades into a view from low Earth orbit, looking down to southeastern North America at dusk. The city lights slowly come on from east to west. The orchestral melody from earlier is back. The camera zooms in quickly to Charleston, West Virginia into a family's home. A young boy, probably 7 or 8 years old, is wearing a fuzzy red sweater with a white snowflake pattern. He's standing beside his kneeling father. He rubs his arms up and down to let us know how cold he is. That sweater is not warm enough. His dad ignites one of those fireplaces that looks like a real wood fireplace but it's just gas, burning under fake logs. The boy stops his overstated gesturing. Both father and son turn to the camera, smile and say in unison, "Thanks, Energy Alliance!"

The camera slowly zooms back out of the home, up into the sky and back down into another house, this one is in Atlanta, Georgia. Two children, one boy and one girl, roughly the same age, are sitting at a set dinner table. Each is holding a fork in one hand and a butter knife in the other. They pound the table rhythmically with the bottoms of their hands. A frantic mother in a blue dress and white apron walks past them and into the kitchen. The camera zooms in on her cooktop as it sparks into a blue flame. A quick montage of food preparation later and the mom is serving her hungry children at the table. The children get steak. The three turn the camera as if they are noticing it for the first time and say,

"Thanks, Energy Alliance!"

The camera zooms out of their home, back up to the sky and this time down to somewhere in Texas. Instead of into another home, we're taken inside a massive industrial facility. Huge conveyer belts move thousands of bottles of water around the room. Metal dividers sort the fast-moving bottles into smaller more manageable groups. Each group is sorted perfectly onto a cardboard pallet. Robotic arms descend onto the pallet and wrap it in a thin layer of plastic. The arms then load the pallet onto an autonomously driven forklift. This is the last load it can hold. The camera follows the forklift as it drives out of the warehouse and unloads its pallets into the back of a semi-truck. Once finished, the back of the truck closes its trailer automatically. The camera pans around to the cab of the truck to show us there is no driver.

"Boooo!" another voice protests from the crowd.

The truck starts its own engine and drives away from the facility. The scene cuts to the truck pulling onto a road alongside a park. A man in jeans and a red Energy Alliance polo is waiting. The truck stops and opens its trailer. The man takes out one of the pallets and puts it onto a dolly. He wheels it over to a vending machine, opens the back and starts loading in the bottles. Cut to a pretty blonde lady in a pink tank top jogging in the park. She stops by the vending machine, scans her watch and a bottle clunks down. She is sweating and the bottle is wet from condensation. She takes a long drink and turns to the camera. Panting hard, she still manages to get out an enthusiastic "Thanks, Energy Alliance!"

The camera zooms up out of the park and back

into the sky. It then zooms down into a Houston skyscraper, pausing for a moment on the Energy Alliance logo on the side of the building. We're in a posh office with a mahogany desk and red carpeting. The office is wrapped in windows with an impressive view of the Houston skyline. A man with silver slicked-back hair in a suit and red tie walks onto the screen. His jet-black eyebrows sit just above his piercing blue eyes like woolly worms arching their backs mid crawl. He has a gold Energy Alliance logo on his lapel.

"Good evening; I'm Titus Dunbar," he leans back casually on the front of his desk to let us know he's *approachable.* "I'm the president and C.E.O of the Energy Alliance. I want you to know those people weren't thanking the board of directors or even me."

I'm pretty sure the actors were thanking whoever cut their check.

"No, they were thanking all of you: the men and women out there working our campuses all across the American Republic." Mr. Dunbar leans forward and tents his fingers. That's how we know he's being very sincere. "We are one family at the Energy Alliance and I want each and every one of you to know just how important you are to this family." It's nice to be cared about.

"By now, your supervisors may have told you about the derecho heading toward central Appalachia. Our meteorological experts tell me this storm will greatly impact our operations in northern Kentucky, West Virginia and Virginia." The video cuts to weather radar map–the same one Gina showed me. "

Wind speeds of this storm are expected to gust

over one hundred and twenty miles per hour. It is not yet known how much rainfall will accompany this awesome windstorm." The audience whispers their concerns amongst themselves. The camera cuts back to the Energy Alliance CEO at his desk. Mr. Dunbar continues, "With as much consideration as permitted by our tight timeframe, I have decided to suspend all mining operations indefinitely in the affected areas. Ground transportation will evacuate your families and non-essential personal at all company towns and well pads."

The concerned whispers turn into agitated murmurs.

The video continues to play over the audience voices. "Those evacuated will be taken to your regional headquarters for debriefing. Our regional offices are already hard at work to find you new jobs after this crisis is over. You have my personal guarantee that the Energy Alliance will work as hard for you as you have for us."

"Bullshit!" a man in front stands up and throws a can of something at the screen. It thuds into the canvas spilling its contents as it rolls down the stage.. The murmurs turn into a roar. A few voices stand out.

"Are we losing our jobs over this?" a lady speaks out.

"How long is the storm here for?"

"We better get PTO!"

"Thanks for *nothin'* Energy Alliance!"

The video on the screen pauses.

A man in our row stands up and looks down our aisle. It's Lucas Sykes, a hydro tech that works in the water treatment building at The Watershed. "Did you know about this, Gina?"

"I'm sorry, Lucas. I only found out this afternoon." Gina shouts over the crowd, which was now losing its collective shit. I guess there were a lot of people coming into today's meeting wholly uninformed. Lucas throws up his arms. A voice from the PA attempts to stifle the crowd.

"Everyone, please remain calm. After the message from Mr. Dunbar, you will break into groups to discuss the situation with your supervisors. You are all still employed by the Energy Alliance and are expected to conduct yourselves professionally. Those who do not will be escorted out of the conference center and fined accordingly."

The threat to their accounts is extremely effective. Those that stood up sit back down. Whoever is controlling the video hits play.

Mr. Dunbar continues, "Not all of us are going to be evacuated to safety. Many of our family members will be staying behind to secure our campuses. Those who have been selected to stay, please stand."

Uh-oh. I slouch down.

Tobias pokes me in the shoulder. I raise my hand to smack his finger away but am picked by my armpits up to my feet from behind. Silas has betrayed me. One by one, a few dozen people stand. I get the feeling we were the quiet ones during the crowd's brief uprising. As I feared, the murmurs begin again a bit more hateful than before.

Mr. Dunbar goes on: "These brave men and women will be staying behind to weather this treacherous storm. It is they who will be securing your campuses and maybe even your current positions." The crowd quiets a bit at that. "I fully intend to resume gas mining operations in the affected areas as soon as it makes sense. Many of you will be called back to pick up where you left off. The men and women standing before you will work tirelessly to get you back to work as soon as possible. Please show them your appreciation and wish them good luck in their work."

A few of those left seated politely applaud. I look up at Silas. He is waving with one cupped hand as though he had won a beauty pageant. I resist the urge to backhand his testicles.

"The board and I would like to personally thank those who are staying behind. You will each be receiving hazard compensation in the amount equal to two weeks' pay. Right about... now." Mr. Dunbar points one finger gun toward the camera and into the audience.

Mine and the others' watches simultaneously vibrate and "ding!" I receive a notification on my watch and the balance on my account rolls up with exactly two weeks' pay. The man is magic, and I'm feeling flush.

This announcement did however eliminate whatever niceties the crowd was willing to extend. Dismissive scoffs and boos descend on those who remained standing.

"I will now turn the all-hands meeting over to the campus directors. I leave you with this: the Energy Alliance family is strong. We will not only get through this storm, but we will come out better. We have to. Our country depends on us, and I depend on you. Sincerely, from all of us here in Houston and from the entire Energy Alliance: thank you and Godspeed."

The video operator shuts down the projector leaving us in total darkness for a moment before the auditorium lights fade up. A small man in a suit clearly too big for him creeps onto the stage. He wears the same red tie that Titus Dunbar was wearing It's our regional director, Jerry Xun. He steps up to the podium.

"G-Good evening," he stutters. The microphone crackles for a moment and returns his greeting with some screechy feedback. He clears his throat.

"Thank you all for being here and thank you, Mr. Dunbar, for those inspirational words." Mr. Dunbar can't hear him of course. That was a prerecorded video with some impeccable timing from Financial Management. "I want you all to know that I, too, will be standing with you through this storm. If anyone has any troubles or concerns, please feel free to contact me. I count on all of you. You sure can count on me." He gives us two very rehearsed thumbs up. The crowd obliges him with a bit of applause. Mr. Xun is earnest, but in our eyes he's mainly just the onsite voice of corporate. He's Gina's boss. I've never worked with him directly. Gina does a pretty good job of shielding her employees from him and his tendency to micromanage. Not that he could micromanage the watershed anyway.

Mr. Xun nods, content with the crowd's response. "Okay," the microphone crackles again, "everyone, please go to your assigned meeting rooms. Supervisors, you have been sent a schedule of the evacuation procedures. Please go over this in detail with staff. Thank you."

Most of our team was sitting together anyway, so we file out to head in the same direction. Gina leads us to our conference room. There are twenty-two people on our team. There used to be fifty-one, but more than half of us have been reassigned or laid off. Mostly, it's the roustabouts that get laid off. Engineers and techs are normally safe.

We pile into the small conference room. A projection screen sits at the front of the room as does a holographic projector in the middle of a large rectangular table in the center. Not everybody has a chair, but the lot of us piles in anyway. Gina walks up to the front near the screen and Zeke sits down to her right.

"I'll keep this as short as possible. I'm sure those of you who are to be evacuated will want to get home to your families and start packing. Tobias, will you turn on the projector?"

"Sure."

Gina powers on her watch. A brightly colored menu illuminates the air just above her wrist. She taps a few commands into the air and gestures a sweeping motion toward the projector. It mirrors Gina's display onto the wall. She pulls up the evacuation schedule.

"I want to start by apologizing to those of you who I couldn't talk to personally. You deserve better than to find out about this from a video, but *I* only found an hour ago. Our preparations have to move fast," she says.

She leans forward and rests her elbows on the table. "I understand that some of you may not be happy with our choices of who stayed behind, but understand that these men were chosen based on their ability and past work history. I also did not want to break up any of you from your families."

"You chose them because they don't have families to take care of?" Sam Bisset, a veteran roustabout, questioned Gina. He looks over to me and back to her and shakes his head. "You don't know what it means to have a family if you thought you were doing the right thing. I'd rebuild this place myself if it meant I could send scrip home. Anybody here will tell you, they'd rather work so their families can eat than to sit at home and starve with them."

Gina straightens up, but her expression is blank.

"You're right, Sam," Gina says. "I don't know what it means to have a family, but I do know that when I was a little girl, if my Daddy were around, I wasn't afraid of anything. Your daughter will appreciate having you with her during the storm."

"Goddammit, Gina, you're *still* a little girl!" Sam slams his fist onto the table. He stands up from his seat sending his chair wheeling behind him into the wall. Zeke also stands up.

"You're dismissed, Sam. Go home. Get packed. Be with your family." Gina doesn't flinch. She points to the schedule projected behind her. "The first buses should be arriving soon. The earlier you're packed and ready, the better. The last buses will be crowded."

Sam eyes Zeke, then Gina. He leaves the room without saying another word.

"Tobias, you can go, too if you want. I know you need to be out early." Her tone is much softer.

Tobias shakes his head and takes out his tablet from his messenger bag. "I'm in no hurry."

"Moving on, then. Levi and I met to discuss what needs to be done to do to secure The Watershed. We need twelve of you to work tomorrow to help out.

Levi, please go over the procedure," Gina says.

"Uh, sure," I say a little surprised to have the room. I lean forward in my chair. "So, I was thinking we need three teams of four to secure each area. One team will work to extract algae from the human wastewater impoundment, another will pump out the fracking water and the third will handle the water treatment facility. I'llsupervise the work at the impoundments and Silas'll supervise the security of water treatment." Silas clicks his tongue and gives me the "ok" with his hand. "I've already set the shutdown sequence to stop gas extraction at midnight tonight. I figure I'll shut down sewage remotely when the storm gets bad." I look at Gina for confirmation. She nods.

"We didn't choose the twelve we need to work," says Gina. "I wanted to give you all a chance to volunteer. You will get paid for tomorrow, but you will have less time to organize for the evacuation. Those who do work will have to crowd in on the final busses out. It doesn't matter what your previous job was. Everyone will have a chance to volunteer."

"Uh, I have a problem with that," Silas interrupts. "I need hydro techs for my team only. No offense to the roustabouts, but I need people who know the equipment." A few of the remaining laborers shift uncomfortably.

"That makes sense," Gina confirms.

"I get four, right? Sorry, Ira."

The water treatment facility only had six staff members including Silas. Old Ira was the only roustabout that worked there. If he wasn't the oldest person on the entire campus, he was close. I only ever saw him sweeping or clearing out trashcans. Or chain-smoking out behind the building.

"S'alright, Silas. I'm tired of working for your scrawny ass anyway." That gets the room to laugh and the tension to let up. Old Ira likes to kid, but there was for sure more than a hint of the truth to that. "I don't want to work in that muck either. You kids can keep playing in it if you want. I'll head home now." He slides up out of his chair. "Takes me a while to climb that damn hill, if that's all right with you, Ms. Gina."

"Sure thing, Ira." Gina smiles.

"You're a good girl. Don't let no one tell you otherwise. Take care, boys." Ira winks at Gina, pats Silas on the shoulder and leaves.

"That's the last person to call me a 'girl'," Gina warns the room

The remaining men and women talk amongst themselves and thankfully decide without drama. Gina dismisses the last four roustabouts to prepare for their evacuation.

"Great. We'll start our preparations at 6 AM, tomorrow; and aim to be done by 2." Gina stands to the side of the projection screen and points up to the schedule. "As you can see, ground transportation for the evacuation will run on two-hour cycles starting at 4 AM and will run continuously until everyone is evacuated or it is no longer safe to do so." She swipes at the projection above her watch to show us some new text. "Those of you with trailers will need to have them cleared by 6 PM tomorrow. At 6 PM, the trailers will autonomously return to the depot in Charleston." Gina reads directly from the text.

"Any belongings left in your trailers after 6 PM will become the property of the Energy Alliance.

Belongings you wish to take with you will need to be packed into clearly labeled boxes. You can purchase boxes at the general store, which will remain open from now until the evacuation is complete. Moving trucks will be sent to gather your belongings on the same schedule as the busses. Once evacuated, you and your belongings will be taken to company housing in Charleston where you will be permitted to stay at the cost not to exceed the rental cost of your existing housing. Those of you receiving a downgrade in the square footage of living quarters will have your rent prorated. The duration of your remaining employment will be determined on an individual basis." she looks up from the hologram.

"I'll write recommendation letters for each of you, but I'm afraid that's all I can do. Does anyone have any questions?"

"What about the rest of us staying through the storm? Where will we sleep?" Silas asks.

"I'll brief everyone staying behind separately after we discuss tomorrow's procedures," Gina answered. "If there aren't any other questions, I'll hand the meeting back over to Levi. I'll send everyone a summary of what I just covered."

"Sure. Can I get the projector?" I power up my loaner watch's holoprojector and load the map of the watershed and send it to the bigger projector for everyone to see.

"We won't be doing anything you all haven't done before. We'll work in two teams of four. One team will harvest the algae from the human waste pool and take it to Silas at the water treatment facility." I tap the pool on the hologram projected above my wrist to highlight it for everyone. "We could be in for a lot of rain, so we need to drain the impaired water impoundment. Currently the water level is sitting at a foot and half below freeboard. Our goal is two feet. We've been allocated two water bottles for this task–"

"Two? That's it?" Silas interrupts.

"That's it. And I need two roustabouts per truck to set out the pumps. I'll monitor the levels from the control center. We should have the tank space in water treatment building for the water we drain out, right?" I ask Silas.

"I think so, but if we don't have it already, we can make room."

"Good. Then I'll set the water bottles to drain at the mainline. With the short travel distance, that job should be done early." I tap the other pool illuminating it as well. "The bigger job will be collecting the algae, so once we hit our water level target, we'll need all hands there. When all the algae have been collected from the other impoundment, we're going to tarp up the pools and call it a day." I gesture down on my control interface to activate the simulation. Each pool is slowly covered like window shades being pulled over windows a hundred yards long. "Any questions?"

The volunteers are less than enthusiastic, but they seem to understand their duties. I get a few nods. "You got anything, Silas?"

"Nah, we'll cover it in the morning," he says.

"Okay, everyone but Micah, Levi, Silas and Zeke, you're dismissed. I'll see you at 6 AM sharp."

The room empties. Micah, the big equipment operator with a belly joins us at the table.

"Hey, Micah," Tobias says. "We're having a

bonfire tonight at my trailer. Come by if you can, yeah?"

"Sure. I got some beers."

"Beautiful," I pat Micah on the back.

"Silas, I'm sending you some specific instruction for extracting this final batch of biofuel," says Tobias. "It should save you on hexane. You guys will want every drop in case you're without power for an extended time, and be sure to save a starter in case you want to start growing again." Tobias is the one person in this room that had a certain future and he is still looking out for us. He swipes away something on his tablet.

I'd like to say I'd have done the same, but a pang of guilt told me that I might not have.

"Gina, you'll want to work with Operations after the storm to ration your fuel stores. I'll send you the stock numbers," he adds.

"Thanks."

We're interrupted with a knock at the door. Kayla lets herself into the room.

"Don't mind me. I figured I'd catch a ride up with you to Tobias's, if it's okay, Gina." Kayla says. I pull out a seat for her.

"No problem," Gina says.

"So, where are we gonna sleep when our trailers leave?" Silas asks.

"Here, temporarily. After the storm and initial damage assessment, we'll be assigned new quarters. We can hope for trailers but it's more likely they'll assign us to apartments that have been evacuated. This entire hall's five rooms and *one* bathroom are ours. The Operations Department will clear the office furniture in the morning. They're supposed to help you move your stuff in, too. But we're responsible for getting our belongings down the mountain. We've been allocated a moving truck. It gets here at six. We can take turns moving throughout the day and supervising. Zeke will help each you pack and unload." Gina answers.

"What about food?" Silas asks.

"We also get the kitchen on this floor. We'll share it with whoever is assigned to the other side of the hall. The general store and grocer will stay open and are scheduled to receive supplies as normal. I doubt the restaurants and bars will stay open to only serve a few dozen people, though. My brief doesn't say anything about it."

"Noooo!" Silas put his head down to the table and fake cries into his arms. "Not the bar. Take my house, but please, not the bar." Micah pats his back.

"You'll live," Gina says.

"How?" Silas asks. Gina declines to answer.

<four>

I hop out of the back of Gina's side-by-side as soon as we come to a stop. "I'll see y'all at Tobias's," I say. "I got to go clean up."

I head toward my trailer, shaking the unsteadiness out of my legs from the ride. I breathe in the cooling night air and take a moment to look out across the mountains, now glowing with the setting sun and I realize this will be one of the last times I walk this familiar path home.

The porch lights flick on as I get closer. I scan my watch to the lock and step inside. The indoor lights turn.

"Welcome home, Levi," my personal assistant AI greets me through the house speakers. I customized it to have a soft generic female voice. It's not creepy.

"Thanks, Caroline."

Yes, I named it. *That* might be a little creepy.

"I guess this won't be 'home' much longer, eh?" I ask her as I step into the mudroom to kick off my boots.

"Your trailer is scheduled to depart at 6 PM

tomorrow evening. Please have all of your belongings packed and removed from the trailer by that time. Any belongings still–"

"Stop. I know already."

"Ok."

I sit my boots on the rack and disrobe entirely, putting my work clothes into the hamper just inside the doorway. I still can't help but track a bit of dirt into the kitchen. It's a messy job and though I only spent the morning in the field, mud and dirt get everywhere all the time. Neither are welcome in my trailer.

"Caroline, please have Daisy vacuum the kitchen immediately" Daisy is my robotic vacuum cleaner. Aside from vacuuming she also has a little spritzer for odor control.

Yes, I gave her a name, too.

"Starting the vacuum, now." The little cylindrical robotic vacuum emerges from its charging station and whirs to life combing through the kitchen dutifully. Daisy technically isn't mine either. She's a part of the trailer and will also be leaving me tomorrow.

"Also, turn the fan on in the bathroom and start the shower. Water temperature to one hundred and fifteen degrees."

I step face-first into the shower and let the water wash the stink and stress of the day down the drain. I breathe in the water vapor to clear my sinuses. The day finally catches me and I'm tempted to blow off the party to sleep, but I can't. I'm not sure when I'll see Tobias again and the others need to know I'm with them. I scrub my skin raw and force myself out of the comfort of the hot water.

"Shower off, Caroline."

I get dressed and decide to put some wax in my hair. Kayla might notice. I put on my watch and check the time: 9:06 PM. Damn long day, and tomorrow will be longer.

I search my barren kitchen for anything to take the party. I have a bag of chips to contribute and it's better than nothing. At least it's unopened. I could share the half of a bottle of Old No. 7 that's left, but I think I'll need that later.

Tobias lives a few trailers down, and there's a faint glow of a bonfire coming from behind his backyard. It outshines his porch light. I'm not the first or the last to arrive. Gina, Kayla and a fair number of moths have also been attracted to the fire. Zeke has manned up to the grill and Micah is carefully supervising. I sit the chips on the card table next to them.

"Fellas. Tobias not coming to his own party?" I open my own bag of chips and cram a handful into my mouth.

"He went over the hill to check his distiller." Micah points to a footpath leading into the woods with his beer bottle. It's too dark to see more than a few feet down it.

"Got another one of those?" He grabs a beer from the cooler at his feet and pops the cap off with the end of the card table before handing it to me. We clink bottles.

"Was that you, booing the self-driving truck in the meeting?"

"Yup."

"Thought so." I take a sip of beer. "How's your dad?"

"Oh, he's alright. Moved up to Mechanicsburg to closer to my aunt."

"Good he has family." I lean in close to the grill to check Zeke's work. He's Some hot dogs are just starting to turn brown, but the burgers are still looking pretty raw. Zeke delicately brushes sauce on some chicken thighs. It gets me more excited than it probably should.

"Lookin' good." I can't cook for shit.

"Damn right, it does. Back up, though," Zeke says. I do as I'm told.

"I was just admiring your work. When do you think they'll be done?" I ask.

"Dogs in a couple minutes. The rest will be done when they ready."

"Right on." I tip my beer to him and move. He seems a bit touchy and I try not to piss off anyone cooking for me. Feeling brave, I walk over to the fire and sit in the empty lawn chair next to Kayla.

"Convince Gina to do the request to fix my watch, yet?" I ask.

"I don't know. Did I?" Kayla looks over to Gina.

"Fine." She throws her the hand not holding a bottle up in the air. "I'll only do it because of the storm. I figure you'll have enough stressors. Money shouldn't be one of them."

"Yes! Thank you! You're such a nice boss.

"Try kissing my ass before you ask for favors." She's a bit touchy, too. She said she's worried about my stress, but hers seems more concerning.

"So, Kayla. I need to thank you for helping me out so many times," I say.

"I'm listening." She turns back to face me, tilts her head and smiles with her eyes. We make eye contact. My mind goes blank. She really is listening. It's time to say words.

"He's trying to ask you out," Gina says.

"Gina! What the hell?!" I ask. Kayla laughs.

"Hey, babe, you want a burger?" Zeke asks from the grill.

"Yes, Ezekiel. And my name's not 'babe'." Gina turns back to me. "Am I wrong?"

"Uh...no."

"So, after the storm, he'll take you out for a drink," Gina adds.

"Lettuce and tomato?" Zeke asks.

"Please!"

"Appreciate your help, boss, but I can do this myself." I say.

Kayla frowns. "The bar and restaurants will be closed after the storm."

"We'll find a place." I sheepishly take a sip from my bottle.

"Sure thing, Levi." She smiles again and I feel like dancing.

"Hey, finally! You two are so cute." I turn around in my chair to the voice. Silas had walked up behind us unbeknownst to anyone. The three of us turn to his voice. He's carrying his fiddle. He pats me on the shoulder and takes the last seat by the fire. The wind shifts and the smoke blows right into my face.

I pick up my chair and move it to the other side and closer to Kayla. "Play something on that thing," I say to Silas.

"In a minute. It needs tuned, and I need a drink. Where the hell is Tobias?"

"Evidently messing around with his distiller," Micah says, walking over from the table to stand around the fire with the rest of us.

"I still can't believe we're shutting everything down." Silas says twisting the knobs at the end of his fiddle. "Did Xun tell you anything?" he asks Gina.

"Nothing you didn't hear in the meeting."

"That guy's weird," Silas says. He runs his bow across his fiddle and nods, satisfied with the tune.

"He's harmless," Gina says. "Got a tough job."

A moment later, Tobias emerges grinning wildly from the woods his path lit in front of him by his watch. He's got large Mason jar in each hand filled with crystal clear moonshine.

"The guest of honor has arrived!" Silas announces.

"Oh, I'm not the guest of honor. I'm the host if you need to call me anything," says Tobias.

"I wasn't talking about you, donkus," Silas sets down his fiddle. "I was talking about the moonshine."

"Oh, right." Silas relieves Tobias of his jars. "Hey!" He chases Silas over to the card table. They quickly get to work pouring shots.

"Food's ready. Come eat!" Zeke says from the grill.

"Can I get you something?" I ask Kayla and stand up. She's reading something on her watch, the back of the projection set to privacy mode.

"I'll have the chicken and some coleslaw. Thanks," she says without looking up.

"Sure." I get up to fix our plates. Gina joins me to collect her own burger. "Seriously, thanks for taking care of the watch problem," I say to her.

"No worries. With the logistics of the storm damage, this will slide on through."

I get our food and return to the fire. It's died down a bit from when I first arrived. I hand Kayla her food. She shuts down her projector and takes the plate. "Thanks."

A few bites later, Tobias and Silas pass out shots. I take a whiff of the glass. It smells like mix of turpentine and acetone with a hint of cinnamon.

Tobias steps on the other side of the fire and raises his glass. "Thanks for coming, everyone. You're about to try 'Tobias's Apple Brandy 3.0."

"3.0?" Micah asks.

"Yeah, 2.0 wasn't worth sharing and 1.0 was a total failure," he answers.

"1.0 was good poison," Silas adds. "Old Ira used it to fuck up the rats behind the water treatment building."

"You boys aren't doing a good job selling this." Zeke says.

"Don't worry, Zeke. *This* one is good; I promise," Tobias says.

"Good luck out there, Tobias." I raise my glass.

"To, Tobias," Silas echoes.

We raise our glasses. And we drink. And we cough and hack and make other noises of disgust.

"Jesus Christ, Tobias! This is horrible!" Gina says through a shudder. Ugh, she's right. It's all burn. I chase it with the rest of my beer, and shake my head to refocus my eyes.

"Whew!" Tobias yelps. "Sorry, guys. This is as good as it's ever going to get. No more moonshine after this. I'm retiring."

"Well, as 'horrible' as it is, it's an improvement over the last batch," Silas says and puts an arm around Tobias. "*And* it's free!"

"I don't think it was *that* bad," says Micha.

"But it ain't *good* either," Zeke says. Tobias shrugs.

"Suck it up, you pansies. I'm pouring more." Silas collects our glasses and retreats to the table. Tobias runs up to his back porch and grabs another log for the fire. He tosses it on and goes to get his own plate.

I finish my hot dog. "I'll stick to beer for now, Silas."

"Me, too," Kayla adds.

I walk over get two beers out of Micah's cooler.

"I'll send you some scrip for these." I say to him. "Don't let me forget," I say to him.

"Don't worry about it," Micah says. "You let me keep my job. A few beers is the least I can do."

No one wants to be unemployed. I'm starting to think we should have pushed to keep as many people as possible through the storm. I return to Kayla and the fire. She's now sitting by herself, staring directly into the flames. I hand her a beer.

"You all right?" I ask.

She takes a sip. "They really got us, don't they?'

"What do you mean?"

"The Energy Alliance has us all convinced we're better off here protecting their assets for money that they create so we can buy their goods. The secession was supposed to be a reboot for our state. But it set us back to the 1800s."

"Yep."

"Yep? Just 'yep'?"

"I don't' know what to say. I mean, I agree with you, but like I said, we're stuck."

Silas is finally drunk enough to start playing his

fiddle. He plays the intro of a song I can't quite remember before he starts improvising. Micah pulls a harmonica out of his pocket and tries to follow Silas. I turn back to Kayla.

"It's not like we have a lot of options. The Energy Alliance is the best employer most of us can get, but you could probably do anything working in IT," I say.

"There aren't as many opportunities here as you'd think and no one pays as much as the Energy Alliance. I'd have to leave West Virginia." This is a tired conversation I've had a thousand times with so many people, but not with her.

"Where would you go?" I ask even though I already know the answer.

"The Democratic Socialist Republic of America," she says tiling her head with each word in the new country's name.

The southern and Appalachian states weren't the only ones to secede. The west coast has always had its own ways. And they went the whole other direction.

"For the UBI, right?" I ask. "Then what would you do?"

"I'm not sure. Try and build something on my own, I guess. Maybe an app or software as a service. I don't have the time or energy to invest into something like that and do my job here. Even if I did, the company would just take it. They made me sign an NDA that says anything I build while I'm employed belongs to them. I don't feel free. But if I was there, and had the UBI, I'd at least have time. Look at this."

She loads a document with the DRSA letter head

and logo–an eagle with a rose its beak–on her watch's projector and spins it around so I can see. That's probably what she was looking at earlier. I skim the long diatribe against the American Republic and ovation of opportunity and freedom that universal basic income brings the citizens of the DRSA.

"Isn't houselessness out of control over there?" I ask.

"It's going up here, too, Levi."

"I also hear crime is a major problem."

"Again, ain't getting better here. Do you know what the Alliance's second most popular product is?"

I lean back in the lawn chair. "Oil?"

"Nope."

"Coal?"

"Personal security."

"Jesus."

"*This*. This is what late-stage capitalism looks like. I want to be *free*, Levi."

I stand up out of the lawn chair and stretch with a groan. "You know what freedom looks like to me?" I ask.

"What?" She leans back in her chair and takes a sip of her beer.

"It looks like good food cooked with fire." I point to Zeke and Gina standing by the grill. "Like a couple of idiots trying to play bluegrass." I point to Micah and Silas. They take a bow in my direction without dropping a note. "Some bad moonshine." I walk over to the table and kick back my refilled shot glass. My guts scream at the burn. I ignore them, shake my head and grit my teeth. Kayla laughs.

Tobias throws another log on the fire.

"Levi, I hear what you're saying, but–"

"I hear you, too. But we're not solving nothin' tonight. So, how 'bout a dance?" I grab her by the hand and pull her up to her feet.

<five>

"Good morning, Levi. The time is 5:30 AM. Would you like to snooze the alarm for 10 minutes?"

"Yes, for the love of Christ, Caroline, snooze. Confirm. Fuck." My head is pounding from the base of my neck to right up behind my eyeballs. Every heartbeat sends a new wave of pain. I consider throwing up but think better of it. God damn Tobias. I count in my head: two beers plus three (four?) shots of moonshine. Yep, that's at least five drinks with two of them being unknown homemade swill. I borrowed too much happiness.

I feel too gross to go back to sleep. Instead, I use the time to rally myself psychologically to get out of bed. I can't be late because of this. This is not allowed to affect my work. I am not that guy.

"Good morning, Levi. The time is 5:40AM. Would you like to snooze the alarm for 10 minutes?"

"No, Caroline. I'm up. Sort of."

I stagger into the kitchen and chug a glass of

water. It hits my stomach like a pound of hamburger. There are no quick solutions for a hangover. If there were, I would have found them. I've thought about this a lot.

See, water or Gatorade or whatever won't cure you because a hangover is more than just dehydration. Now, it is true that you are dehydrated and that's because when you drink, your body suppresses a hormone that helps you absorb water. And of course if you're not absorbing water in your body, you're going to piss it out and become dehydrated. The more dehydrated you become, the more your head hurts.

However, the real chemical bastard to watch out after a night of drinking is acetaldehyde. Your body creates this poison as a byproduct of metabolizing alcohol. A small concentration of this stuff makes your skin feel clammy and you get nauseated. If you make a lot of it, you're in for a long fucking morning. There is no known cure for the havoc of acetaldehyde.

"Shower on, Caroline. Eighty degrees Fahrenheit." I disrobe and step in slowly. A cool shower won't wash away last night's sins, but it does clear some of the brain fog.

"What's the time, Caroline?"

"The time is 5:50 AM," the A.I. responds. I have time, but not much. My workplace is right outside my front door.

"Caroline, shower off."

I get dressed and turn on my watch. The system map reads green except for gas extraction–it's red and reads "shutdown". The timer worked. I leave my trailer and walk over to the pools. The sky is overcast, but just about ready to let the first rays of morning light through the cloud cover. A cool breeze blows through the trees. The branches bend just a bit up top. The roustabouts from last night's meeting are already here and waiting for instruction.

Gina comes out of the control center with a cup of coffee in each hand. She hands me a cup and greets me with a flat "Good morning."

"If you say so. I feel like death."

"You ready to get started?"

The coffee is all I'll get for sympathy.

"Yeah, I think so." I navigate to vehicle management on the hologram. "I'll call up the water bottles so we can get started on the fracking water. I need to check with Tobias to make sure it's okay that the other team can get started on the algae."

"Sounds good. Zeke and I are going to move my stuff down to the conference center soon. You can go next if you want," she says.

"I'll let Silas go. I want to make sure everything starts smoothly."

"Okay. Is there anything I should know before I leave?" she asks.

"Gas extraction has stopped as scheduled."

"I saw that. I checked the HMS just a few minutes ago. It's weird seeing it off. Does that mean the main pipeline is empty?"

I take a sip of coffee. "Well, the main line isn't empty but *our* line is. The main line is the *big* line that goes clear across the state. I just disconnected our system from it by shutting down the entrance and exit valves. The entrance valve is at the one at the far end of The Base. When it's open, it allows our operation to join the main line. The exit valve is over there." I point to the valve behind the control center.

"That valve, when open, allows the gas that we extract to flow back into the main line. This two-valve system, when closed as they are now, isolates our campus from the main line so no gas extracted from us flows into it. But that doesn't mean the main line is empty. It just has *less* gas in it. I can show you a full map of our system and how it's integrated into the statewide pipeline transport network you like." I pull the greater system map on my watch.

"No, no, that's okay. I trust you. The moving truck is here anyway." The truck came rumbling up the gravel road and parked itself in front of Gina's trailer while I was talking. "I'll check in with you after I'm moved. There are pepperoni rolls in the control center if you get hungry." With that, she shuffles off toward her trailer.

"Alright, thanks," I say to her back. Gina doesn't give a damn about the technical makeup of the system she's in charge of supervising. She didn't bother to learn much when Silas and I were building it, either. It bothers me. I like her, but I sometimes wonder what her function here is.

"Caroline, call Tobias," I say into my watch's microphone. I shut down the holographic emitter and switch the display to the watch face.

"Mornin', Levi," Tobias answers.

"Tobias, what the hell did you feed me last night? I'm struggling."

"Don't blame me. You're just getting old," he says.

True enough.

"Where you at? I thought you'd be out of here by

now."

"I'm still at home packing up. I'll be leaving soon, though. Did you know they're sending a quadcopter for me? I'm not even going to Charleston. They're routing me directly to Houston."

"Wow. Did they say why they changed plans?" The company doesn't throw money away. There's no way a low-level employee would be airlifted out without good reason.

"They just said it was an extra precaution. I'm suspecting that the severity of the storm might not be exaggerated. You and the others need to be careful."

"Don't worry about us, buddy. We'll be alright." I'm not sure I believe my own words. They hang in the air longer than I intended.

"Did you need something?" Tobias asks.

"Yeah, we're ready to start our prep and I want to get the guys harvesting the last of the algae. Double-checking with you first."

"Everything's set. Silas should able to handle any potential problems if you have them." I start the walk over to the pools catching the eyes of team. I wave.

"Thanks. I'll let you get finished packing. And hey, if I don't see you, take care, man. Remember me if you think I can help out with anything down in Houston."

"Absolutely," he says. "Take care, Levi."

I hang up the call, re-load the HMS and swipe over to the field controls. A pop up tells me the water bottles will be here in just over a minute. I use the controls to raise the screen underneath the human waste impoundment. The screen lifts the algae up, separating it from the wastewater. Well, from most of it anyway. Solids inevitably come up with the screen. Once up, the screen can run like a conveyer belt sending the algae to pile up at one end of the pool.

"Morning, guys," I say in my best I'm-not-hungover-voice. I count eight. Everyone is here. A few greet me back.

"Alright, you four are on fracking water. The water bottles will be here in a minute. I'm having one truck at each end of the pool. When it arrives, fill it up. I'll monitor the flow rate and water levels from the control center. Call me if you have questions."

They break off from the group and head to either end of the fracking water pool as instructed. Everyone seems somber. I have no idea how to lighten the mood.

"The rest of you are on algae collection. You can get your shovels, rakes and wheelbarrows from the water treatment building. I'll start the belt when you get back. The others will likely finish before you do, and when they do, I'll have them join you. Don't overwork yourselves."

One woman, Janine, scoffs and over her shoulder.

"Question?" I ask.

"Nope."

"Okay, then." I better let Silas know they'll be coming. "Caroline, call Silas" It rings several times.

He finally picks up. "Don't make me work, Levi. I'm dying."

"Are you still in bed?"

"Most of me is. I managed to slide off the mattress but my right foot is still hanging on."

"Oh, boy. Well, I just sent a crew over to get tools out of your building. We're going to start collecting algae. You got fifteen, maybe twenty minutes. If you're not ready, I'm telling Gina."

"Don't tell Mom, please. I'll get up." He groans. "How are you not hungover

"I *am*. I'm just not being a bitch about it." It's somewhat comforting to know that I'm not the only one feeling last night's bad decisions.

"*Har har*." I hear some water running on the other end. "Oh hey, did you take Kayla home last night? You two were looking *pretty cozy* by the fire."

I take a sip of my coffee. "I ain't tellin'."

"I guess that means 'no'."

"Go to work, Silas." I hang up on him.

Things did go well.

The water bottles come up from the gravel road, and park themselves on either side of the fracking water impoundment as I had requested. My teams get to work unpacking their respective trucks and preparing the vacuums to suck up the water. I think back to the video from last night when the door of the semi-truck closed itself automatically. This process, too, will likely be automated on a newer model of a truck at some point.

As the algae harvesting team comes back, tools in hand, I start the conveyer belt with the HMS before swiping over to the ComFlow app to send a text to Gina to let her know we got started. ComFlow is our internal file sharing, communication and collaboration app.

I wave to the teams of laborers at each pool and walk back to the control center passing Gina's trailer along the way. Zeke is loading boxes into the moving truck.

As I enter the control center, a sharp gust of wind slams the door behind me. I flinch at the sound and rub the side of my aching head. I adjust the blinds to only let in the smallest bit of natural light. Light is not welcome right now. I grab a pepperoni roll off the table. Bread is welcome. So is more coffee.

I refill my cup, collapse into the office chair and thank God for the fact that I shouldn't have to move for a few hours.

<six>

I slipped into a daze and did my job on autopilot from our little wooden shack most of the morning. The guys outside doing the real work hadn't needed me to do anything except give commands to the autonomously driven trucks. I was not so impaired that I couldn't push a few buttons to make the lights on the monitor blink the way I wanted them to.

My watch buzzes. It's Silas.

"What's up?" I answer.

"Yo. You're next up for moving. Zeke and the truck are headed to your trailer soon. Oh, and thanks for volunteering me to get moved early, asshole."

"Maybe if you got to work on time–."

"Whatever." He groans with another stretch.

"What's moving into the conference center like?" I ask.

"Moving is easy. Zeke did most of the work. The conference center rooms are tiny though."

"Same as the meeting room we were in last night?"

"Yup."

"Christ." I exhale. "How's water treatment?"

"Everything was going smoothly when I left. I'm going to grab a bite and then I'll be back up. I found a few extra 1200 barrel tanks to store the water from the impoundment, but we're not going to be able to churn out a lot of extra fuel out of the algae being brought in, even with Tobias's new plan."

"Hopefully we won't need to use any biofuel at all. I'm going to double the number of workers on algae soon. The fracking water impoundment is close enough to the target level to call it a day."

"Right on. I'll catch up with you later. Bye-bye!"

I get out of the chair and stretch out my lower back. My head gives me one last throb as the blood redistributes itself throughout the rest of my body. I shake my sleeping right foot awake before hobbling outside. With the help of the now steady wind, the door, again, slams behind me.

The air outside is hot and the wind is tipping more than just the tops of the trees. I catch a glimpse of the top of the last tank truck as it rumbles down over the hill. The teams assigned to man the water bottles are heading to the water treatment building get their tools as to help the other team currently busy sifting and shoveling algae.

I activate the intercom app on my watch to speak to everyone through theirs. "Take twenty for lunch. Everyone is on algae after. Silas is on his way." I get a few waves and the algae team tosses down their tools. The crowd disperses, and I walk to my trailer.

A stack of flattened cardboard boxes, a roll of bubble wrap and tape gun are waiting for me on my porch. I grab the tape and a box and prop open the door. By habit, I kick off my boots. I look around. This is no longer my home.

"Good afternoon, Levi." My AI is as welcoming as ever.

"Howdy, Caroline." I tape the box into shape and take a look around. The trailer was furnished for me, so all the big stuff stays except for the mattress. They make us buy mattresses. The kitchen is as good as anywhere to start. I grab the bubble wrap off the porch and start wrapping glasses and placing them into the box as carefully as I could.

I've moved a couple times in life: once when I was a kid out of our hometown when Dad got the job in Charleston, then again for college, and one more time when I got the job here. This feels different, though. I felt worse about it yesterday, but I'm not really going anywhere. I'm just leaving this trailer and for a small room a walkable distance away. Things aren't changing that much, yet. I'll get an apartment after a while as long as we can get gas extraction restarted. I will miss living in a smart home, though. The apartments are regular, dumb rooms.

"Caroline, will you miss this trailer?"

"Sorry, Levi. I don't understand the question."

"That's okay."

"Ok, then."

"C'mon in, Zeke. Don't worry about your boots."

Zeke enters, ducking in under the doorframe holding up a plastic bag. "You care if I eat here? I made sandwiches from the leftover chicken from last night," he says. "I got one for you, if you want it."

"Sure. I thought I had some chips leftover, but I

seem to have lost them."

Zeke pulls up a chair to my tiny kitchen table and unloads his bag. "I got those, too. You left them at Tobias's."

I sit down to join him. I don't deserve my break, but if everyone wants to feed me today, I'll let 'em.

"How's moving going?" I ask after a bite.

"No problems. You're my third one today. I think I got these trailers figured out." He looks around mine. "Smart of you to pack the kitchen first. When we done eatin', I'll put the boxes together and you pack 'em. While you doin' that, I'll load the furniture. You just keep filling boxes and I'll load 'em, too. We'll be done in no time."

"The furniture ain't mine. Why does it go in the truck?" I ask.

"I'm to load all company furniture into the same moving truck and the guys at the conference center load it onto a bigger one." He unwraps his sandwich and takes a bite.

"Can't the trailer just drive off with the furniture inside? It could be its own moving truck."

"You'd think, but there ain't no way to secure the furniture inside. It'd slide all over the place when movin'," he says.

"Makes sense."

Zeke grunts and goes back to his lunch. I do the same. I know the chicken is good, but my stomach is still churning and I have to force-feed myself. I am almost positive that I won't throw up.

"I gotta call Gina real quick," I warn Zeke. "Caroline, call Gina."

"You named your computer 'Caroline'?" Zeke smirks.

Shit.

"That weird?" I ask.

"Hey, Levi." Gina answers.

"Naw. Just sad. We got to get you a real girl. Keep working on Kayla. Gina said she likes you." Zeke takes a big bite of sandwich taking out nearly half of it.

Wait. Shit. Why did I call Gina? Zeke said Kayla's name, the word 'likes' followed by 'you'. And 'you' in the context of his last sentence meant 'me'. I already had a feeling, but this was real third-hand confirmation.

"Gina! Levi named his computer 'Caroline'," Zeke says through his very full mouth.

"Hey, why'd you tell her?"

"I hope you didn't call just to tell me that," Gina says.

"You need to hook him up with Kayla proper. I'm worried about him," Zeke says.

"I can handle all that on my own, Zeke. Thanks," I say. "And Caroline *is* a nice name for my computer." I play off my embarrassment and finally remember why I called Gina in the first place. "I *called* to tell you that Zeke and I are just getting started here and Silas will be back up to the 'shed to supervise soon."

"Great. I'm still at The Base getting settled into my room. I'll be back up soon, too. Any trouble with prep?" she asks.

"Nope. Everyone's on algae as planned, after that they'll tarp up the pools and you can dismiss them."

"Great."

"Yep, talk to you later."

"Bye, sweetheart!" Zeke says. Gina audibly sighs on the other end.

"Goodbye, Ezekiel."

Gina hangs up and Zeke gives me a big smile. He might be right that if I had a real girlfriend, I might not have to name my computer. I decide to poke Zeke about his.

"So, you and Gina, huh?" I ask.

"She wants to be discrete, but we ain't being as discrete as she thinks. Gina's a good woman, but she thinks everyone is dumber than they are," he says.

"What do you see in her?" I'm genuinely curious. I barely see Gina as feminine, let alone attractive.

"Somethin' you don't." I don't think Zeke likes the way I asked that. He paused long enough to let me know he wasn't going to elaborate.

"Are you worried about dating your boss?" I ask.

"Women always boss men. Mine just happens to boss me at work, too. There's no rules against it. The company doesn't care. Why should I?"

"No reason to, I guess."

Zeke nods. "Enough girl talk. Let's get your shit down the mountain."

Our work is efficient. Zeke kept a pace that made me move quicker than I wanted. He loaded the furniture into the truck by himself (including the sofa) and took away my boxes as fast as I could pack and label them. All in all, it took two hours to load everything I owned into the truck. I'm not sure if Zeke is that good or I just don't have that much stuff. It's probably a bit of both. Zeke comes back into the trailer after the last load carrying a tablet.

"You probably ought to take one last look around to make sure you didn't leave anything behind. When you ready–" Zeke reads from the tablet. "I need you to sign here to acknowledge we got all your stuff out of the trailer and you know that anything you left inside becomes company property. When you sign, you also relinquish your access rights to enter this trailer.".

I do as he suggests and walk through every room. I've lived here for nearly six years, but now without all my stuff, it's just an empty box on wheels. I woke up yesterday morning confident I had another two years left in here.

"Caroline, run Daisy one last time in the entire trailer. The floor is dirty."

"Ok. Starting the vacuum, now," Caroline responds. Daisy comes out of her charging station and starts her rounds. I bend down and give her a pat as she passes by.

"You be a good girl, Daisy." The vacuum doesn't respond. It can't. But I'll still miss it. At least I can keep Caroline. She stays on my watch and every terminal I get connected to, but I also liked to imagine that she was always there taking care of my house while I was gone. I live alone. You think some weird-ass thoughts when you live alone. I feel Zeke's eyes on my back. I stop petting my vacuum cleaner.

"You're a weird dude, Levi." Zeke clears his throat. "You ready?"

"Yeah." I stand up and scan my thumbprint on his tablet. "Let's go."

I close the door behind us and Zeke closes the back of the truck. We hop into the cab. He gives a voice command to the onboard computer: "Conference Center".

"Destination confirmed," the computer responds in a voice far more mechanical than Caroline's and we rumble down the gravel road.

“I’ll be damned. Look at that.” Zeke points up through the windshield. A quadcopter bigger than my trailer is flying away having just taken off from the base of the mountain. Its large metallic body is propelled upward by four enormous pads of rotating blades on each of the body’s corners. A cloud of dust kicks up underneath formed by the tens of thousands of pounds of downward air pressure. A line of busses filled with evacuees has backed up the main road out of campus, waiting for it to clear.

“That must be Tobias,” I say. “I talked to him this morning. The company sent the quadcopter to get him. I guess they sent a big one so he could move his things, too.”

“Man, you couldn’t pay me enough to get on of those things,” says Zeke.

“Afraid of flying?”

“A little. I don’t like being driven by computers, neither. I don’t even like this truck. Certainly don’t want to be in something that can just drop out of the sky.”

Autonomous vehicles are everywhere, but you if didn’t grow up around them then they understandably come off as creepy. My dad still shivers whenever he has to ride in one. I don’t mind them. They were pretty common in my hometown. Zeke grew up in the hollers so I doubt he was exposed to public transportation. His family didn’t have much money so I doubt the family car had AI, either. Statistically; the roads have never been safer and logically, there isn’t much reason to be afraid. Although, fear isn’t often logical.

Zeke didn’t have much time to be scared of the truck. It stopped in front of the conference center right before Tobias's quadcopter flew out of sight. He jumps out of the vehicle as soon as it comes to a stop. A roll of thunder booms overhead and the clouds open up a bit to let out some drizzle. The opening act of the storm is weak but enough to give me pause. A man in work gloves with a team of four behind him meets me under the canopy of the conference building's entrance.

"Levi Pickering?" he asks.

"That's me."

"You're assigned to conference room 203 on the southeast wing. Do we have your permission to unload your belongings into that room?"

"Please do."

"Sign here." He holds up a tablet and I scan my thumbprint. He turns to the men behind him.

"Let's do this before the rain picks up." He turns back to us. "Zeke, you can take a break if you need it, but we could use your help if you're willing."

"I ain't tired, yet. But I'm going to eat off your catering table after," Zeke bargains.

"Deal," the moving team leader agrees. He opens the truck with a scan of his watch and the men get to work unloading the truck.

My mind goes to the rain. I better check on the team at 'shed. I step inside the building away from the noise and out of the weather.

"Caroline, call Gina," I speak into my watch. The other end rings once.

"Hello?" she answers.

"Hey. It's starting to rain if you haven't noticed. We probably should give up on algae collection and tarp the pools. Silas said the last of the algae isn't going to matter much in terms of extra fuel production anyway."

"I was thinking the same thing. I'll give the order. The roustabouts need to get ready to be evacuated, anyway."

"Okay. Zeke and I just got down to the conference center. I'll monitor the progress from here."

The impoundments' covering mechanisms are mostly automated. Motorized tracks run on either side of the pool just above where the water level would be if the pool were filled to capacity. The tarps don't stay connected all the time, though. We keep them rolled up on spools in the water treatment building, so, they'll need to be wheeled out and connected to the motorized track. Then we can use the HMS to unspool the tarps and monitor the whole process. It works without issue most of the time. Sometimes it snags.

"Hey, if you're done with Zeke, send him back up here with some two by fours and plywood. I want him to secure the control center. This shack won't make it otherwise," says Gina.

"Will do. Do you need me to work from the 'shed anymore today?" I ask.

"Probably not, but check with Silas after you get moved."

"Yep. Seeya."

"Seeya."

The thought of climbing the hill in the rain and then back down again in whatever worse weather is on the way is not appealing. I am finally starting to feel human again after last night's transgressions and I'd rather spend my newly recovered energy making the best of my new space.

I get off the phone with Gina and give Zeke his

new instruction. Apparently, he'll head up after making good on the deal he made to raid the movers' catering table. I'm not sure how many calories it takes to fuel a man of his size, but I assume it's a lot.

Back outside, I check in with the movers' team leader. They had made quick work of the truck and only a few boxes remain. I decide to help out with the last of the boxes. It is my stuff after all. The movers' team lead makes me scan my thumb on last time before leaving me to my boxes.

There's next to no walkway remaining in the tiny conference room. Rather than unpack the boxes, I decide to make some furniture. I cut out the sides of four boxes and tape them together to make one big box. I secure the big box to two more at the bottom to make a wardrobe. Then I unpack my clothes and hang my shirts from the tall end. I organize pants and fold them neatly to sit underneath.

I cut up one box to make a "U" shape out of it and put it beside the door. That will serve to hold my muddy boots. I don't have Daisy to clean up mud anymore. I miss her already. Instead, I wander outside into the hall to find a janitor's closet. I borrow a broom and address the situation the movers created on my floor.

For a makeshift kitchen, I'll need a pantry. Two stacked boxes facing outward will suffice. I unpack my dishes and use my dish rack to prop up a few plates and cups. I store some utensils in the bottom box. I don't have any food to put in my cardboard cupboard save for that bottle of Jack. I stare at it hard.

"What the hell," I say to nobody and pour a shot

in a coffee mug and plop down on the bed. I might not have Daisy or Caroline, but I organized this place pretty well.

I kick back my shot, and my watch buzzes. It's Silas. Damn, I forgot to watch the HMS. The time tells me I spent the last hour obsessing over my new cardboard hovel.

"Hey?" I answer.

"Levi, you got to get up here. There's been an accident." Silas's breathing hard. He's outside. I can hear the wind and rain. "You know that old tree behind the control center? The wind took it down on top of the building. The entire thing was smashed. Gina was inside! She's not answering calls. I called the hospital to get an ambulance up here. Zeke is going ape-shit tearing through debris trying to get to her."

<seven>

I rip my parka from my cardboard wardrobe and run down the hall. I need to get transportation to The Watershed. I run around outside the conference center looking for help. There's no one outside for good reason. It's raining *sideways*. Drenched, I turn around and go back into the building. Hopefully, my AI can do this faster than I can. I think about my words carefully.

"Caroline, open Job Board. Create new job. Title: Emergency Transportation from the Conference Center to The Watershed. Bounty: 10 Scrip. Time: ASAP. Push notification to all Energy Alliance team members at The Base at Burning Springs that my authority grants me with a link to the newly created job. Sign job: Levi Pickering, Senior Hydraulic Engineer."

The Job Board is an internal app that lets us post odd jobs that need doing outside the scope of normal job descriptions. We pay each other in scrip and the company takes a cut off the top. This will technically cost me 12 scrip, but I need to get up there and I don't think I can run in this rain. I could send for a water bottle and ride up in the cab, but the water bottles are parked at the depot on the next mountain over from the well pad. It'd take 30 minutes to get here at least.

A long minute later, I get a notification that the job was accepted. To my surprise it's Micha. I monitor his location on my watch. When he gets close, I go back out into the rain. He pulls up on his four-wheeler and motions for me to get on.

I explain the situation as quickly as I can, shouting over the engine and the storm. It's not an easy ride. Micah's ATV only has one seat. I scoot as close to him as I can and with one hand, I hold onto the ATV's rear basket. I pull the hood of my parka down with my other hand to shield my eyes from the rain. I can't see where we're going. I doubt Micah can see very well, either. We bump up the gravel road. I can't anticipate potholes. We hit them hard and I bounce tensing my grip on the wet rear basket a little more each time. My parka provides little protection from the rain. My jeans provide even. I'm cold.

A blast of wind forces the ATV to strafe right. Micah overcorrects left and we swerve on the gravel and I'm raised off the seat saved only by my grip on the basket. Micah regains control. A rush of adrenaline tenses up every muscle in my body. My legs shake but I make them clench the bike's seat as hard as I can.

"Lean uphill and against the wind!" Micah shouts through the squall. I do and we crest the last hill. An ambulance has beat us here, parking itself in front of the former control center. Silas didn't exaggerate. The building is now no more than a pile of busted lumber. God, I hope Gina isn't still under that.

I point to the pile to direct Micah. A small crowd is standing around the ambulance in the rain. I get off the four-wheeler, admittedly relieved for myself to be back on solid ground. Now closer, I recognize the crowd to be the roustabouts that were working the pools earlier, plus Silas.

He walks up shaking his head.

"Is she okay?" I ask.

"They got her out, but it's not good. She was unconscious. They're working on her now inside the ambulance. From what I saw, she has a pretty serious head injury. And lots of cuts and bruises. Lot of blood, Levi."

"Jesus, okay. Where's Zeke?"

"Inside the ambulance. He was standing next to the control center when the tree came down. His arm's cut up pretty bad." He runs his fingers through his soaked wavy hair and flicks the water out. "I... I didn't know what to do, man."

"You called for the ambulance. That's what you should have done."

Our ambulances are basically mobile hospitals. They're equipped with everything a field surgeon could need. I check the impoundments behind me. The fracking water pool is covered but the human wastewater impoundment isn't and it's taking on water. The tarp for it is still spooled and parked outside the water treatment building.

"Is there any reason the human wastewater pool isn't covered?" I ask Silas.

"The laborers just got out the tarp before the tree came down. I think everyone is stunned."

I clap my hands twice to get everyone's attention.

"Alright, I know we're all worried about Gina, but that pool is taking on water and everyone knows what will happen if it floods. We got to get that tarp hooked up!"

The soaked through roustabouts look at me wide-eyed with their shoulders slumped in exhaustion. "Let's get it done and get to the water treatment building out of the rain. I'll see about ground transportation so no one's walking down the mountain in the rain. Silas, if water treatment's secure, we could use your help."

"Yeah, of course. Let's go, people!" Silas shouts over the rain and leads the crowd back toward the impoundment.

I put my hand on Micah's shoulder who's still seated on his four-wheeler. "Micah, if you can, I'll take all the help I can get right now."

He lifts up the visor of his helmet. "No problem, Levi. Where do you need me?"

"Go with Silas. I'll be there in a minute."

I walk through the rain over to the water treatment building, stopping outside the building underneath the awning and flip off my hood. With a shiver, I wipe the water out of my eyes. Silas and the roustabouts have already moved the spool into position. I activate the intercom on my watch.

"Let's get this thing hooked up. I'll activate the motors. I'm going to crank the speed to get this done quickly. I want teams of four spread out evenly on either side of the impoundment ready to undo any snags. You've got to act fast otherwise the tarp might tear." And if that happens, and we keep getting this much rain, we'll end up with a waterfall of shit flowing straight down the mountain.

The tracks are pretty reliable but only up to certain speeds. There are fail-safes that shut down the motors in case the tarp gets jammed, but I don't want to rely on the sensor alone. I'd rather a human smooth the tarp out before we have any problems.

I load up the HMS on my watch but minimize the pool controls, for now, to check the trucks at my disposal. Yep, just as Gina said yesterday. I just have the one. That will have to be everyone's taxi when we're finished. I order it to drive up.

I get a notification indicating the tarp has been connected to tracks on the remaining uncovered impoundment. Silas gives me a wave and a thumbs up confirming the successful docking. I motion for him to come over and wait for everyone else to get into position.

Everyone's in place. I switch back to the pool controls on the HMS and activate the track motor on the hologram. The tarp begins to unspool and I flip my hood back up and run out into the rain toward the impoundment. My boots sink into the earth and water splashes up my pant legs with every step. My socks get soaked through.

Rain drops beat at the light projection emitted from my watch breaking up the display, but not to the point that it's unreadable. No warnings, yet.

"Caroline, increase the tarp deployment speed to twice default."

I catch up to everyone and follow the tarp as it clanks down tracks passing each spotter along the way. I pass Silas and slap him on the back to get him to follow me. We run up ahead of the tarp, and I look down into the pool. It's still below freeboard, but it's rising. My readout tells me its gained nearly an inch of water in two hours.

The tarp catches up to us and we walk in pace beside it as it snakes along the track. A warning flashes on the flickering display and I turn around to see Connie, a roustabout, decoupling the tarp in front of her from her side of the track. I pause spool on the HMS, wait it for it go green and start it up again.

"That's one!" Silas shouts over the rain pounding on the ever-expanding tarp.

"The more tarp rolled out, the more snags there'll be," I say. "I'll turn the speed back down."

Our work is slow, but the snags are few. Finally, Silas and I reach the end of the impoundment and watch the tarp secure itself to the bank. We trudge toward the shelter of the water treatment building, and I signal for everyone else to do the same.

"I guess with Gina down, you're in charge, now, yeah?" Silas asks.

"For now. I'll need to report to Mr. Xun and he'll decide what to do next." I exhale as the rain finally starts to let up. "Is she going to be okay?"

"I don't know."

We walk in silence the rest of the way to the water treatment building.

Micah and everyone else is standing outside. "Good job, guys. Let's get out of the rain. Do you have anything for the guys to dry off with in the building?" I ask Silas.

"Um... probably not much. I'll see what Old Ira left in the cleaning storage room."

The water treatment building is nothing grandiose, but it is the largest building at The

Watershed. From the outside, it looks like a big silver aluminum barn. Inside, pipelines of 12" poly come in from underground that leads into giant 1200-barrel tanks tall enough to reach the ceiling. Those tanks have even bigger pipelines emerging from the bottom allowing water to flow through the filtration system. The filtration system is not tall but it is wide. Rows of 12" polylines lead water to more tanks we call separators. Inside these tall cylindrical tanks, water, oil and sand are all separated. Ultimately all of these different layers of filters scrub water for two different uses: human consumption or drilling. Silas's team keeps the water flowing in here and mixes up fracking water as needed.

The space in the back of the building is reserved for Tobias where he refines biofuel from the algae. The algae are run through a different set of transparent pipeline so it adds some fluorescent green to the otherwise dull gray interior. Unfortunately, it also comes with the smell of the human waste the algae grow in. This is something Silas has complained about daily since Tobias's arrival. This building is the heart that pumps water to our campus, but right now, it's just a roof to keep us dry.

"Guys, thanks for everything, today," I say.

"Are we done?" Connie asks. The stout blonde is soaked through, water dripping form her clothes joining the puddle on the tile floor formed the water the lot of us tracked in. Silas returns to pass out the few towels he'd managed to find.

"Uh... yeah. I'll call the water bottles up so y'all can get a ride back down to the base. No need to walk in the rain," I say.

"How's Gina?" Connie asks.

"We don't know–"

"Will she be able to write the recommendation letters she promised?" Some of the other roustabouts nod with the question.

"I'm sure she will when she recovers," I say.

"So, she will recover?"

I look at Silas. He shrugs.

"You'll get your letter, Connie. I'll write it myself if I have to. You'll all get your letters." My watch dings with a notification of the water bottle's arrival. "We have one truck to serve as a taxi. It's outside, now. Y'all can go in fours back to The Base. I set it to go in loops to the apartments. Let the folks that worked on algae this morning go first."

"I'll walk," Connie says. Two more follow her out.

"I'm going to head out, too, Levi." Micah says, helmet in hand. "Keep me updated on Gina." We shake hands.

"We'll go last," I say to Silas. He nods. I let my shoulders relax as my adrenaline runs out, but my neck stays tense. I shake the other roustabout's hands and dismiss them. I turn back to Silas. "Can we use your office?"

"Sure."

We walk to the back of the building to Silas's small, windowless office. 1start to feel light pounding at the base of my skull. Oh, right. I took a shot of Jack before all this started. Sometimes, one is all it takes to relieve and or compound the day's stress. At least one more will be required when I get back to my room.

"I'm honestly surprised at how well you handled this." Silas says.

"Thanks, I think. I feel like all did was get wet and push a few buttons."

"Tarp's down. No one mutinied. That counts for something."

"Mm." I don't have the energy for banter. I peek out the window to see the truckload of workers follow the ambulance down the hill. They must have stabilized Gina well enough to travel. "I should check in with Mr. Xun. You can listen in, if you want."

"Ok."

"Caroline, call Jerry Xun," I speak into my watch. I've only called him directly one other time before this. It was during my orientation six years ago, and my father was sitting beside me then. I've met him in person many times, though, but only had small talk. I've never had to work with him directly.

"Hello?" Mr. Xun answers.

"Mr. Xun, it's Levi Pickering."

"Of course, Levi. I've been... expecting a call from you. *Just a moment.*" There was a long pause. "Sorry about that. How... how's Gina doing?"

"Oh, you know about the accident already. I'm not sure of all the details, but she's not well, sir. Silas Banks is with me. He was up here when tree came down."

"Hi Mr. Xun. I didn't see the accident, but I did see Gina when she was taken to the ambulance. She has a head injury sir," Silas says.

"She is on the way to the hospital by now. Ezekiel Allen was also injured, but not seriously," I look to Silas, he nods with confirmation. "He is with Gina, now." It makes sense that he'd already know about the incident, now that I think about it. As the campus director, he probably gets a notification if an ambulance is deployed.

"I'm glad Ezekiel will be okay..." he trails off the last word of his sentence to nowhere. I think I hear him tapping on his desk. He is obviously distracted, but onsite accidents are rare. I expected a thousand questions, but now I only have half of his attention. Silas and I's eyes meet. He shrugs.

"Yeah, me too," I say. "So, considering the accident, I took the lead on securing The Watershed. Despite everything, we were able to execute our plan as intended except for the control center of course. It was completely destroyed. Would you like me to go over the details?"

"I would, but not tonight. Let's have a meeting in the morning at say... 10:30AM in conference room 301. Unless there's something specific you need tonight."

"Um... no, I'll meet you in the morning. "

"Great. See you then," and Mr. Xun hangs up.

"Does he even care?" Silas was clearly sharing my irritation.

"Sure feels like he doesn't, but I don't know him or his job well enough to know for sure." Nor am I sure whether or not he deserves the benefit of the doubt I am giving him. He was distracted, but I can't imagine what would be more important than meeting after an onsite accident. "You ever work with him before?" I ask Silas.

"Not directly," he says. "He comes up here every so often. I've given him tours of the water treatment building before, but he mostly just harasses Tobias."

"Maybe, but that still seems weird to me."

"Has he ever seemed normal to you?" Silas grins

and gives me two big thumbs up, mimicking Mr. Xun's awkward speech from last night. I shake my head.

"Let's get out of here. I need a hot shower," I say. "Maybe not as bad as you do, though."

"C'mon man, it's Tobias shit slime. That stink sticks with you."

<eight>

I take a bite of the sandwich I nipped from the movers' table and kick my feet up on the bed, my hair still wet from the shower I absolutely required. I wash the bite down with the sip of whiskey I promised myself. I miss my trailer, but this room of cardboard furniture is welcoming enough for now. I down my glass to get some much-needed courage.

"Caroline, call Kayla," I say into my watch.

"Hey, Levi," she answers. I hear some voices in the background and then the sound of a door closing.

"Hey. Did you hear about Gina's accident?"

"I did. Zeke called me from the ambulance. I'm at the hospital with them now. Gina is awake but really high on morphine. You should come see her."

"I don't think so. Have you looked outside?" The hospital is at the far end of the company town. And again, I am without transportation.

"Aw, c'mon. I'll have Gina send you her car. She's high enough to agree to that. The hospital's kitchen is stocked with well... hospital food but at least it can be warmed up."

She already knows how to manipulate me. I sigh.

"Alright, I'll come, but only if you can get Gina to send the car *which I don't think you can do*. I've had my fill of the rain today." Gina is so protective that goofy little car. As far as I know, she's never even turned on the AI let alone allow it to drive autonomously. She would have to be very high (and concussed) to go along with this.

"Deal." She hangs up without another word. A few minutes later, I get a text:

"The car is on its way."

"Really?"

"Yeah, get ready."

"Ok."

Good enough. I put on my sneakers–boots are too wet and caked in mud to wear again. On the way out, I stop in the bathroom to take care of some business and check the mirror. I look and feel ragged. I splash some water on my face and straighten my hair with my fingers before leaving. A small crowd has gathered in the conference center's entranceway in front of the windows. Silas is among them. I walk over.

"Oh good, you got rid of that stink," I say to Silas's back. He turns around to give me a look of death. I look passed him.

"What's everyone looking at?" I ask.

"It's after six. We're watching our trailers leave." I check my watch: 6:07. He's right. It's time.

"That's depressing." I look out the window. Trailers are driving away one by one in procession. I can't tell one from the other. Mine might have already gone by. After the last one leaves, I see

Gina's side-by-side pull up and flash its lights. I get a text from the car.

"Hey, I'm going to the hospital to see Gina and Zeke. Do you want to come along?" I ask Silas. "Kayla is there, too. She somehow got Gina to send the car for me."

"Pass. I just want to go to bed," he says. I empathize. Silas looks as bad as I did in the mirror.

"Alright, man. Get some rest. I'll hit you up after my meeting with Xun to let you know what our next steps are."

"Later." He walks off toward his room and I run outside to the car. It's still raining but the wind has died down. The first storm front must have passed.

Gina's car drove me to the hospital without trouble. Compared to Micah's ATV, Gina's side-by-side is a limousine. If I keep my job, I think I'll start saving to buy one these things.

The hospital is the second largest building on campus next to the convention center. It's equipped to provide healthcare to the campus at its peak population and is located at the far end of town because it also serves the public, not that there are many people outside campus to be served.

I walk passed the ambulance that carried Gina down here and enter through the sliding glass doors. Two hallways blocked by double glass doors are on either side of the reception desk that sits in front of a giant Energy Alliance monogram. A waiting area with a couple dozen chairs are off to the side of the desk. I look through the windows on one set of double doors down a long hallway. There's no sign of anyone. My loneliness is unsettling. I call Kayla.

"Hello?"

"Hey, I'm down here at reception, but nobody's here. It's spooky. Please come get me."

"Ha! Okay, I'm on my way."

A minute later, she comes out a set of double doors opposite to where I was standing. I turn around and we make eye contact. Her long curly blond hair is let down, draping over her shoulders. She was clearly rained on recently and looks a little disheveled. She forces a smile and I float. Some of my energy is restored.

"I hope you didn't get too scared," she says.

"I feel better, now. Thanks."

"Gina's up on the fourth floor. They gave her the penthouse suite since there's basically no one here."

"Lucky her."

Kayla leads me down the long white hall to some elevator doors. She presses the button.

"The hospital definitely feels weird being empty, but I kind of like it," she says. "It reminds me of this time in middle school when my youth group got to stay overnight in our church. We were almost entirely unsupervised. The church was big and had lots of different rooms for Bible school or meetings or whatever. Different cliques separated and took over their pick of rooms. Of course, some couples separated off completely."

"That doesn't seem very pious to let a bunch of teenagers stay overnight together." The elevator arrives with a "ding". We get inside and Kayla pushes the number 4.

"It wasn't. I'm not sure whose idea it was. I guess maybe they thought all the Bible lessons during the day would keep us from sinning at night. Threats of hellfire are no match for hormones."

"How'd you do? Did you find a choir boy to hide in a closet with?" I grin and raise my eyebrows.

"Maybe," she turns her head side-to-side waiting for my reaction.

"Nice," I say.

She goes on. "I don't think anyone actually slept that night. Being in this empty hospital reminds me of that." I'm tempted to ask her if we can find a closet.

"I fully intend on sleeping tonight," I say after too long. "After the day I had..." I stretch my arms up to the top of the elevator.

"I can imagine. We're lucky no one else was hurt." The elevator stops and opens its doors.

"How is she? Really?"

"She'll be okay."

Kayla leads me down the hall to room 406. I make a mental note of the room number. She knocks twice on the door and we go inside.

Gina is sitting upright in her hospital bed. She has a sling over one shoulder to help hold up one of her arms. She also has several stitches across her forehead. She turns to us. Her eyes are glossy. Zeke is sitting in a chair beside her bed, his arm is bandaged from his shoulder to his wrist. I put my arm on his good shoulder to greet him.

"Hey, Gina." I ask.

"Oh, Levi, you didn't have to walk here in the storm," Gina says concerned. I look at Kayla. She quickly shakes her head "no".

"It's no trouble, Gina. I wanted to check on you. How are you?"

"I feel great! *But* that was scary as shit," her speech is slurred. "I was looking at the monitor and then BOOM!" She slams her good arm onto the bed.

"Easy," Zeke says.

"I blacked out and woke up in the ambulance. Did you get the impoundments covered?"

"Yeah, the guys did a great job, but don't worry about it. Just worry about getting better," I say.

"Did you talk to Jerry?" She means Jerry Xun, and she ignored my advice to not be concerned with work.

"Briefly. I'm meeting him tomorrow. Did you?"

"No, but the doctor did. They're still not evacuating me. I'll be staying here for a few days. Zeke'll look after me." She grabs Zeke's hand. Both the situation and the morphine have combined to take down whatever qualms she previously had about public displays of affection. I glance at Kayla.

"How's the arm?" I ask Zeke.

"More banged up than I thought. The scratch went down to the bone. It's sore now, but it'll heal quick. I can be back to work tomorrow if you need me."

"We can't do anything until after the storm passes. You're needed here more, anyway." Zeke nods. Gina looks at me vacantly and then down at her hand. She pulls it back slowly. The room goes silent save for the rain on the one window overlooking the forest behind the hospital.

Kayla breaks the silence. "Let's go get some food," she says to me.

"Sure. Gina, call me if you need anything. I'll visit again tomorrow."

"Will do," he says.

"C'mon, let's check out the kitchen. It's on the second floor," Kayla pulls me away, back down the hall back to the elevator. I rub my eyes with one hand. Kayla leans her head down from one side to look up at my face.

“Are you okay?” she asks.

“Yeah. It’s weird seeing Gina like that. I wasn’t there when the accident happened. I was still getting moved into the conference center, but I could have been. It’s dumb, but my head is filled with a lot of useless thoughts that are making me second-guess myself. Maybe I should have just dumped my boxes in my room and went back to work. I feel guilty for sending her up there. But then if I did that, I could have easily been sitting there myself when the tree came down. Admittedly, I’m relieved that I wasn’t.” I suddenly feel self-conscious and unsure as to why I’m dumping all of this on Kayla.

“That’s a little neurotic.” She blinks three times.

“Hey, I said those thoughts were useless.”

“You do know there’s no way you caused that tree to come down or knew it was going to happen, right?” she asks.

“I do.”

The elevator arrives and we take it to the second floor. We come out in front of another desk not unlike the one at reception. Kayla leads me past it to the right. We enter a large cafeteria with a dozen long hard plastic picnic tables. On the far end is a counter with a set of stainless-steel double doors behind it.

A woman in scrubs with a ponytail is sitting by herself at the table closest to the counter. She’s wearing large ear covering headphones and eating from a tray. She looks up at us, clearly confused. She takes off her headphones.

"We're visiting Gina Green up on the 4th floor. We just came down for some dinner," Kayla says to the woman.

"Do you need help in the kitchen?" she asks.

"Nah, we can handle it. I'm from IT. I've done maintenance on the control systems back there," Kayla answers. I wave to the lady.

"M'kay," she shrugs and puts her headphones back on.

Kayla grabs a tray from underneath the counter and slides me another. We stop in front of the doors. I look through the windows into the kitchen. A scanner similar to the one that let me into my old trailer sits to the right of the door.

"Have you ever been in here before?" Kayla asks.

"Nope."

"The system works just like the general store except the food is much worse and everything is prepackaged. We scan our watches to get into the kitchen. All the food and drinks have RFID tags. Take whatever you want, but you'll be charged for it automatically when you leave. You can use a microwave inside for one scrip per minute. I'll pay since I dragged you out here."

"No, no. I owe you one remember? Last night, I'd said I'd buy you dinner for convincing Gina to write off the bill to fix my watch."

"You did. But this is a pretty lame dinner. I want something nicer than hospital food."

"I can't think of when we'll get a better opportunity."

"If this counts as your 'thank you', then I'm not helping you ever again."

"Harsh. The food can't be that bad." I hold my

watch up to the scanner and the doors slide open. We walk in together. Three of the kitchen's four walls are lined by freezers with glass doors that you'd see in any supermarket. Refrigerators with bottles of everything sit on either side of the door we just walked through. The wall to the right is lined floor to ceiling with microwaves. A machine with two outstretched arms sits underneath. It's on tracks that clearly give it the ability to move alongside the wall.

I grab a bottle of beer from the refrigerator next to the door and sit it on my tray. Kayla does the same and we work our way to the selection of frozen dinners. I grab a Salisbury steak and she gets fish sticks. We get to the dessert rack and I pick up a slice of blackberry cobbler. I turn to Kayla.

"Because this is a special occasion, I'll let you get dessert, too."

"I was going to regardless of what you said." She grabs a chocolate brownie and a cup of ice cream. I act shocked.

"Hey, what's this little thing for?" I lightly kick the machine underneath the microwave.

"He nukes our food." She frowns. "Don't kick him."

"I figured, but how?"

"Give him your tray."

I balance my tray on the machine's arms and its LEDs light up. Two previously unseen claws extend from the front of the arms and two more extend from the back. Together, both sets of claws slide toward each other to secure the tray. The robot then swings its arms 180 degrees so my tray faces the wall of microwaves.

The last two swing open. The machine raises itself up from a jack concealed inside its fat little body to an open microwave. The claws retract and a third arm juts out from the center of its body and guides my frozen dinner inside. The microwave door closes and the timer starts. The robot then glides over to the next open door and slides in my slice of cobbler. As before, the microwave door closes and it turns itself on. The little robot does not microwave my beer, fortunately.

The robot descends back down on its jack and Kayla hands it her tray. It repeats the process. Once mine is done, it raises itself back up, collects my tray, picks up my food from the different microwaves and serves me.

"Thanks, little buddy! You're pretty neat!"

It doesn't respond, but it does go back up for Kayla's food and brings it down to her. Kayla takes her tray from the robot and smiles at it. It returns to its starting position.

We return to the cafeteria, trays of hot food in hand. I get a notification of the bill on the way out: a pittance. I'm flush with hazard pay. We sit down and start eating. It's terrible, but warm. Warm is what I need.

"So, how'd you convince Gina to let her side-by-side come get me?" I ask Kayla.

"Oh, I didn't," she says.

"What do you mean? Did you hack the car or something?"

She laughs and takes a sip of beer.

"No. Most *hacking* is actually social engineering or some disgruntled employee causing chaos with the access rights they already have. Like when someone leaks important emails or whatever. Why is it that people with no IT knowledge assume that everyone with any programming experience at all can hack anything?"

"I don't know. I just use software. I don't build it." I raise an eyebrow, frown and turn my focus back to my food. I'm an engineer. I understand the world of technical specializations.

"Sorry." She tilts her head. "I actually have authorization over everything with AI on campus so I can troubleshoot something when it breaks. I just put Gina's car in 'maintenance mode' and as a false test, I told it to go pick you up."

"That's a little shady. And technically I think what you just said is that *hacking* is causing chaos with the access you already have. That's exactly what you did. You did hack the car. Gina would be pissed if she knew you did that."

"Ok, yeah that's what I did, but I mean something like that is a layman's interpretation of hacking. And Gina wouldn't be as mad as you'd think. She's protective of her car, but she likes you more." She smiles again and looks up at me without lifting her head. I return her look with a skeptical one of my own. She continues.

"Look, Gina's hard on you, but it's a show. She's way more relaxed with people that don't work for her."

"I know. I've worked with the woman for six years, now, and I've seen her with her guard down. It just doesn't happen very often. People tend to go along with Gina to avoid conflict. Whenever there is an issue, it's usually petty and she squashes it quickly. Since the storm, though, people actually have been pushing back on her. You should have been there for the first part of our departmental all-hands meeting. One of the veteran roustabouts got pretty heated, and if Zeke hadn't been there–." I notice Kayla looking down at her watch and suspect she was only half paying attention to what I was saying.

"Am I boring you?" I ask.

"Oh, no, sorry. I just noticed it's nearly eight o'clock. I planned on calling my brother in Marietta."

"Really?" I shake my head. I sigh. "Alright. I can take off or give you some time if you need to make the call."

"No, stick around." She narrows her eyes. "Can I use your watch?"

"Why?"

"I got a bit of an ongoing joke I like to play on my brother. See, he's a computer nerd like I am but he's a total conspiracy nut. He thinks the Alliance, the U.S. Government, the DRSA: pretty much everybody is out to get him. So, I try to throw him off by making audio-only calls from random Energy Alliance phone numbers. If we're lucky, he'll answer with a diatribe about how he knows our plan and he won't let us get away with it. It's worked more often than it should."

"That's ridiculous." I'm getting the feeling Kayla likes to manipulate more than just machines. Whatever. I still have to eat my cobbler. I take my watch off and hand it to her.

"Knock yourself out," I say.

"Thanks, but you have to give the voice command to make the call. Here's the number." She activates the holoprojector on her own watch and reverses the image to show me her brother's contact card. I ask Caroline to make the call. It rings several times on the other end.

"You named your personal AI, 'Caroline'?" Kayla asks.

"Yeah. What'd you name yours?" I say, honestly over whatever earlier embarrassment I had.

"Not telling," she says with a smile.

"Nice try, Kayla," her brother answers.

"This is employee number 885641. We know what you've been doing. This is your only warning to stop. Cease all operations or we will be forced to take extreme measures," Kayla says in her not-entirely-unconvincing attempt to sound intimidating. I look up from my cobbler.

"Now, you're being pathetic. I can see the watch you're calling me from is literally beside your own. And you're not that good of an actress."

"Wait, how does he know that?" I try to interject. This sibling rivalry may have some real- world security implications if he got onto the Intranet.

"Bullshit," she says. "You might have tunneled into my network, but there is no way you got into GPS tracking." She ignores my concern.

"Who's with you? Oh, your watch's ID is tied to your boyfriend. I told you to only call me when you're alone. And you're in the hospital. Are you hurt? What happened?" His bravado is gone and his questions are hurried.

"Relax. And no, I'm not hurt. We're here visiting Gina. There was an accident. She's okay. And Levi's not my boyfriend."

I slump down and take another bite of my

cobbler. The blackberries therein are far kinder than my date.

"That's awful for Gina," he says. He lowers his voice to a whisper "And awful for me that I just unknowingly admitted I tunneled into the Energy Alliance Intranet to Levi."

"Believe me, Levi didn't want to know what you've been up to either," I say in the third person.

"Oh, God. Now who's with you?" Devin says, panicked. "Kayla, this is your fault and you're paying for any legal fees. Don't tell them anything about me."

Kayla giggles. She childishly pumps her fists into the air. She leaves one hand up waiting for a high five. I leave her hanging for a few seconds before patronizing her with a muted slap on the hand.

"What's your name, kid?" I ask him.

"Longinus," he says.

"His name is Devin. Longinus is his net handle," Kayla says.

"Dammit, Kayla. Why don't you–"

Devin is cut off by an alarm I've never heard before coming from my watch. It's blaring. Kayla hands the watch back to me. The holo emitter turns on automatically and loads up the HMS.

"What's that sound? Is everything okay?" Devin asks. I scan the readouts in front of me. The entire map lights up with one warning after another.

"No, everything is definitely not okay," I say.

<nine>

"Are you screwing with my display?" I ask Devin.

"I'm not doing anything. I disconnected from the Intranet as soon as I heard your voice. What's going on?"

"This can't be right," I say to Kayla. "I'm reading a gas build-up at the exit valve, but it's not possible. I shut down the entire system last night."

Kayla looks at her own view of the HMS. According to her readout, everything is fine. She sits her watch down on the table and activates the secondary projector to beam a keyboard onto the table in front of her. She pulls up an all-black command line window and taps at the keyboard.

"Devin, if I find out this is you and you're fucking with us, I'm going to kill you. I'll be impressed. But then, I'm going to kill you," she says.

"I'm not doing anything! I swear!"

I turn back to my HMS to try and rectify some of the issues I'm seeing, but nothing happens. Every command I give returns a message: "Access Denied".

"My dashboard isn't responding to commands either," I say. "I'm reading that the entrance valve was opened, but the exit valve is closed off. So, pressure is building up at The Watershed, but these pressure levels, the blow-out preventer should have triggered. I'm trying to release the exit valve to let the gas escape but it's not responding. I can't issue an emergency shut down of the entrance valve either. I'm getting a few unrelated warnings from other systems, too," I say.

"I don't know why I'm not getting the same warnings on my HMS, but I can see the problem if I look at the readouts directly from the sensors on the console. Your pressure readout at the exit valve accurate. I'm not sure about the other stuff. What else should I look for?" Kayla asks.

Fuck.

"Forget the other stuff, for now, we've got to release that pressure. Can you open the exit valve?"

"I'll try. How much trouble are we in?" she asks.

"Minimally, if you can't release the valve, a secondary fail-safe should activate a relief valve that will blow the gas into the air. So, a small environmental disaster is a best-case scenario. If that fail-safe is also not operational, then the pressure will build up until the pipe explodes. And gas will continue to flow from the main line to fuel the fire until we can close the entrance valve at this end of The Base. So, open the exit valve and then close the entrance valve as soon as possible."

"Oh my God. Okay." She taps at the holo-projected keyboard faster. The pressure readings on my dashboard keep climbing.

"Caroline, urgent call to Jerry Xun. Join the call

with Silas, Zeke and Micah Zimmerman," I speak into my watch.

"Micah, here." He answers first.

"Hey, Micah. It's a joint call, please wait."

The others pick up in time. I look to Kayla and hold out my hands to ask her for more information. She holds up one finger and doesn't break focus.

"Everyone, we've got an emergency. Mr. Xun, Silas, I need you both to open up your HMS, and tell me if you are receiving any unusual readings."

"It reads just how we left it, Levi," Silas says. "What's going on?"

"I'm not seeing anything unusual either. Aside from gas production shut down, but that's as ordered," Mr. Xun confirms I'm the only one getting the warnings.

Why is it just me? Okay, I have to think. I look at my own flashing readout and take stock of the issues one by one. If Kayla can't open the exit valve from here, then we may be able to open it manually. I check the rate of the pressure build-up. It's fast. Too fast for anyone at The Base to get to on time.

"Silas, is anyone up at The Watershed right now?" I ask.

"I don't think so. We should have been the last people to come down. Are you going to tell us what's going on?"

"Mr. Xun, I need you to confirm that no one is up at The Watershed. If someone is, I need to know who."

"Okay, Levi, but you have to tell us what is going on, now," he says.

"About five minutes ago, I received an alarm and several warning messages on my HMS. For some reason, I'm the only one able to see these warnings. The most urgent problem being reported is that our campus's gas pipeline has been reconnected to the State's main line. Gas is flowing into our campus but our exit valve is closed and is ignoring my commands to open back up. Gas is building up at that valve very quickly and our BOPs aren't triggering. If we have someone up there, then they may be able to get to the exit valve in time to open it manually, but–"

"They may be the one causing all of this," Kayla interrupts.

"Who is with you?" Mr. Xun asks.

"It's Kayla Pierce, sir, from IT. I'm troubleshooting the system as we speak. Mr. Xun, this looks like sabotage. Also, Levi, I can't open the exit valve through my administration panel. It says I don't have access. I can't close the entrance valve, either."

"Shit. We can't get to the exit valve in time, but we can minimize the damage." I get up from the table. "Kayla, keep digging. Find out anything you can. Zeke, meet me out front. We're going to the entrance valve to shut it down manually. We can at least cut the gas off at the source."

"I'm not seeing anyone at The Watershed on the campus-wide GPS readout. If someone is up there, then they're not wearing their watch. I'll alert security. Keep me informed, Levi," Mr. Xun hangs up.

"Kayla, I need Gina's car to get to the entrance valve."

"Zeke, get the keys from Gina just in case," says Kayla. "But I'll set a command for the car to take you to the entrance valve from here. It will take off as soon as you guys get in the car."

"On my way," Zeke confirms. I nod to Kayla and run out of the cafeteria, keeping one eye on the pressure readout at the exit valve.

"Caroline, add Kayla to the conference call."

"I'm here," she says through my watch's speakers.

"This entire situation is impossible! I checked those fail-safes myself. If the entrance gate valve is open, the exit gate valve *has* to be open. It's a paired system," Silas says.

"I know, Silas. Keep trying to open the exit valve remotely. Kayla is trying to restore our access. We're a couple minutes away from a leak if we're lucky. If not, just hope we can get that entrance valve shut."

"Jesus Christ. Okay, I'll keep pushing the button," Silas says.

I get to the elevators but run down the stairs. I hear Zeke coming down behind me.

"Micah, we have another problem that I need you to look into. Kayla can confirm, but I'm reading that a water bottle is at the watershed collecting fracking water from the water treatment building."

"There's *no way*. I shut everything down at water treatment, too," Silas says.

"Micah, do you see anything on your Vehicle Management System?" I ask.

"No, Levi. I'm reading that there is one vehicle at the well pad and it's shut down," Micah says.

Zeke comes out of the stairwell and hands me the keys. The lull in the storm is over, and the full force of the derecho is again upon us. Rain, carried by the wind, douses us as soon as we leave the building. I shield my eyes from the rain with my forearm. Gina's car starts up as we approach.

Zeke jumps up into the back of Gina's side-by-side in the rain. He grabs onto either side of the roll bar and motions me to get in the cab with his bandaged arm.

"Are you nuts!? Get in the cab! You'll fall off if you ride up there in this!" I shout up at him over the noise of the wind.

"I told you I can't fit in the damn cab! Don't worry. I ain't gonna fall off," he shouts down.

I don't have time to argue with him. I get in the cab and it takes off in the direction campus entrance where the valve is located.

"Kayla, see if you can confirm the issue I'm seeing with the water bottle," I say over the pounding rain on the roof of the side-by-side. "If it's true, Micah, you got to get up there and do whatever you can to stop it."

"Ok, Levi," Kayla says. "Hypothetically speaking, though, if you wanted to do everything that we're being alerted to, could you?" she asks. I turn up the volume on my watch. I can barely hear her.

"Are you asking if I have authorization over these systems? Yes, I normally do," I say.

"I thought so. Our control systems are being hacked. Whoever is in the system couldn't stop you from getting the alerts because they are sabotaging gas production from your account."

"My account? How?"

"I'm not sure, yet."

"Can you stop them?" I ask.

"I don't think so. I've already severed all links to the Internet, but commands are still coming in.

Whoever did this must have uploaded a virus. The commands have already been issued and are coming in programmatically. I can't cancel or alter them on your authority."

"You have my permission!" I shout.

"I know, but you have to give the commands or use the system to authorize another account. There's a permission lock even for IT admins and everyone else. Not even Titus Dunbar could override these commands. On your authority, commands from your watch have also have been disabled. You can only give commands from the control center."

"The control center was smashed by a tree!" I say.

"I know," she says.

"You're not helping!"

"I know. I'm sorry. I'm just using you to think through these things. A lot of this doesn't make sense. Your account shouldn't have the authorization to lock everyone out like this, but it does," she says.

"Okay. What about the truck?" I ask.

"There's an infinite loop running to give commands to the truck to retrieve fracking water from the water treatment building and pump it into..." she pauses as if confirming what she's reading. "It says Disposal Well #1 (Defunct), whatever that is. It's been running since 6:30PM. Another command was issued four minutes ago."

"Oh my God," Silas says.

"They're trying to cause a landslide," I say. Before we built the water treatment facility, we dumped fracking wastewater into a disposal well. It's inefficient and not so great for the environment, but it was cheap and it helped us get gas production up faster while our waterworks were in production. "Micah, you have to–"

My words are cut off as the side-by-side suddenly veers left, hard. It throws its emergency brake whipping the backend around. I slam into the passenger side door.

"Ah! What the hell? The car just stopped!"

The car accelerates forcing me back in the seats. I take the key out of my jacket pocket and scrape at the lock, forcing it in with a final lunge. I slide up and reposition myself in the driver's seat, turn the key and slam on the breaks. I stop just short of running us into a ditch.

"Kayla, what happened?"

"I... I don't know. They must still be in the network somehow. They figured out what you're trying to do and got to the car AI through the VMS."

"You still up there, Zeke?" I ask having remembered he's still on the conference call.

"Fuck no! I got bucked off when the car did a U-turn."

"Shit. Are you okay?"

"Not great, but I can walk."

"Okay, sit tight. I'll come back to pick you up."

I turn the car around and floor it. The HMS flashes red, warning that the pressure at the exit valve has gone critical. As I feared, the fail-safe to open the relief valve didn't fire. An explosion is imminent. It isn't a matter of "if" anymore but "when". The most we can do is cut off its fuel source.

I stop just shy of where Zeke is standing when it happens. The exit valve explodes shooting ignited gas in every direction at The Watershed. Like a volcanic eruption, a fireball leaps up from the top of the mountain into the storm clouds. It rains shrapnel on the peak where I spent the last six years of my life. The side-by-side rattles rocking me just a bit in place. Wait, no. That shouldn't have happened. The explosion wasn't that big.

"Guys, that was an earthquake. The truck has pumped too much water into the disposal well," I say into my watch.

Silence.

"Did you hear me? You need to evacuate now!" I shout.

Nothing.

"Caroline, call Kayla!" I scream into my watch.

"Cannot complete the request. You are no longer connected to the Energy Alliance Telecommunication Systems," Caroline responds.

Too many things are happening at once. Think. My team has the same pieces of information I have. I need to trust that they can piece it together. The fires at The Watershed are no longer the biggest issue. The landslide is. I need to get out, too. I have this car. Should I just drive away? Should I go back to the hospital in case they do need warning? My panicking is interrupted by a knock on the window. I slide it down, letting the rain into the car.

Zeke looks at me expectedly. He's soaked with rain, his bandaged right arm now soaked with a mix of mud and blood.

"I don't know what to do anymore. That shake wasn't from the explosion. It was an earthquake. They're trying to bring down the whole mountain. They've shut down the telecom server. I can't warn everyone."

"You got to take this car and get the hell outta

here. There are people outside the campus that have no idea what's going on, either. Go warn them."

"O-okay. What about you? You've got to get out of here, too," I say.

"I'll get back to the hospital and make sure Gina and the others get out." He pounded twice on the door and took off running off in the rain.

"Zeke, you don't have time– wait!" I shout after him, but he disappears into the storm. I consider going after him, but there really is no time. He's right. People outside campus need to be warned.

I make the tiny car speed through mud and the rain. A second quake hits just as I get to the entrance to the campus. This one is longer. Two guards are standing outside their booth at the gate. I relay the details of the situation as fast as I can. Fortunately, Mr. Xun has already alerted them to the emergency situation. I pass off the responsibility of warning people outside campus to them. I have other plans. They open the gate and I ensure they get in their own side-by-side and leave.

I check my watch for the time. At least that function wasn't hijacked. It's been seven minutes since I parted with Zeke. He should have got to the hospital by now. I try again to call Kayla, but no luck. The telecom server is still down. I can't wait here. I'm directly downhill from where the land will slide.

There are multiple ways to get into the campus from different access roads. Each road has a similar guard station that leads up to another well pad that runs adjacent to the one above the Base. There are similar access roads that let the water bottles travel around the mountain from one well pad to another.

And at every adjacent well pad, there is a shack with a control center with the same style terminals as the one we have at The Watershed. Kayla said that my account should have normal access to the pipeline network from the control center. Getting to a different control center on another mountain might be our last hope.

The derecho has other ideas. The rain batters the tiny car. Visibility was next to nil and the faster I drive the less I can see. I could no longer trust the AI's electronic eyes to help me. The wind blows steadily on the side of the car, threatening to throw me into the ravine below. Debris from wind-damaged brush litters the country road. I swerve around and pull onto the first access road.

The gate is open and the guard booth is empty. I leave the car to look inside the booth check the terminal. No luck. The telecom network is down from here, too.

I get back in the car and start the slow climb up the access road to the well pad. The rain has turned the dirt road into a muddy, shallow stream. The tiny car's tires find only the slightest bit of traction, but we inch our way up. I check my watch. It'd been sixteen minutes since Zeke and I parted. I don't have time for this. I can hike faster.

I check the car for anything to help me move forward. Luckily, Gina stashed a disposable rain parka, a flashlight and an umbrella in her glove box. The umbrella is useless in this wind. I grab the parka and pull it over my already rain-soaked clothes, take the flashlight and leave the relative safety of the car.

Water fills my sneakers the second I stepped

down into the stream flowing down the road. I might as well be barefoot. I hop up to the bank above the road and get moving one squishy step after another. After some floundering in the wind, I find I could guide myself up the mountain with one arm in front of my face to block the rain and the other shining the light in front of me.

A faint orange glow coming from uphill motivates me to a run. The light has to be coming from the fires at The Watershed and the fact I could see it meant that I was nearing the well pad. Fueled by panic, I get careless with my footing and turn my left ankle sliding down the bank. I pull my foot up and test it on the ground. It's unsteady but doesn't hurt much. I can keep moving. My run turns into a skip and I crest the hill to see that Hell itself has taken the campus.

It's night, but where I am standing is fully illuminated from the fires to the west. Ashes, wind and rain blur my vision, but this well pad is adjacent to the campus and used to offer a view I once admired. I fall into the mud.

I was right. The forced injection at the disposal well above The Base caused a landslide. Waters from the pools we had secured a few hours earlier now flow freely down the mountain. Mixed with the gas leak, a steady river of fire and human waste surges through town. The water treatment smolders above it all having suffered from secondary explosions when Tobias's biofuel tanks were exposed to the fires. The river of liquid earth and fire had washed over The Base igniting or outright destroying every building and vehicle in its path. There is no sight of the offending water bottle.

The conference center wall facing uphill collapsed, yielding to the landslide as it claimed the entire first floor. The flames took the rest. That building was designated to shelter over forty people from the storm but now it may be their tomb.

The earth and fire didn't stop at the conference center. It continued to take the apartment complex, the general store and way on down at the far end of The Base, it took the hospital, too. Nothing was spared. Every building, every home was crushed or burned and I had no way to know if anyone made it out alive.

I check my watch. Twenty-seven minutes have passed since I parted with Zeke. I don't know if that was enough time for anyone else to escape. I don't know what I need to do next. I can't catch my breath. All I can do is let out some sort of muted sob. The rain is freely flowing down my parka.

I limp over to the well pad's control center to get a respite from the rain. I turn on the console and try to call Kayla. Nope. The server is still down. I load the HMS. All warnings had stopped. There was no longer anything to report. The watershed's sensors, the entrance valve and everything else had been destroyed.

My pace is slowed as my ankle begins to swell. The pain from the injury fights its way passed my depleted adrenaline, and I lose my footing several times as I squish down the bank. I find the car right where I left it.

I get in and reverse my way down to where the road is a bit wider so I can turn around. The car slides down the slope of the mountain effortlessly. I slam on the brakes, but the car keeps sliding. At some point, while I was up the mountain, the wind must've felled the tree. And I can't help but to drive right into it.

My head hits the steering wheel. The airbag goes off. I feel warm. There is a ringing sound. Everyone else back at The Base probably died.

I think I'll go ahead and die, too.

<ten>

I remember being hot and seeing the light of the sun. The car wasn't ventilated. The air was thick and humid. And I was thirsty. Too thirsty. I felt a rush of cool air when the car door opened. Someone pulled me out. I remember they said something, but I couldn't talk back or if I did, I don't remember what I said.

I'm not well, but I'm not dead. My head is heavy and throbbing. I'm alone in a nice bed in someone's bedroom, but I should probably be in a hospital. I figure it's afternoon due to the sunlight coming in through the bedroom's one window. The mattress is thick and the bed sits little too high off the ground to be convenient.

There's an ornate white dresser in the room with gold handles and floral wallpaper covers the walls. A large wooden crucifix is mounted on the wall above the foot of the bed. A carving of Jesus is nailed to it. I stare up at Him, and He stares up in agony.

A bandage wrapped around my head and covering my left eye. I have another bandage on my right arm and an IV drip in my left. I follow the line to a bag of clear liquid. Whatever's in there isn't helping my dry tongue. My ankle is also wrapped. I have no idea the extent of the damage these bandages conceal.

I sit up in the bed and test my body. My arms and legs move well enough. Neck is stiff but not broken. I crack it left and right to get some mobility back in it. I test my voice to but all that comes out is a wheeze. I knock on the wall behind me.

A moment later an older woman comes into the room. She's not old, just older than me. She's wearing a long denim skirt, white blouse and has tears in her eyes.

"You're awake! God is good! How are you? Can you remember anything?" she asks.

I make a drinking motion with one hand to ask for water.

"Of course." She returns a minute later with a glass. She hands it to me and steps back to keep her distance. I drink the whole glass and try my voice again.

"Th-thank you." I clear my throat loudly. "Not just for the water, but for saving me." I put my hand up to the bandage over my eye.

"Please don't touch your bandage. You've got an orbital wall fracture. Your eye is also badly damaged."

"Are you a doctor?" I ask.

"I used to be a nurse."

"Where are we?"

"You're in our home. We would have taken you to the hospital, but it was destroyed in the landslide." She leans against the wall and crosses her arms. "We didn't have enough fuel to get you to Parkersburg and you might have died waiting for an ambulance. So, we brought you home and treated you the best we could. You've got a pretty banged up arm, too, but I don't think anything is fractured. Just cuts and bruises. How do you feel?"

"I'm in a lot of pain, but just in my head. My arm is fine."

"I reckon you have quite a concussion. I gave you some painkillers when you got in and were semi-conscious. I'll get you some more." She takes my glass, leaves the room and returns with a couple pills and another full cup of water. I eat the pills and finish the glass. I'm hit with a pang of anxiety that I just willingly popped two pills a strange woman has given me.

"Please ask if you need more," she says.

"Thanks. What's this?" I point to the IV.

"Saline, but you've also had a few doses of antibiotics. I've kept you fed for the past two days with the IV. Do you think you could eat now? I can take it out and get you some food. We've managed to get some fuel, so we can talk about taking you to Parkersburg after you eat, but first I think you ought to answer some questions we have."

"Okay." That makes sense. I am a stranger to her.

"I'm going to get my husband, first. Please wait here."

"I don't think I could go anywhere yet if I wanted to."

I prop the pillows up behind me. My movements reveal hidden pains from the accident and the stiffness of having lain down for what did she say? Two days? Surely, an ambulance could have gotten here by now even in the aftermath of the storm. Did they even try to call for help?

I feel the pain of memory and a sense of urgency to reach out. I look down to my bare left wrist. My watch is gone. The woman returns with a short scrawny man with a long scraggly black beard. He squints at me.

“My wife says you can talk. How you feel?” he asks.

“Seems like I’ll live. Thanks to you all.”

He grunts. “Them bandages and pills ain’t cheap, you know.”

“I’ve got Energy Alliance scrip. I’m happy to pay for y’all’s kindness,” I say.

He grunts again. This was a more approving grunt than the semi unimpressed one when I thanked him with words. I look over at the woman standing in the doorway.

“I didn’t get your names. I’m Levi Pickering. I am, or was, the Senior Hydraulic Engineer at the Energy Alliance Burning Springs Campus.”

“I thought so,” the man says. He reaches behind the door and pulls a shotgun into the room.

“Woah, there.” I raise my hands in defense.

“I think you better tell me everything you remember about how you wound up in that car. And I don’t think I have to tell you to not do anything dumb.”

“I’m wounded, in a bed and can only see out of one eye. I assure you. I’m no threat. And I wouldn’t be a threat if I were healthy either.”

“I suppose you don’t know anything about this.” He pulls out an old Android phone from his pocket and taps on it a few times. He tosses it to me. A press release from the Energy Alliance is on the screen.

BURNING SPRINGS, WV – June 17, 2032 – The Energy Alliance (NYSE: ENA) board of directors would like to extend our condolences to the families of those lost in the tragic June 14 landslide that claimed thirty-four lives. Out of respect to the families, we will not be releasing the names of those confirmed deceased at this time. The Energy Alliance is providing every resource possible to West Virginia law enforcement to bring those responsible for this heinous act of terrorism to justice. One perpetrator, Kayla Pierce, age 33, is already in custody. Levi Pickering, age 31, and Devin Pierce, age 22, are wanted for questioning. If anyone has any information on the whereabouts of these individuals, please contact your local law enforcement or Energy Alliance Security center.

I slumped back into the bed. This was too much to unpack. I reread the press release. Thirty-four dead. That means out of the forty-three who stayed behind nine survived. Kayla is in custody, but alive! At some point in my reading, I began crying out of my one good eye. I wipe it with my bandaged arm.

"Look, this is all a big misunderstanding. Kayla, Devin and I did nothing wrong. We were actually trying to stop the disaster. I was locked out of the system–"

"The headlines say you're a terrorist," the man interrupts me.

"An anonymous whistleblower leaked a conversation between you, Kayla and Devin Pierce talking about hacking the Energy Alliance Intranet. They also say there's evidence that your account gave the orders to dump the fracking water into the disposal well that caused the landslide," the woman says.

"That's not right. See my account was hijacked. As for Kayla and Devin, Devin is Kayla's brother and yes, he did hack the network, but he's just a kid pranking his sister. See, Kayla works in IT. Devin was proving he could crack her network. There's no way they'd cause the accident. Hell, Kayla was right in the line of the landslide. I'm surprised she survived."

They don't flinch at my words and I'm struggling to find better ones. I look down.

"Wait! Why are they saying we did this? We've got no reason to destroy our workplace and kill our friends in the process. I worked there for six years. I was devastated when they told me we were ceasing operations before the derecho got here. We have no motive."

"There's a lot of conjecture as to why you did it, but right now the most popular is that you and the Pierces were paid off by Titus Dunbar to deliberately cause the landslide all in order to crash the company stock price," the man says. "Dunbar sold the majority of his stock before the storm. At the same time, a Chinese fiduciary company made a short play against the stock and profited more than three hundred million dollars. From an outsider's perspective, the landslide would have looked like it was caused by the derecho, but then you all were outed by the first whistleblower when they leaked that data."

"The first?" I ask.

"Yup, there were two. The one about your phone call with the Pierces was the second one. The one before was just a log of commands issued from the control system. That log is what made you the suspect," he says.

"You say the leakers are anonymous? Who could they be if only nine people survived the landslide?"

"Some say the second one is you trying to come clean and rat out Dunbar in a bid for amnesty. But you've been in this bed for three days. Some say the first was the Pierce boy also trying to take down Dunbar," he says.

"What do you think?" I ask.

"I think you're a dumb bastard caught in something you don't understand." He smiles revealing a set of teeth that never knew braces. "Look, no one's been by here yet. There's too much brush in the roads, but they will be. And when they do come, I ain't gonna hide you."

"I understand, but I don't intend to run, either. I haven't done anything wrong."

"Good." He nods. "I'm Isaac and this is my wife, Myrna." Myrna grabs the shotgun from Isaac, gives me a nod and walks out of the room. "There's something you might be able to help us with."

"Y'all saved my life. I'll help you however I can. Though, I'm not sure how much good I'll be to you all banged up like this."

Isaac went on to explain what he and Myrna were doing when they discovered me in the car. Looting. Their house is not far from the Energy Alliance campus and they had been watching the evacuation and pieced together it was for the storm. As soon as it was practical to go out after the weather had calmed down, they went scavenging. Having discovered the abandoned guard post, they drove up the access road in their pickup truck and found me in the side-by-side. Later, Isaac went back and took the generator from the command center as well as the computer and anything else that wasn't nailed down. He wants to hook the generator up to his house to supplement his existing one, but he's having trouble. There's a microcomputer locking him out of the generator's controls. He tried to use my watch to unlock it to no avail.

Myrna returns and disconnects my IV. She still moves cautiously around me, but clearly she is not as tense as before. I thank her graciously.

"Your ankle is sprained, but not badly. Will you please try to stand?" she asks.

"Sure." I swing my legs to the side of the bed and ease myself up. Blood rushes down from my head, redistributing throughout the rest of my body. I feel dizzy. I lower my legs to the floor and let one hand rest on the bed to steady myself. The tape on my ankle works well. I can put some weight on it.

"How does it feel?" Myrna asks.

"My ankle is fine, but my head is not."

"That makes sense. You likely have a concussion and you haven't eaten solid food in a couple of days. If you think you can, I'll help you walk to the kitchen. I put on a pot of tomato soup that should be ready."

"Thanks, I think I can walk on my own."

I follow Myrna, easing myself out of the room and down a hallway. I keep one hand sliding on the wall past hanging photos of a younger version of the couple posing with younger woman. Their daughter, maybe. We come to a modest kitchen also decorated with floral wallpaper. Another crucifix adorns the windowless wall at the head of the dining table with only two chairs. They must not often have company.

Myrna dips a ladle into the pot on the stove and pours the soup into a bowl. She smiles warmly and puts the bowl in front of me. She serves herself and brings a loaf of bread. I pick up my spoon.

“Please, let us say grace before we begin,” she says. I freeze. She bows her head. “Thank you Lord in Heaven for this meal and its nourishment of our bodies. Thank you for sending us Levi so that he may heal from his injuries and please guide him in his healing and in his tribulations to come. In Jesus’s name, Amen.”

“Amen,” I echo trying not to sound hollow. The woman saved my life. I’ll be at least appreciative. I let her take the first bite of soup. I focus on the spoon and dip it into the bowl, clanging it clumsily against the side. I swing my head side to side to get different views of my soup to compensate for my loss depth perception. It doesn’t help.

“Thank you for including me in your prayer,” I say, trying to hide my frustration over my inability to use a spoon.

“Absolutely. I think you’ll need it.” She breaks some crackers into her soup.

“Can’t hurt. I’m not sure what’s going to happen next. I suppose I’ll be arrested.”

“Well, before that, you’re going to eat this soup and bread. And then you’re going go outside and help Isaac with the generator. You said you’re an engineer, right?” she asks.

"Yes, ma'am. A hydraulic engineer."

"Does that mean you can do plumbing?"

"I'm not a trained plumber, but I know my way around pipes and valves. Did you have something else you'd like me to look at?"

"Cleaning your wounds and having an extra mouth has unexpectedly depleted our stores of freshwater. We have a new water filter that needs set up."

"Sure. I'll hook it up to whatever faucet you'd like."

She nods and we finish our meals in silence. She cleans up the table, but I sit still letting the soup settle my uneasy stomach. It wasn't much to eat, but it did energize me a bit and helps curb the nausea from the pain pills. I'll take Myrna's advice and just worry about the immediate future. I need some time to think and heal, and there's a fog sitting on my head. I'm disoriented either from the opiates, concussion, trauma or all three. I ease myself up from the table.

"Are you ready to go outside? Your shoes are by the door. The generator is on the opposite side of the house. Do you think you can walk there?" Myrna asks.

"I'll try."

I walk over to the door on the opposite side of the kitchen and find my shoes on a rack with many other pairs. They've been cleaned and dried. The rack looks stretched, warped no doubt from my new vision impairment. I fumble my shoes. My body feels centered, but I'm aiming too far right for everything. I'm having to concentrate far more than normal. It's as if my one good eye has migrated to the center of my forehead, but the rest of reality hasn't changed to reflect my new false sense of orientation. If I didn't have the muscle memory in my hands to tie my shoes, I never would have made it out the door.

The sun is out and the air is humid. The house sits on top of a mountain surrounded by trees. The wind damage from the derecho is evident everywhere. Old trees from across the hillsides lay dead against their younger brothers. Even some of the young trees have fallen. Isaac and Myrna's yard is covered with brush. I walk around the side of the house to find Isaac removing a board that was covering a window.

"Hey Isaac."

He looks over and grunts as he sends a nail flying behind him. He points to the generator. "I have it connected to the house's fuse box, but I can't bypass the computer to start it."

"That's how it was designed. No one but authorized Energy Alliance personnel can enable these," I say. He walks and I limp over.

"Well, you are Energy Alliance personnel, ain't you?"

"I can try to turn it on, but lately I haven't had a lot of luck getting these systems to do what I ask. If you give me my watch back, I'll see what I can do."

He reaches into his pocket and hands me my watch. It's powered off. Turning it on will likely alert anyone at the Energy Alliance looking for me to my exact location via GPS. I shouldn't be scared, but the logic of it doesn't stop the feeling of dread. I don't' want to be here, but I don't want to be arrested, either. I'd already resolved not to run. I know I haven't done anything wrong, but I'm about to. It's a fireable offense to authorize the use of company equipment to a non-employee.

"I can get into a lot of trouble for this."

"You're already in a lot of trouble, ain't ya?"

"That's true, but this might cause trouble for you, too. If Energy Alliance Security shows up here and they find this generator, they'll press charges."

"When they show up, I'll just throw a tarp on it. Once you turn it on, you can remove the security lockout. It ain't connected to the net. I already checked for that. So, no one is gonna know it's here except you, me and , and Myrna ain't gonna sell me out. Are you?" he asks.

This redneck is a lot smarter than he looks. His plan might actually work. The only other way he'd get caught is if someone checked the command logs coming from my account. Those logs are already screwed up from when my account got hijacked. It's not exactly the perfect crime, but his chances of getting caught are pretty low considering all the heat that's already on me.

"No, I won't say anything. Consider this a thank you and a plea to you to not point your shotgun at me again," I say.

"I didn't point the gun at you. I only would have done that if I intended to kill you," he says.

I turn my watch on and let it finish its boot sequence. I hold it up to the generator's computer. The holo emitter projects the generator controller's interface into the air. A popup window prompts me to login. I put my thumb on the watch face. An error message appears on the screen: "Energy Alliance Personal Assistant not authorized."

"It doesn't like your watch even with your log in," says Isaac. He frowns.

"I'm not surprised. I haven't been able to access any system with it since the hack." I shut off the projection. "You said earlier you grabbed the terminal from Well Pad Two's control center, right? It's a long shot, but I might be able to access my profile to re-authorize this watch for field use. Although, I imagine IT has suspended my account if they think I'm a terrorist. But it's worth a shot."

"Sure, I'll set it up. But work quick when we turn it on. There's enough fuel left in the old generator to run the terminal, but not for long. I'd rather not have to siphon fuel out of the new one if I don't have to."

"No problem. I just need to access my profile settings. I'll know right away whether or not this idea will work," I say.

Using the side of the house for balance, I follow Isaac back inside. I hadn't been on my feet for very long, but I'm drained. I need time to recover, and I'm not sure if I'm going to get it.

"I'll set up the terminal on the kitchen table. You can sit down," Isaac says.

"Thanks."

I rub my bandaged ankle. It's holding up well enough, but stiffness tells me that the muscles are swollen. Isaac returns with the terminal and plugs it into an outlet underneath the kitchen table.

The screen boots with the Energy Alliance logo and prompts with a login screen. I enter my credentials and am given access to the control panel. But this screen is different than what I normally see. This panel has access to employee profiles, financial records, GPS employee monitoring, HMS access to every campus across the American Republic. I have access to *everything*.

"Holy shit," I say.

"Holy shit, indeed." Isaac leans over my shoulder to get a closer look at the screen.

"Don't swear in this house, boys," Myrna says looking in on us from the hallway.

<eleven>

The amount of data, options and control this screen offers is overwhelming. I stare blankly the flood of icons, and scratch the back of my head.

"No time to play now. Time is fuel, Levi," Isaac says.

"Right, the generator," I answer.

I navigate to my profile on the control panel and select "Connect Energy Alliance SmartWatch". I select the device currently connected to the terminal–my watch. I fire up its holo emitter, and just like that, I have access to everything the terminal has on my watch. At least for now, I am a superuser over all Energy Alliance systems. I power down the terminal.

"I thought you said you were an engineer," Isaac says.

"I am."

"Then explain why you access to all that data."

"I can't. I can only speculate that it has something to do with the hack. I guess it's still ongoing. Energy Alliance IT must not have figured out a way to restore the systems, yet. My profile was the one that was hijacked. I guess the hacker found a way to give it executive privileges and just left it after the landslide."

"Seems like you should be able to get the generator working," Myrna says from the hallway. "Levi, when you're done, come back to the bedroom and I'll change your bandages."

"Oh... sure," I say.

"C'mon, I'll help you outside," says Isaac.

Isaac lets me use him as a crutch and we hobble back to the generator. The air has changed. These people saved my life, but they are thieves and I just showed them something immeasurably valuable. I can't run. I saw the gun once. They could coerce me into anything.

Isaac reopened the hatch on top of the generator. He looked at me expectedly, noticing my hesitation. He threw up his arms and shook his head.

"What's a matter? You were ready to do this before."

"Uh... nothing, sorry. I'm just lightheaded." I say and hold up my watch to the computer inside the generator. I'm prompted with the same login screen as before. I push my thumbprint to my watch face. This time, I get a "Success" message and the generator whirs to life. My watch's projection loads the generator's control panel.

"Can you shut off the authorization requirement?"

"Let me see." I fumble through the control panel's submenus and eventually find the right setting. "I think I got it, but we should probably test it."

I power down the generator from my watch's

projection and log out. Isaac flips the power switch on the computer inside the hatch, waits for a few seconds and then flips it back on. The generator starts up as intended.

Isaac nods and smiles out of the corner of his mouth. “That oughtta keep the lights on.”

Well, that’s the first crime I’ve committed for these people. Let’s hope there won’t be too many more. When I re-authorized this watch’s access rights, I briefly saw in another window that the GPS was enabled. I can safely assume that Energy Alliance Security is on their way. They might be coming to take me to jail, but I might be better off there than here. I should be able to explain away anything Isaac and Myrna make me do as coercion.

“Myrna wants to get you cleaned up. Want me to help you get back inside?”

“No, thanks. I think I can make it.” I hobble back over to the side of the house to use it as a crutch. I need to find a moment of privacy so I can try to make some calls. I have to let my dad know I’m alive.

“Don’t be such a hard ass,” says Isaac. He comes over between the wall and me and grabs my arm. He guides me all the way back to the bedroom I woke up in. Myrna is waiting. She’s prepared two large basins of hot water and a pile of clean bandages. Having already laundered the clothes I was wearing the night of the accident, she folded them neatly and set them at the corner of the bed.

“You can use the shower and get changed, later, but we’ll need to wash your face here,” she says.

“Actually, Myrna, before we begin I was hoping to make a phone call.” I tap on my watch. I considered waiting for an opportunity for when I was alone, but I was about to be more vulnerable than ever. I don't want to get drugged up to the point they could steal my watch again. Hell, for all I know, these strangers might be capable of cutting off my thumb so they could get access to my biometric logins.

"Sure, Levi. I–"

"Caroline, call Dad." I didn't let her finish her sentence. I had the element of surprise and I was going to use it. It rings on the other end. Myrna's eyes go wide. Isaac is standing still in the doorway.

"Don't say anything that would get us into trouble, please," Myrna says.

"Hello?" my father answers.

"Dad! It's good to hear your voice. Listen, I'm al—"

"I don't know who you are, but you must be a special kind of piece of shit to call here and impersonate my dead son."

"I...what?"

"It's bad enough that in his death, he's being accused of terrorism. I don't need prank calls on top of everything else I'm going through. Did you know they locked up his girlfriend!? She's facing the death penalty! They're even trying to extradite her brother from the United States."

"Dad! What the hell? I'm—"

"Energy Alliance security will surely track this call and when they find you they will—" The line goes silent.

"Dad!? Dad? Hello!?"

"They cut off the call," says Isaac.

"Mm," confirms Myrna.

"What the hell was that about? He wouldn't let

me talk."

"You ain't too bright, are you, Levi?" asks Isaac.

"Easy, Isaac," Myrna says.

"I'll leave you, then. I hate watching when you're with patients."

"I'll be fine. Go get the boat ready, please."

"We going to Marietta?" he asks.

"I think so," she says and turns to me.

"Alrighty." Isaac leaves the room.

"Let's get those bandages off of you, dear. We'll start with your ankle."

Myrna pulls my bad leg into her lap and starts to unwrap the bandage. I jerk my leg out of her hands and get up off the bed. It hurts to do so, but my situation is changing too fast. What the hell was that about? Dad thinks I'm dead and wouldn't let me explain where I am. Kayla is facing the death penalty.

"Fuck! That was a warning!" I say out loud.

"Yes, it was," Myrna says. She pats the bed, telling me to sit.

"I can't go home."

"No, you can't."

"But they're on their way here."

"Yes, they are."

"What am I supposed to do now?"

"Sit down on the bed and let me look at your ankle."

The lack of panic in her voice makes me trust her a bit more than I probably should. She has no motivation to hurt me. I sit on the bed and offer her my leg. She undresses the bandage and applies a bit of pressure around the joints and rolls my ankle, testing its motion. I wince.

"It's sprained, but I think it will be fine in a week or so. I'll clean it before rewrapping it. I'm afraid you'll have to skip that shower I offered. Well you don't' have to. That's entirely up to you."

"What do you mean?" I ask.

"Well, you have decisions to make. I can offer you means to escape, as well as the medical care you need, but not for free, of course. If you choose to escape, you won't have time to shower." Myrna's hands work fast, removing the bandage. "But, if you choose to stay and wait for Energy Alliance Security, then you can shower, but you'll run the risk of being wet, naked and injured while getting arrested. It wouldn't be how I would like to go down, but that's up to you." She smiles. I shake my head. Her warmth is contagious. Myrna puts a new bandage on my ankle as fast as she removed the old and begins undressing the bandage on my arm.

"Why should I trust you? You're a thief."

"It's true. And I pray for forgiveness every day." She shakes her head "Levi, don't you think it's odd that a couple of hermits way out here have enough medical supplies to triage a man with a concussion and a broken eye socket? You've had serious injuries with no sign of infection, as far as I can tell. You seem to be recovering well, no?"

I flex my ankle inside the new bandage. "It is strange. But I've only been conscious for a few hours and most of that time I've been high on painkillers. I haven't exactly had time to suss out my circumstances."

"My husband and I are part of a network of former and current healthcare providers that traffic medical supplies to underfunded hospitals and organizations who provide care to those who cannot afford it."

"I imagine there is a lot of money to be made in undercutting medical suppliers."

"I imagine there would be if we sold them. Look around you. Do you see a mansion? Would a rich thief have a need to steal a generator or a bit of fuel to power her lights?" Myrna sighs deeply as she washes my arm. "But my decisions are not yours to judge. Only God can judge me. I don't think your arm needs a new bandage." She wrings out the sponge into the bucket.

"Let's get a look at your eye." She slowly unwraps the bandage on my head. "Now, we have a boat. Isaac can take you, along with a batch of supplies, up the river to Marietta Memorial Hospital in Ohio. There, you can get the care you need. No one at the hospital will ask who you are once they know I am the one who sent you, and don't offer anyone your real identity."

"Why would you do this for me?" I ask.

Myrna finishes unwrapping the bandage on my face. She carefully pulls each bit of bandage still stuck to exposed tissue off with a pair of tweezers. My eye is swollen shut. I reflexively reach up to touch the wound. She bats my hand down.

"Ah ah. Don't touch," she says. "You are a son of Adam and therefore you are worth helping." She lightly starts sponging the wounds around my eye. With each dab of the wet sponge, a tinge of pain shoots through my face.

"Really, now?"

"Yes, *really*," she says. "It's God's will that I help heal the sick and injured. And I would like your help with that, in exchange for the help I'm offering you."

"How?" I ask.

"I'd like you to use the terminal in the kitchen to export as much of the Energy Alliance medical database as you can onto an external drive. If you refuse, my offer to help get you to the hospital in Marietta is off. You'll have to wait right here with me for Energy Alliance Security." She smiles, again. "I'll still let you take a shower, though."

With a data dump, they'd have inventory records of every Energy Alliance hospital in the country. They'd also be able to determine when to hijack deliveries. She'd have names of personnel and their profiles for recruitment into her network. It's probably their Holy Grail of information.

"It seems I don't have much choice," I resign. "But why would you stay here? Why not come to Marietta with us?"

"To buy you time. I'll have my personal medical supply closet wide open and the terminal sitting on the table when they arrive. I'll lie and lie and lie and lie about you and tell some truths about what we do."

"That's crazy! You'll be thrown in jail."

"Yes, but as I said, you'll need the extra time to escape. And with my capture, people will learn the truth about our network and come to know why we do what we do." She finishes cleaning the wounds around my eye and starts wrapping a new bandage around my head. "I fear the Energy Alliance may not be interested in the truth. Your father was trying to tell you that."

She may be right. Knowing Kayla, I've got to believe she's already shown Energy Alliance Security every bit of data she possibly could to prove what really happened the day of the hack. Dad had to have a reason to say the things that he did.

I glance down at my watch. Maybe with my new access rights over the Energy Alliance database, I could find some irrefutable evidence that could prove our innocence. If I could get to Marietta, I might be able to find Devin. He could help me.

"All right, Myrna. I accept your offer."

"I'm delighted to hear that." She finishes bandaging my eye and helps me change back into my own clothes. I follow her into the kitchen and sit down at the terminal. She goes outside, leaving me to my work.

I log in and navigate through my new superuser control panel. Getting to the medical system is as easy as loading an app on my watch. Conveniently, there's an "export" function in each of the Energy Alliance Medical Information Systems databases. I check the boxes for everything I thought a thief might want, select the external drive as the destination for the export and click "Ok", committing a felony in the process.

I navigate back over to my profile and disable the GPS tracking for my smartwatch. If I'm going to be a fugitive, I might as well do it right. There's no doubt they'll try to follow me once they realize I'm not here. I'm certainly not going to feed them my exact location. Myrna and Isaac come back into the house.

"You finished, yet?" Isaac asks.

"Yep," I say.

"Just a moment, please," Myrna says. She takes a small tablet out of her pocket and holds it up to the external drive. She taps on the tablet, waits a few seconds and looks up.

"Thank you, Levi." She hands Isaac the drive. "It's all here. Please give this to Ravinder."

"Give it to him yourself. You don't have to be a damned martyr," he says.

"You know as well as I do how important that data is and you may need every second I can give you." She smiles warmly at her husband. "With some luck, my arrest will be covered in the media and everyone will learn our story. The sick need to know they have allies. I have thought this through, Isaac. Now, please, go."

"Give us a minute, Levi," Isaac demands.

"Uh, sure." I log off the terminal and hobble outside, closing the door behind me. I check the time on my watch nervously. A long two minutes go by. I know there's some sensitive talk going on back inside the house, but my would-be captors are surely close. Finally, the door opens back up and Isaac steps outside.

"C'mon, the boat's just over the hill," Isaac says. He holds out an arm. I take his shoulder. We walk as fast as we can across their yard toward the tree line. I look back to see Myrna standing in the doorway watching us leave.

There's a steep winding dirt path leading down the hill to a dock. A large fishing boat with an open cockpit and, large back deck and a cabin is parked at the end. The path is too narrow for Isaac to carry me down.

"Find me a walking stick, and we can get down faster," I say. Isaac sets me up against a tree and we survey the ground. There are plenty of sticks to choose from. The path is wrecked with fallen branches. Isaac walks down the path a few feet and picks one up. He makes quick work pruning the switches off with his pocketknife and tosses it up to me.

The stick is a useful crutch for my sprained ankle, but more importantly it helps me feel my way down the path to compensate for my lack of depth perception. My pace is still slow.

"Go ahead and get the boat ready for launch. I'll get there as soon as I can," I say.

"I *will* leave without you if I have to," he shouts back running down the path.

"Your wife won't like that!"

I quicken my pace as much as I can, stumbling all the way. I'll have to risk injuring myself further if I want on that boat. Isaac gets there quickly and starts up the engine. I tank my way through the brush adding a few scratches and bruises to my injury count. At the dock, Isaac helps me onboard. I collapse into the row of seats in the back of the boat happy to be off my bad leg. I elevate my ankle and Isaac unties us from the dock. The boat's control panel looks old. No AI here. Isaac tosses the rope on the floor and gets into the cockpit. He pushes the throttle forward, demanding the old engines work to their limit. They whine in protest before coughing out some black smoke, filling the air with diesel. The nose of the old boat lifts up and we shoot downstream leaving a wake behind us.

"I take it you know the way to Marietta well?" I shout over the noise of the engine.

"I've run cargo up this way, but never with anyone chasing me. We take the Little Kanawha to the Ohio. From there we head upriver to Marietta,"

Isaac shouts back.

"How long?" I ask.

"'bout an hour."

The dock we departed from disappears quickly as we snake the bends in the river. More fallen brush lies on either side of the riverbed. Whole trees lay in the water. Isaac navigates the rivers with ease. There's no chop. A hawk follows the path behind us. It gains on us quickly.

Too quickly.

"Isaac, drone!" I shout.

Isaac turns around and looks up. He pushes the throttle even harder. We drift around a bend to a straight stretch in the river. He slows us down and jumps down the stairs into the cabin. A moment later he returns with the strangest looking gun I've ever seen. He tosses it to me and jumps sits back into the driver's seat. It clearly doesn't fire bullets. It has no chamber.

"Ever use a drone gun?" he asks.

"Nope."

"Just point and shoot. If nothing happens, turn the knob and point and shoot again."

The gun has a single knob that appears to attenuate it to different frequencies. "Sounds easy enough," I say.

Again, Isaac throttles us forward. The drone rounds the bend and I do as I'm told. I point the gun at the drone and pull the trigger. The gun makes no sound, but it does *something*. The drone soars straight up into the sky disappearing into the clouds.

"Neat! What's this thing do exactly?" I ask.

"It scrambles the drone's controls and cuts off the video feed to the user. Most drones will fly straight up whenever they're disconnected from their controllers," Isaac explains. "Did you recognize that as an Energy Alliance drone?"

"It looked like it, but I can't know for sure from this distance."

"If it was, then they know where we're headed. I doubt they'll be able to catch us on the Little Kanawha, but they'll have the Parkersburg police boats after us once we get to the mouth of the river. We might see a barricade."

"What'll we do then?" I ask.

"I don't know."

<twelve>

We boat upriver in silence. I stayed on the lookout for drones, but no more came. The sun is starting to set, and our optimism is sinking with it.

If there isn't a barricade, we might be able to use the cover of darkness to get to the Ohio side without getting caught, but if we're spotted crossing the border then local Ohio authorities would arrest us just the same. We'd be extradited back to West Virginia and into Energy Alliance custody. We need to get to our rendezvous in secret. There is no other way.

I tried to convince Isaac to park the boat and hide out for a while, but he was dead set on getting the hard drive with the Energy Alliance Medical Database dump to Ohio. He said if he could get anywhere across the river, he could ditch the drive somewhere and get a message out to his contact, Ravinder, to come pick it up. I offered to send an export of the database directly to Ravinder over the net, but Isaac didn't want to leave a digital trail linking Ravinder to Myrna or to the Network. Before we left, Isaac chastised his wife for being a martyr, but he seemed to have no problem playing the role himself or making me one, either.

I glance down at my watch. We'd been on the river for nearly half an hour. We will be at the mouth soon. Damnit! Maybe if I was better with technology, I could somehow use my new access rights to shut down the boats or call off the search or something. I wish Kayla were here. If there is a blockade, she could to do whatever she did to Gina's car to the Energy Alliance Security boats.

"I need to cause some chaos with the access I already have!" I nearly scream finishing my thought out loud.

"What?" Isaac asks.

"I have an idea! Do you have a desk?"

Isaac motions an invitation to go inside the cabin. Using the side of the bench for balance, I hobble down the steps and go inside. It's cramped with boxes of allegedly-stolen medical supplies. I sit down a sturdy-looking box and clear off some space on the desk. I take off my watch and activate the holoprojector for the display and the second one for the keyboard.

Good. My master access rights haven't been revoked. I punch around my new control panel until I find the ComFlow icon. I load the administration panel and read through the list of the latest threads coming in. Thousands have been created in the last hour from every department throughout the company. I need to filter these down to a number I can comprehend. The search bar at the top will let me narrow down the list. I type in "Paul Wright".

Paul Wright is the chief of Energy Alliance

Security for West Virginia. The thousands are narrowed down to the tens of threads he participates in. I select one with the title line “Apprehension of Levi Pickering”, dated the day after the hack. The thread has less than ten members, presumably senior members of Energy Alliance Security. Paul Wright sent a message himself a few minutes ago. It read:

“The capture of the terrorist, Levi Pickering and his accomplice, Isaac Abbott, is to be your first priority. He was last spotted in a white fishing boat approximately 25-30 feet in length, license number WV 3758 YW traveling northwest of Burning Springs up the Little Kanawha River. Security personnel are to cooperate with Parkersburg police officers if requested. However, it is in the company’s best interest to apprehend Mr. Pickering without assistance from public law enforcement. ”

At least Parkersburg police won’t be after us. That should make things a bit easier. We’ll need a bit more luck than that, though. Paul Wright’s username is hyperlinked in the application. This is has got to be a feature of the administration panel I am using. I tap on his name and am navigated to his company profile.

Perfect. I tap the “Log In” link at the top of the screen. My dashboard changes to a very familiar one. It’s the normal user interface for ComFlow that I use every day. Except this time, I’m logged in as the Energy Alliance Chief of Security for West Virginia.

First off, let’s kick the real Paul Wright out of his

account. I change his password and unauthorize all of his devices: his watch, office terminals and personal assistant AI.

Now, let's cause a little chaos. I navigate back to the "Levi Pickering" thread and set the priority of the announcement to "urgent". This should send an alert directly to all security personnel's watches who were added to the thread. I title the announcement "CORRECTION and UPDATE" and send:

"Correction: the boat ferrying Levi Pickering has license number WV 8768 YW. The boat is now believed to have turned around and is heading southeast back toward Burning Springs."

I wait for a few more minutes to tick away before sending another message from Mr. Wright's account. This time I give it the subject line "Levi Pickering Apprehended". I write:

"The terrorist Levi Pickering and his accomplice, Isaac Abbott, have been apprehended northwest of Burning Springs. If anyone has coordinated with local law enforcement, please call off all searches as this Energy Alliance company matter has been resolved internally. Congratulations to all officers involved."

I click send and immediately lock the thread stopping all incoming messages and questions. That's going to look suspicious for sure, but I only need to disrupt our pursuit long enough for us to get to Ohio and get hidden.

Paul Wright's account is already receiving direct

messages with confirmations to the announcement as well as congratulations and requests for details. The real Mr. Wright should be none the wiser unless he is physically with someone that received the fake messages. Even then, the lockout should stop him from correcting the information personally. But of course that person could send out an announcement to correct my fake news. Oh, shit, though. I have access to *everyone's* accounts.

I go back down the list of everyone who was added to the "Levi Pickering" thread and log in as the first person on the list and change his password. Then I find the relevant thread for his specific team and forward my fake announcement from Paul Wright to his entire team. Then I return to the original thread and repeat the process for every senior member in that first thread. Now sufficiently proud of my chaos, I decide to fill in Isaac.

I poke my head out of the cabin and explain how and what I did as fast and plainly as I could. I tell him to drive casually and to go the original rendezvous as planned. Driving like a maniac now would only draw unnecessary attention.

Our rendezvous point is a bar on Virginia Street in Marietta called The Marina. It's a drop point that Isaac has used many times before. The bar owner is a part of the Network and happily stores medical supplies when immediate pick up can't be arranged.

This time, though, immediate pick up is required considering the sensitivity of today's cargo: the stolen data (not me). Ravinder, an EMT, will be called to a medical emergency at the bar. I'm to play the role of an idiot that got his ass kicked bad enough in a bar fight to require an ambulance.

Given my injuries, I'm very confident I can play the part.

I decide to stay in the cabin for the remainder of the trip. My appearance is too conspicuous. I have to believe authorities knew I was injured from the footage the drone captured earlier. I also want to monitor ComFlow for any additional chatter that might help us.

I look out the cabin door window to Isaac. He's got one hand on the wheel and the other is clenching his beard, his eyes forward. I think I can trust him and the hospital staff he plans on delivering me to, but I'd like to contact Kayla's brother to let him know I'm coming to Marietta. I need more friends than a syndicate of medical supply thieves despite how altruistic they believe their goals to be. Calling Devin now could be dumb, though.

My father had warned me that the Energy Alliance had been trying to get Devin extradited, so I'm sure the company is surveilling him if they're capable. I'm sure someone at the company is watching my profile's communications, too, waiting for me to contact him to get more evidence against him. I'll need to call him from something other than my watch.

I spend the next few minutes obsessively reading every new ComFlow thread that's been created since I sent the false messages. It seems like at the very least I succeeded in creating some confusion. Everyone wants to know who caught the terrorist, but no one is taking credit.

I rest my eyes by looking out the porthole towards shore and am surprised to see some city lights. We finally made it to the mouth of the river. Out the port side window, I find myself staring directly into a floodlight.

I stumble backward falling down onto the box I was sitting on. Squinting through the light, I can see the side of a much larger ship.

"Parkersburg City Police, prepare to be boarded," a male voice warns over a megaphone. Isaac kills the engines. A few minutes earlier, I talked him out of a suicide run. I now wish he had stuck to that conviction. I'd rather be captured in Ohio than here.

I think.

I power down my watch so as to not project any light out from the cabin. I get as low as I can to get out of view of either porthole or the cabin door window.

Two consecutive thunks hit the deck. I think we were boarded by two officers. The conversation isn't heated. Their voices get quieter over time. Now nothing. I sit motionless, swaying with the waters as they move our boat up and down.

"Oh, come on!" Isaac yells.

A stomp. This is it. My misinformation plan failed. I'm going to be arrested and I am going to have to explain why I helped these thieves and tried to flee to Ohio. Maybe I should just walk out and greet them with dignity. Or I could stay here among the cargo like a rat and cling to hope that this goes any other way.

Several seconds pass as I work up the courage to leave my hiding place. The door still hasn't opened. Wait. A *lot* of time has passed. If they want me, they should have me by now. On second thought, maybe I go with the rat plan.

A few more stomps and then nothing. The boat's

searchlights shut off and I'm back in total darkness save the few city lights I can see out the porthole. Isaac starts the engines and then, we're moving. I count out a minute in my head before poking my head out of the cabin. Isaac looks pissed.

"What the hell happened?" I ask.

"I got robbed," he says flatly. "There's this cop that shakes me down on this route every other time I pass through here. Evidently he got extra excited when he saw the bulletin about a boat carrying a terrorist with my license number on it. Son of a bitch doubled the fine for passing through his waters."

"Oh, thank God that's all it was."

"Yeah, thank God." Isaac flicks his chin at me. "I'm broke *and* the God damn Alliance took my wife, but you're safe. That's what matters."

"Sorry, Isaac, I didn't mean..."

He grunts and pushes the throttle forward. I decide to sit on the stairs to the cabin to get some air. The temperature has dropped since sunset. The Ohio's waters are twice as wide as the Little Kanawha's but they are also twice as choppy. Isaac's boat bounces uncomfortably with our speed. From my blurry, one-eyed perspective, Parkersburg's city lights dance up and down on one riverbank. The other side is dark, comparatively. The farther we travel upriver, the darker both sides become. Marietta is a few miles north of Parkersburg. But those few miles mean traveling in relative darkness in international waters. I count the few lights I do see to pass the time and stave off anxiety.

Marietta's lights eventually find their way into my cyclopean view and soon we're parking at a small dock with just room enough for two, maybe three boats, but ours is alone. Wooden stairs lead up to a deck that wraps around a French colonial-style house. The deck is all lit up and with picnic tables filled with people drinking, smoking and laughing. Country music plays through a speaker system mounted to the side of the building. A flat-screen TV is playing a baseball game. The Reds are beating the Padres 4-1.

Isaac helps me out of the boat, up the stairs and into the building. The bar is dimly lit and smells of booze and mildew. Despite the dinginess of the interior, the bar is at capacity. People of all shapes and sizes mingle. A loud murmur of slurred conversation fills the room. I couldn't be more out of place. Everyone's eyes find me. They look confused or disgusted or both. I guess not many men covered in bandages come to their bar traveling by boat.

A man with a dark complexion and green scrubs steps forward to greet us. Isaac reaches into his pocket and hands him the hard drive. He snatches it out of Isaac's hand.

Isaac frowns at him. "You're welcome."

"This is incredible! I can't believe we have this! But poor Myrna," the man talks fast with a thick British accent. He turns his attention to me. He lifts my arm and looks it over noticing the scratches and looks into my one good eye, getting uncomfortably close. I resist the urge to push him back.

"Stay here at the bar for a bit, Isaac. Have a drink. I'll get Mr. Casey set up at the hospital and give you a lift to the safehouse. I'll be in touch, soon."

"Got a few bucks? Parkersburg police got me again."

"Oh, of course," Ravinder taps his smartwatch on his wrist and Isaac pulls his old phone out of his pocket. "There you go."

"Thanks. First time I've had USD in a while. Normally don't stay on this side of the river long enough to need it."

Ravinder nods to Isaac and grabs me by the arm. "C'mon Mr. Casey. Let's get you to the hospital."

"Mr. Casey? What?" I ask.

"Ooh, it seems you've taken a very bad knock to the head, Mr. Casey. Can't even remember your own name, now? Let's go, now, c'mon. Excuse us." Ravinder starts to pull me through the crowded bar.

"Wait a damn minute." I turn around and lean forward to shake Isaac's hand. "Thank you, Isaac. And thank Myrna for me as well. I'll find some way to repay you once I get out of this, I promise."

He grunts and holds up his phone to my watch. His contact information loads into my address book.

"Good luck, Levi."

"You, too," I shake his hand again. "Alright. Let's go," I say to Ravinder.

"Yes sir, Mr. Casey. Right this way."

Ravinder leads me to an ambulance parked outside the bar. It looks ancient. We get into the back and he insists I sit down on a gurney secured to the right wall. This van is half the size of the ambulances we have (or had) on campus. A driver sits in the cab. Ravinder starts unwrapping my bandages around my ankle.

"Wouldn't it make sense to leave those on until we get to the hospital?" I ask.

"Medically, yes. But we have to make you look like you were just in a very nasty bar fight, so the bandages should come off. Also, drink this please." He hands me a flask. I unscrew the cap and take a sniff. It smells cheap. I take a swig. It's terrible, but not as bad Tobias's Apple Brandy 3.0. I should find a way to contact Tobias. I finish the flask as Ravinder removes the bandage from my head.

"Did you finish your drink?" he asks.

"Yes." I hand him the empty flask.

"Good. Sorry about this."

Ravinder sucker punches me in my one good eye. I recoil back and tear up. The pain from the one good side of my face radiates to the broken side.

"What the hell, man!? I've got a broken orbital wall on the other side. You could have killed me!" I scream at him.

"Bar fight, remember?" he says.

"Am I not fucked up enough already!?"

"Well, yes, but your wounds don't look very fresh. Myrna is a great nurse, I must say. You don't look nearly as bad as you should, considering your accident was only a few days ago."

"If you hit me again, and you might need to see Myrna, yourself."

"Oh, come now. No hard feelings. Lay back and let's get you strapped you in. We'll get you to the hospital and before you know it you'll be well enough to make good on your threat."

I wipe the water away from my one good but now increasingly swelling eye. I'm getting sick of being strung around by circumstance and injury. Ravinder's bedside manner was a far cry from the calm warmth I woke up to in Myrna's bedroom. But as much as I want to hit him right now, Ravinder isn't my enemy. I don't think. He straps me securely to the side of the ambulance.

"Alright, Robert. Let's get on then." The driver turns on the lights and we leave the bar's parking lot. "Now," he turns back to me. "Your name is Grant Casey. You're a wealthy investment banker from New York here on business. Tonight, you went to The Marina Bar and Grill and you got into a roe with several locals that you did not get a good look at. You'll receive the best care Marietta Memorial Hospital can afford to give you with the supplies bought with your very generous donation. If anyone asks you to fill out any forms, tell them to send the forms to your assistant, Myrna."

"Got it, but why would an investment banker be in this podunk town on business?" I ask.

"No one cares, Mr. Casey. Just relax."

I think I hate Ravinder. But I will take his advice. I lay my head against the plastic pillow and try to ignore the smell of my wounds coming from the right side of my face. Today's journey and stress are not good for my recovery.

Fortunately, the town is small and the trip is mercifully short. Within minutes we're parked and the ambulance doors swing open. I'm lifted and wheeled through the hospital's emergency room.

I'm too bruised and tired to fight or be suspicious anymore. My head is split. I can only see out of one eye. I can't walk. I got sucker-punched by an EMT. I've been branded a terrorist and most of my friends died in a river of fire and shit. I close the eye that still works. I'm so fucking done for today.

<thirteen>

"Mr. Casey! Please stay awake! You can't sleep now!" I hear a woman shout.

"Ugh. Okay. Why not?" I ask.

I open my eye to see a woman in green scrubs with her hair pinned under a cap leaning over me. Her eyes are as green as her scrubs. A surgical mask covers her mouth. Fluorescent lights on the ceiling pass over her head as she and two others push me down the hallway on a gurney.

"You may have a concussion. We need to put you through the protocol before we can let you sleep. It could be very dangerous for you to sleep now." She leans in close and looks into my open eye. "Good. Can you tell me what happened?"

"I'm here on business and I got jumped by a group of guys in a bar. They robbed me." I recite the story Ravinder gave me, expounding a little. I didn't have any identification on me and a robbery would explain why.

"That's awful. I'll have someone contact the police right away."

"No, no. That's okay," Shit. Nice story, Ravinder. Of course, the hospital would have to call the police. "I don't want to press charges. Uh, actually, could you just call my assistant, Myrna? She could help you get my information sorted."

The woman squints down at me through her protective eyewear for a long second as she processes what I'm saying. Finally, she nods.

"Sure, thing, Mr. Casey. My name is Doctor Elizabeth Rowley. We'll take good care of you." She looks over the right side of my face. Another woman takes my blood pressure and another takes my temperature. We turn into an elevator large enough to hold us all. The fog over my head is thick and this feels like a dream. I've never been hospitalized before. I wonder if this is what Gina experienced, too. I hope she's still alive.

I'm wheeled out of the elevator and down another hallway into a private room. They help me out of my clothes and into a hospital gown. It's not a pleasant experience for anybody. They raise the back of my gurney to prop me upright and Dr. Rowley pulls up a stool next to me. She dismisses the nurses.

"We can speak freely," she says, running her fingers over my fractured eye socket.

"Who brought you in?"

"Ravinder," I answer.

She pushes a button underneath a speaker on the wall. It's an old intercom system built into the building. I guess they don't have personal communication devices.

"This is Doctor Rowley. Please have Ravinder come to Mr. Casey's room." She releases the button and looks back at me. "Is it just the right side of your face?"

"No, I sprained my left ankle, too. Also, I haven't eaten anything since this afternoon." I look down at my watch. It's nearly midnight. The doctor directs me to look back up at her and she shines a flashlight into the swollen right side of my head. I try to be still.

"Can you see the light?" she asks.

"No."

"We'll need to get an x-ray and an MRI, but I think you have an orbital wall fracture. You likely have significant damage to your right eye."

"That's what Myrna said."

My least favorite EMT enters the room. Ravinder hands Dr. Rowley a piece of paper. She reads it over.

"Is this real?" Dr. Rowley asks.

"Seems so!" Ravinder smiles brightly and shifts his weight from his toes to his heels. "The lads in IT are pulling the data now. It's Christmas morning down there. They called in Eric, too. Also, given Mr. Casey's condition, he might be exactly what they've been waiting for."

"I don't think I like the sound of that," I say.

"It's good news," Dr. Rowley says to me.

"How is our VIP?" Ravinder asks.

"He's hungry, but he may need to be prepped for emergency surgery," Dr. Rowley says giving me a glance and half a smile. "We need to know the extent of the damage to your right eye. If it's bleeding or infected, we'll need to operate immediately. I'll go order the scans." She stands up. "A nurse will be in to treat your ankle and get you some ice for your black eye. That looks fresh, what happened there?"

"I was told I needed to look like I'd been in a bar

fight." I give Ravinder the most threatening look my disfigured face can muster.

"Again, sorry about that. I didn't know Elizabeth would be your doctor. Didn't want to take any chances."

"Good grief," Dr. Rowley shakes her head, and walks out. Fortunately, Ravinder follows her. I swing my legs up onto my bed and lean back to take the opportunity to rest my eyes.

My moment of peace is short-lived. A quick knock at the door and the nurses from earlier enter. One is pushing a wheelchair and the other is carrying an ice pack. As Dr. Rowley promised, they work together to put a fresh wrap on my ankle and ice the eye Ravinder blackened. Afterward, they help me into the wheelchair and I'm wheeled out.

We enter a room with what I assume to be an MRI machine. The machine has a single plastic arch mounted on two tracks that span the majority of the room. A table sits at the far end of the track. I assume that's the scanner's control panel.

The nurse pushing my wheelchair reaches down underneath the seat and pulls a lever. The two wheels at the base separate into four which slide up the backrest and secure in place with a click. She then reclines the back of the chair and raises the footrest effectively turning my wheelchair into a gurney. The nurse then wheels me into place underneath the arch while the other goes to the control panel.

"We'd like to start the scan now, Mr. Casey. Please lie as still as possible. It will only take a few seconds. Please, let us know when you're ready."

"Go ahead," I say.

The nurse at the control panel taps on the terminal. A chime plays, and a tiny electric motor whirs to life inside the arch just above my head. It inches forward down the tracks. A bright blue light shines into my eye as it passes. Seeing through the spots it left, I watch the straight blue line of light traverse its way down my body. It stops just past my feet. The blue light turns to red and the arch reverses taking a second pass. I anticipate the light's arrival and close my left eye before it can blind me again. The arch stalls for a moment before returning to its dock back against the wall. Another chime plays from the terminal.

"All set. The doctor has been sent your results and will be in to discuss them with you shortly. Would you like to sit up?" the nurse at the terminal asks.

"Yes, please, and I'd also like some water."

"I'm afraid that I can't give you water. Your stomach needs to be empty in case you need to go into surgery." Both nurses work to get me out from between the machine's tracks and sit me upright.

They leave and I'm left in the room alone. I decide to take the opportunity to check ComFlow for any news. Surely, they've pieced together I haven't been caught by now. I wheel myself over to the desk and boot up my watch's holoprojector. Paul Wright managed to get back into his account. A new thread titled "CEASE COMFLOW COMMUNICATION IMMEDIATELY" has been created. The first and only message reads:

"Refrain from using this communication channel moving forward. The fugitive, Levi Pickering, is still at large and is using ComFlow to spread false information."

I hear Dr. Rowley enter the room behind me. I power off my display.

"Am I interrupting something?" she asks.

"Just checking some messages," I say.

"I see. I take it *that's* how the billing department got paid?" she asks glancing down to my watch. I instinctively grab it, with my opposite hand shielding it from her

"It is." I remove my hand from the watch's face. "It only works for me, though, I'm afraid. Biometric access and all."

"Relax. I'm no thief."

"Aren't you?"

She puts up her palms and shrugs. "I understand why you'd see us like that, but you're going to have to trust us if you want your face fixed."

She sits down at the terminal on the opposite side. She taps on the surface. With each tap the terminal responds with a beep or a boop. A holoprojector from underneath the surface of the table emits a perfect replication of my body, hospital gown and all, lying down, but hovering a few inches above the table. The projection spans the length table effectively creating a digital holographic clone of me about three quarters the size. It has the same injuries.

"Woah," I can't contain my awe or feelings of disassociation.

"Pretty neat, huh? This scanner cost us almost our entire annual budget." Dr. Rowley pushes another button on the console and the projection loses its gown. It has no genitals. I assume that's to preserve my sense of dignity. Dr. Rowley taps on the console again and a frame appears over the projection's left ankle magnifying it within the area of the frame.

"The anterior talofibular ligament on your left ankle has been partially torn. Normally the treatment is rest and ice for two weeks, but we'll cut down the recovery time with stem cell injections," she says.

"Great."

"Now onto your eye." Dr. Rowley taps on the console and a similar frame appears over the right side of the projection's face. The view magnifies over the wound. The shape of my face has changed as the right side has sunk down. The bottom of my eye socket is so smashed, I can see where my cheeks begin. I cringe.

"Jesus Christ," I say. "Am I going to stay like this?"

"We can fix this," Dr. Rowley says assuredly. "As we thought, you have an orbital wall fracture. With reconstructive surgery and stem cell therapy, you'll look even better than you did before."

"Good."

"As for the eye itself, however..." She presses a few more buttons and the skin and skull disappear from the frame revealing a replication of my right eye. Or what used to be of it. It looks like a collapsed bag of red goop.

"I'll get another opinion, but it appears that your cornea has been irreparably damaged and your retinal blood vessels have completely ruptured. The bleeding is contained within the retina for now." She looks up from the projection and exhales. “You’re going to lose your eye. And to be safe, we need to operate immediately.”

“Oh my God...” I say out loud. My hand instinctively goes to my face. I spent the day trying to compensate for my lack of depth perception and it hadn’t been easy. I had moments where things simply disappeared from my right side altogether. I’d been favoring my left due to my ankle sprain but the truth is that I felt way more handicapped on my right. That can’t be my new normal.

“Are you sure? There’s no other way?”

“No. The remnants must be removed, and soon. Before infection sets in.”

“So, what happens after surgery? A glass eye?” I ask.

“If you like, but we have another option. But it comes with some conditions.”

“Here it comes. You know I could go to jail for a long time for what I’ve already given you people. What more do you want?”

“We need a personal commitment,” she says.

“I don’t understand.”

“We have a prototype for fully functional retinal prosthesis. Essentially, we would give you a glass eye wrapped in a new mechanical retina and connect it to your optical nerves.”

“You mean like a robotic eye implant?” I ask.

“I’m not sure anyone would use the term ‘robotic’ but I think you understand.”

“And I can see with it?”

“Theoretically.”

“Theoretically?” I ask.

“We’re not sure exactly what you’ll see or even if

it will work at all. We do know that once it's implanted, you'll need some significant rehab to get it functional. Your brain will work with the prosthesis to interpret light sent through your optic nerve, just like your brain does with your normal eye. You'll have an advantage since your left eye is functioning normally. Normal, biological eyes are sympathetic and the brain compensates when one eye is weaker than the other. We suspect the nature of the prosthetic is not much different. But we're not exactly sure how smooth that process will be."

"You sound like you're not sure of a lot of things with this."

She bites her lip. "It'll be the first time this surgery has been done by anyone, anywhere as far as we know. You'd be the first patient."

"I think I can guess how you acquired this unique piece of untested medical technology," I say.

"The company you work for has a wealth of resources." Of course, they stole it from the Energy Alliance. They have no idea what they have their hands on, and they want to Frankenstein it into me to learn how it works.

"Anything else I should know?" I ask.

"Yes. The prosthesis is network connected."

"To the Energy Alliance Intranet, I presume."

"We believe so, yes. We think the purpose is to share medical data from the eye to report its status. But there are also projectors in the prosthesis. Not outward-facing holoprojectors like the one on this table but it appears that information can be displayed on the *inside* of the retina."

"Like a heads up display?"

"Yes. To display information garnered from

optical input. Augmented reality."

"That's amazing," I admit.

"So, you'll do it?"

"Hell no! I'm not going to have an uplink to the Energy Alliance Intranet implanted into my head. And for all I know you could be lying about the severity of my injury just to get me to agree to be your test monkey."

"You have my word that no one in the Network would do anything like that. We're healers. I swear to you," Dr. Rowley says unblinking. I sigh taking her words at face value.

"Still, who knows what kind of personal data I'd be sharing. That's too much risk," I say. Techs at the Energy Alliance are already looking for any signs of me accessing the network. The fact Paul Wright got back into his account proves that. This implant could turn me into a walking security camera for them.

"It's not connected *all the time*," Dr. Rowley says. "It's at the user's control and you need a login."

"You sure about that?"

"Yes. Our biomechanical and information technologists have figured out the input functions. They're not sure how the user administers them once the eye is implanted, but we've managed to connect and disconnect the prosthesis from the network through our own makeshift control panel. Once we are connected, though, we can't get passed any login requirements."

"I'm surprised your Network doesn't have any credentials into the Energy Alliance Intranet."

"I didn't say *that*. I said we couldn't get passed these login requirements."

"The credentials you do have don't have enough privileges," I say. But mine for sure do, at least for now. "I'm guessing you want me to try mine and report back to you what I see?" I ask.

"*That's* the commitment we're looking for. With the medical data collected from your personal use and your instruction on how to input controls into it, we can manufacture copies. We'll cure blindness for a price everyone can afford. With the profit, we'll never want for any medical equipment or medicine or anything else again. We could truly practice medicine for no profit motive," she says.

Her green eyes are wide. I look into them for a moment and exhale through my nose.

"Look, Doc, it's been a long day. I get that I don't get enough time to sleep on this but can you give me some time to think? This seems like something that might be a bit hard to reverse if everything goes tits up."

"I don't recommend waiting that long. Your right eye needs to be removed. The longer we wait, the greater risk you run for internal bleeding or infection. I'm afraid you need to decide now."

"Of course I do," I say.

I look up into the fluorescent lights and hold my hand up to the damaged side of my face, tracing my fingers around the swollen flesh concealing the mush that used to be my right eye.

"Alright, its time to cut the bullshit," I say after a long pause. "Do you know who I am?"

"Yes," she answers.

"Do you know what I can do with this?" I tap on my watch.

"Yes."

"Does everyone here?"

"No."

"Does the IT department that works on the eye know?"

"Yes, and it's why you have this opportunity at all. The access you used to get us the medical database is needed to fully operate the prosthetic, *and more importantly to us* help us understand it.."

"Before I agree to this, I have more questions. Go get your senior tech on the eye and let's tinker with it. Getting my vision back is definitely enough of an attractive prospect for me to reconsider my position. But I want to minimize the risks. Also, please lend me a phone. I need to make a call."

"Sure. Eric is already here. I'll have him come up. We can wait a couple hours longer before proceeding with surgery but no more." Doctor Rowley taps on the terminal in front of her and the disturbing projection disappears. In its place, loads an image of the phone's dial pad. "Punch the number in here. It's on speaker. I'll knock before we return to give you your privacy. Use the room as long as you need it."

Dr. Rowley leaves. I place my watch on the table in front of me and turn on both of its holoprojectors: the display and keyboard. I can't wait any longer. It's nearly 1AM; hopefully he's awake.

"Who is this?" Devin answers. I hear techno music on the other end and a door close. The music goes quiet.

"A good friend of your sister's. Are you safe?"

"Holy shit. Yes, I'm fine, but not for their trying. I've got contacts that have been protecting me," he says.

“Glad one of us has friends. I’ve hit some good luck and made some new ones myself, otherwise, I’d be in there with her.” I do my best to avoid specifics in case anyone was listening. “Is this a secure line?”

“As good it gets. I kept it open thinking you’d call eventually. It’s forwarded through a VPN that hits different servers on each call. I ring up the number myself every five minutes and leave the line busy for two to three minutes to flood anyone who could be listening with nonsense metadata. You’re in through an old fashioned call waiting line.”

“Smart. I think.” Truthfully, I only have a vague idea of what he’s talking about. “How’s Kayla? Have you heard anything?”

“The Energy Alliance let her call me after she got arrested, but it was just so they could try and get information on my whereabouts. She’s okay for now. Have you been watching the news?”

“I haven’t found the time,” I say flatly.

“Kayla’s found herself a new friend, too. Titus Dunbar, of all people, is propping her legal defense.”

“Wow. Why would he do that?” I ask.

“Got me, but it might be doing more harm than good in the court of public opinion. People are saying he’s the mastermind behind a plot to destroy the Burning Springs campus to tank the Energy Alliance’s stock price.”

It’s the same story that Isaac told me yesterday. Dunbar shorts the stock using an offshore investment company and then hires Kayla and I to wreck the campus during the derecho. The storm gets blamed for the damage covering up any wrongdoing. The stock price tanks and he gets paid.

“Listen, I’ve got a more immediate problem I

need to talk to you about. Do you know where I am?" I'm still being intentionally vague with my whereabouts. Devin said the line is secure but after a day of being chased, I still feel the need to be careful.

"I do. You're surprisingly close by. How'd you get here?"

"I'll tell you later. Can you come over here? I need you to help me look at something."

"What? No way!"

"Look, Devin. It's important. I'm hurt and tied up with these medical supply smugglers–it's a long story. I exhale and look at my watch. "But also, and I'm not sure how, I have access to the entire Energy Alliance Intranet."

"You do!?"

I give him the abbreviated story of how I got here. After I finish, he pauses. Says nothing for a while.

"Dev–"

"Ack! Fuck! Fine. You're in a big place. How will I find you?"

"I'll send someone, but come quick. It's an *emergency*." I emphasize the word "emergency" hoping he'll put it together to come to the ER. I'll ask Dr. Rowley to have Ravinder bring him up.

"Understood. I'll be there soon." He sniffs and hangs up.

The terminal's display flashes red and changes back to a dial pad. I turn my attention to my watch's holo display and log into the medical database. I search for "retinal prosthesis". Sure enough, the database has all the information I could ever want to read about the implant.

<fourteen>

Devin had checked in with the name "Longinus" complaining of stomach cramps. He frightened the receptionist with histrionics who alerted security. Evidently, Ravinder had to convince a security guard that Devin was no threat. And because he checked in, he created the start of a paper trail that would have to be removed. I know all of this because Ravinder enjoyed telling me what an idiot my friend is and how much he had to work to do to get him up here. Fortunately, Ravinder left after telling me this.

Devin is short, wiry and well dressed. He looks as though he could have come from a nightclub. Seeing him so well-groomed gives me a bit of a pause on my own appearance. The nurses redressed the wounds on my head, but I am far from my best self and I can't shake the imagery of the projection Dr. Rowley showed me earlier.

But really, I'm too exhausted to care much about my appearance and tired of feeling vulnerable. The painkillers Myrna gave me wore off hours ago and my face is hot and throbs with every heartbeat.

Devin looks at me with pity, and I see a little Kayla in his face.

I tell him everything I've been through after I hung up on him the day of the hack. My voice gets weaker and my throat swells as I talk. He doesn't interrupt or ask questions. He paces the floor, stopping intermittently to look through the blinds into the hospital parking lot. I'm not a hundred percent sure he's been listening. He turns to me and licks his gums.

"Do you realize what you have here?" He points to my watch.

"I think so. But I need your help to make the best use out of it."

"Can I see?"

I pull up a table next to my hospital bed and take the watch off my wrist. I lay it down flat and activate the holoprojectors for the keyboard and display. I log in and show him the control panel.

"This is incredible! With this level of access, we should be able to see all the different network traffic that happened during the hack. This is how we prove our innocence!"

"Only if the Energy Alliance is interested in the truth, but I can't focus on that right now. I need to decide whether or not I'm going to take this implant." I pull up the files on the retinal prosthesis. "Here."

Devin quickly reads through the first screen. "It looks like just another interface to the Energy Alliance Intranet, but it functions like an actual eye?" he asks.

"That's what they tell me."

"Do you want to do it?" he asks.

"I don't know. I want my sight back, obviously, but I don't want to take it and immediately tip off EAS to my location. If I do take it, it's not like I can just pop it out of my head if I change my mind."

"You're probably running the same risks by using your watch. It's just different data, but it's talking to the same systems. Leaving a similar trail."

"I already thought about that. I used the administration terminal to disable my watch's GPS. So far, it's worked great. All settings I've changed on the terminal have stuck."

"That's because you're the only one who has access to edit your profile or alter its permissions," he explains as he fidgets around the room. "I've been trying to crack back in ever since the day of the hack, but I haven't had any luck. All security holes I've used in the past have been patched. Whoever wrote that thing knows the Energy Alliance Systems inside and out."

"Hm."

"Anyway, if you decide to take the implant, just make sure it's not connected to the Intranet. It should function fine without network connectivity. I've got to believe the Energy Alliance has every admin and developer trying to crack back in." He pauses and grinds his teeth. "I bet they're even forcing Kayla to work from her cell."

"That's probably true," I say. The Alliance is notorious for using penal labor. Unskilled or otherwise. "She's tough though, man. She'll be okay."

"I know. When they do eventually get back into the network, they may gain control of the eye. And you don't want that," he says.

"No, I don't."

Devin walks back over so he can see the documents on the projection. We sit in silence reading as much as we can. I shift in my bed.

"So, you think I can manage the implant like I do my watch?" I ask.

"This says it's assigned to you just like any other personal device. I'd need to read through the rest of the documentation to know everything, though."

"Sure, keep reading. I'll call the doctor. She said she'd bring in her senior technologist for us to ask questions." I press the intercom on the wall. "Could you please tell Dr. Rowley we're ready to talk?"

A minute later, Dr. Rowley and a really fat guy with salt and pepper hair and a long gray beard enter the room. He walks over and I notice he's carrying a plastic container. He shakes my hand. His is wet and his fingernails are yellow. He smells like cigarettes.

"We're very excited to have you here, Mr. Casey," he says.

Devin nods to me evidently pleased that I have an alias. "I'm Longinus." He reaches out to shake the man's hand himself.

"Nice to meet you. I'm Eric DeVoss." Eric looks to the projection emitted from my watch. "I see you found the documentation on the prosthesis. I've been reading it since you got in. It's exciting stuff for us."

"I'm a freelance software developer and I'm starting to wrap my head around it, too," Devin interjects. "My friend is concerned about being connected to the Energy Alliance Intranet."

"Understandably so, but we couldn't get

connected even if we wanted to. We have a login for the Intranet but it didn't grant us the access we need. It stopped working altogether a few days ago."

"The day of the cyber attack?" I ask.

"Yes."

"Is that it?" Devin asks, pointing to the container Eric is holding.

"Yep." He places it on the table in front of us.

"How much have you tested it so far?" Devin asks.

"We got to the source code and understood it well enough to figure the retina's basic functions. We even built a dummy terminal to get a dump of its output. It's extensive. To really understand it, though, we think we need to be connected to the Energy Alliance Internet as it was intended."

"Can we power it on?" I ask. "I assume it has a wireless network connection like other Energy Alliance tech. My watch should be able to pick it up."

"Sure." Eric opens the container. The prosthesis looks like an eyeball with a gray iris wrapped in a thin clear squishy-looking bag. A short black cable winds out the back of it. There's a black box at the end of the cord with a tiny switch. Eric flips it. Small, red and white text flashes in front of the eyeball projected onto the bag.

"What's its power source?" I ask.

"When implanted, it's mostly biochemical. You'll power it by eating, just like every other part of your body. This box here powers it when it's not implanted. The retina also has a film of millions of microscopic multi-band antennae to pull energy out of radio waves to supplement the biochemical power," Eric explains.

"My watch has the same. It also has solar panels. The battery life is great. I have to charge it on a power station about once a week." And I'll need to soon. My battery is at 20%.

A notification pops up on my watch's projection. It reads, "Energy Alliance Ocular Enhancement detected." I tap it, and a device profile page loads up showing me a list of features and settings. Eric walks around the table to get a better look at my projection. He leans over resting his gut on my bed. I scoot over to avoid touching him.

I read down the listing to GPS and tap it to "Off". Another notification: "Are you sure you wish to disable the GPS? Some AR features will also be disabled."

"Exactly what AR features does this thing have?" I ask the room.

"We're not certain of all of them, but we know you'll be given some additional information about your surroundings. We have found some functions specifically designed for fieldwork on oil and gas drilling sites."

"Oh, right. Some of the guys back at Burning Springs used that. My friend Tobias carries around a tablet. He'd hold up the camera to whatever he needed data from and data would be displayed on the tablet's screen overlaid onto an image or live view of what he was pointing the camera at. He'd tap on his tablet to call up whatever data he wanted. How can you interact with the eye?"

"That's something we don't know. The projection is inside the retina. Only the user can see it, and it can't be interacted with," Eric answers.

"Your watch," Devin answers. "The documentation says there's a companion app you need to download onto your watch. Download it, pair the eye with your account and you should be able to control the HUD."

"What if I don't want to use the AR or pair my account and just use it as a normal eye?" I ask. "I mean, it can't be that useful outside a well pad right? I'd rather just have it disconnect from the network altogether."

"It does look like it can be disconnected at any time. Just change this setting," Devin answers having scrolled down deeper into the documentation. "But the AR might have some uses not related to working a well pad. There's no reason to assume that it's only meant for gas work."

"If you do that, our deal is off," Dr. Rowley says flatly. She's remained silent until now. "Remember our goals, too. We need the raw data collected from how you use the eye. Otherwise we won't be able to replicate the software to run the prosthesis. I assume that network connectivity is required to log that raw data. Right, Eric?" she asks.

"Right," he answers.

"Well, you said your goal is to cure blindness," I say. "Here's the deal the way I see it. I'll take the prosthesis, but the GPS stays off at all times. I'll upload data onto the network while I rehab to get my vision back and I'll provide exports of the data whenever you like, but that's it. My vision isn't worth compromising my freedom."

"Eric?" Dr. Rowley asks.

"Sounds good to me," he says.

"Devin?" I ask, mocking Dr. Rowley.

"I don't love it, but you've been using your watch the same way so that should be fine," Devin answers.

"Great. What now?" I ask the room.

"We prep you for surgery," answers Dr. Rowley.

"First we need to install the software," Devin says. He taps on the projection. Following as closely as I can, I watch him pair the implant to my account and install the partner app onto my watch. "There you go. You should be ready to start using the eye when you wake up. Assuming the surgery goes well." He scrunches his face.

"It will," Dr. Rowley says.

I power down my watch's projectors and ensure the biometric locks are in place. I hold it out to Devin. "Can you take care of this for me? I want it back the moment I wake up. We can work on what we discussed earlier."

"Uh... I don't think you can trust this with me." He holds up his hands defensively. "I'll explain later. Your watch is probably better off with Eric."

"I think it's best kept in the safe with our security," says Doctor Rowley. The coldness she expressed earlier has left her voice. "Levi, you're trusting us with your life when you're undergoing surgery. Your watch should be your last concern, but I can promise you'll get it back. You already gave us everything we need off of it until we start collecting data from the implant. The rest is your business."

"Thank you." I hand her my watch. She puts it into her jacket pocket.

"We need to get started immediately. I'm afraid I'm going to have to ask you two to leave," she says to Eric and Devin.

"I'll be around if you need anything. Sincerely, thank you for doing this," Eric shakes my hand again before leaving. I discretely wipe my hand on the bedsheets.

"Call me on the same number when you're up and ready," Devin says.

"Will do."

As soon as Devin is out the door, Dr. Rowley uses the intercom to call for the nurses. She also orders the front desk to alert the anesthesiologist to set up in Operating Suite A1. I guess that's where I'll be heading.

"Do you have any questions?" she asks.

"Yeah. How the hell are you going to attach that thing to my brain?"

"Very carefully," she nods smiling with her eyes. She sits down on the stool next to my bed. "A team of eight surgeons, five them AI, will be working for the next twenty hours or so to build a bridge from the wires on the back of the prosthesis to your optical nerve. The prosthesis is then placed along the same muscle lining as your old eye. Then a cosmetic surgeon will begin to reconstruct your orbital wall and cheekbone. As I mentioned before, stem cells will be used to regenerate all damaged tissue."

"Will the eye move like my other eye?"

"We think so. The software team found functions that listen for the movement of your extraocular muscles. But again your orbital wall has been damaged. It's likely the muscles that move your eye have also been damaged. They will also need to be rehabilitated."

"What about the color? Am I going to have one

gray eye?"

"I'll get you a Sharpie."

"Funny."

She tilts her head. "I don't think the iris can change colors, but I'll ask. Is that a deal-breaker?"

"No, but I'm sure I'll have a lot more questions after the surgery."

"So will we." She raises her eyebrows, looking through me. "Are you ready to go?"

"I guess."

Dr. Rowley opens the door to let the nurses back in. They help me into a wheelchair and push me down the hallway into the elevator. Dr. Rowley follows closely behind. We go up to the seventh floor down another long hallway and into a vestibule. A sign beside the door reads "A1".

Through a second pair of glass doors opposite to those that we entered, I see the operating room is crowded with steel and plastic machinery. One man is tinkering with a machine next to the bed. Another comes into the vestibule to greet us.

"Welcome, Mr. Casey. My name is Doctor Tsi-Ang. We're very excited to have you here, today." He talks to me like it's my first day of school. He may also have some sort of disorder where he can't control the volume of his voice.

"You and everyone else. *I* am very excited to get some sleep," I answer, my voice a little sharper than I intend.

"Mr. Casey has had a very long day," explains Dr. Rowley.

"Ha! Ha! Of course! Let's let Mr. Casey get some rest."

"I'll come to see you as soon as you're awake and

ready," Dr. Rowley says.

"Thanks. Take care of my watch."

"I will." She squeezes my shoulder and leaves. The two nurses follow her out, leaving me alone with Dr. Tsi-Ang. He presses a button on the wall and the doors leading into the operating room swing open. He pushes me inside giving me a better look at the equipment.

Up close, the machines look even more bizarre. Two robotic arms loom over the bed. Five human-like fingers sit at the end of each robotic arm's hand, but each would-be fingertip has even more protruding digits as if each finger has its own separate tiny hand.

"I see you're admiring my assistants. State of the art machinery! I assure you're in lots of good hands, Mr. Casey!"

Maybe shock or sleep deprivation caused it but for some reason I didn't fully acknowledge the terrifying situation I am now in. I start to sweat. Those little robotic hands will be doing things *inside my skull*. And this man, seemingly more fit to serve juice boxes to five-year-olds is running this shitshow. He helps me up onto the bed. The robotic arms rear overhead, ready to pick me apart.

"This is Dr. Whitehead. He's here to help you relax," says Dr. Tsi-Ang. The man beside the bed gives me a nod and quickly sticks a needle into my right arm. I flinch.

"Please sit still, Mr. Casey. You wouldn't want any unnecessary scratches now, would you? Ha! Ha! Try counting backward from twenty for me, will you? Out loud, please." He reminds me of the Count from Sesame Street. I really am in kindergarten.

"Twenty. Nineteen. Eighteen." I do as I'm told and continue counting staring at the nightmarish claws above my head. My face throbs with every number I count down. Soon, and in rhythm, the ceiling starts to shift above my head, turning clockwise and bouncing back to where it should be.

I'm looking down on the campus from the adjacent mountain. Every building and everybody is drowning in a river of fire. I can hear them screaming my name. I scream back, but my voice is silent. I look down at my hands. They are not wet with rainwater, but with blood. The heat from the fires burns my face. I reach up to protect it, but I can't raise my hands.

I can't do anything. I can't save anyone or even myself. But I do know that I did this. I caused this landslide of fire. I killed everyone, and I meant to do it.

<fifteen>

I try to open my eyes and raise my hands to my face. Half is still covered in bandages and I can't get underneath them to scratch the itchy flesh they're protecting. It's fine. The itch is so far away, I don't care. My body is radiating with a warm comfort only opiates can provide. I rub out the sleep from my left eye and stretch my jaw. A line of heat crawls up to my ear and with effort I rotate my head. It's heavy.

"Oh, good, you're awake. How're you feeling, Mr. Pickering?" a woman asks.

"Good. Stiff. How long have I been out?" I tilt my head side-to-side to crack my neck and sit up.

"If I had to guess I'd say you've been here for about thirty-six hours," she says.

I lift myself up and look toward the voice. A blonde woman in a gray skirt and jacket sits in a chair leaned against the wall at the foot of my bed with her legs crossed. She dangles one of her high-heeled shoes off her toes letting it swing in the air. A gold pin of the new United States flag is attached to her lapel. She smiles warmly and looks at me through a pair of gold-rimmed glasses.

"Who're you?" I ask.

"I'm Agent Gabrielle Vaughn. Nice to meet you, Mr. Pickering."

The word "Agent" clears some of the morphine induced fog I was enjoying. "I think you're in the wrong room. Name's Casey. Not Pickering," I say trying really hard not to slur my speech or sound as scared shitless as I am. She doesn't break eye contact or stop smiling. I push the nurse's call button.

"Oh? All these hospital rooms look the same. I must have gotten lost," she says.

She knows exactly who I am and I suspect has the authority to do whatever she wants about it. A knock at the door and Dr. Rowley enters the room. She raises her eyebrows at the agent.

"I'm sorry. Mr. Casey isn't ready for visitors yet," she warns.

"Of course. Sorry to intrude. Here, Mr. Casey." The agent places a card on the table next to my bed. "If you happen to hear from Mr. Pickering, please have him contact me. He's got something we're very interested in and I think we can come to an agreement that would be mutually beneficial."

"You are going to have to leave my patient's room now," Dr. Rowley says.

"Such strict policies at this hospital," the agent says and walks toward the door with slow deliberate steps, each accentuated by the clack of her high heels. She flashes a smile to Dr. Rowley that seems more threatening than polite. "Do reach out soon, Mr. Casey."

She closes the door behind her. The doctor and I

exchanged nervous looks. We listen to her heels clack down the hallway and wait until they're out of earshot before breaking our silence.

"Who was that?" Dr. Rowley asked.

"No idea. She was here when I woke up. Said her name was Vaughn." I pick up the card in front of me. "FBI."

"Shit. I'm going to have to make some calls," she says.

"Sorry if I got you into trouble."

"We knew the risks when we took you on and have contingencies. How do you feel?"

"Okay. I've got to piss and my face is itchy."

The doctor laughs. I was ambivalent about her at first, but Dr. Rowley is growing on me. She reminds me of Gina.

"You don't have to pee. You're wearing a catheter."

"Oh." I wince.

"Don't worry. It's standard for major surgeries. Now you're awake, I'll order it removed." She looks down at her tablet and taps on it. She reaches into her poket and hands me my watch. "Here. I decided to keep it on me."

"Thanks. That might have been for the best given that agent got passed your security."

"Mm." Dr. Rowley stares passed me. "Are you hungry?"

"A little."

"You should eat if you can. I'll have a nurse bring you some breakfast. When you're up to it, I'd like you to talk to Eric about giving us our first data dump."

"I take it the surgery was a success then?"

"Dr. Tsi-Ang thinks so. The implant is connected to your brain and should already be transmitting data, but we won't know for sure until you use your watch to confirm it. We are eager to see but take your time. Your health comes first."

"Thanks. So, how long before I can take the bandage off?"

"We'll change your wrap after you eat, but don't expect much. With stem cell therapy, your total recovery time should be about a week. I recommend you stay here for the next three days so we can monitor your progress."

"Three days, huh?" I've just been operating out of necessity since the day of the cyber-attack. There are so many people I need to contact, but I need to do it carefully. I should call Devin first. "I know you said no visitors yet, but I need to get Devin back here. I think. If that agent knows I'm here, he might be in trouble, too."

"No problem. I just said that to get rid of her." Dr. Rowley stands up and walks toward the door. "Have Devin come directly to the sixth floor, and not through the ER. Okay?"

"I'll tell him."

"A nurse will be in to change your bandage and remove your catheter in an hour or so." She holds up a stick with a button on the end and hands it to me. "Hit this if the pain starts to come back."

"Thanks"

"Get some rest."

"Sure" I say, but I have had enough rest for now. Doctor Rowley leaves the room. I set the watch on my bedside table and boot it up. The battery is at 100%. She must have charged it for me. A flash of green light surprises me. I turn my head to the right to find its source. The light lingers, but I can't focus on it.

I close my left eye. Green text is projected in the darkness in front of me: "Energy Alliance Personal Assistant connected." I try to look up with the new eye to focus on it. It takes effort. The text disappears, and again I see nothing.

Back on my watch, I check my profile for the implant's settings. Nothing else on my profile has changed. It's probably safe to assume that Energy Alliance IT still can't get access to my profile. Out of curiosity, I re-enable the Augmented Reality feature without GPS of course. Nothing. I assume it's because the eye is covered. It doesn't have a picture to augment. I'll play with it more later.

"Hello?" he answers.

"Hey, I'm up."

"How are you?" he asks.

"Pretty okay. But we got a problem. An FBI agent came to the hospital. Her name is Vaughn. She–"

"Shit! Don't say anything else. Period. I'm on my way."

"Uh... okay, but just come right up to my room. No need to check-in."

Devin hangs up and I get nervous again. There's a knock on my door.

It's a nurse with my breakfast: oatmeal, crackers, and soymilk. I choke down a couple bites of oatmeal and eat the crackers. I hate oatmeal but I'm starving. While I eat, I look through the documentation for the rest of the implant's settings.

There's nothing exciting: just some on and offs for the network, AR, and profile assignment. I also don't see how to get the data dump Eric is going to want. He might have to figure that out himself. Oh shit, that's right. Devin said he installed a partner app on my watch.

I navigate over to my watch's applications and tap the new icon. The text "Energy Alliance Ocular Enhancement Partner" loads onto the screen, but then it opens to a console. I'm staring at a black box with a green cursor. I have no idea what to type. I guess I'll have to go back to the documentation to figure out what I can do from here. Or I can just wait for Eric and Devin. I'll take the doc's advice and rest.

I flip on the TV for any news involving the Burning Springs incident. Nothing. I guess the media have already moved on. I let it play. Eventually the talking head's voice fades into the background and I doze off.

I wake up to find Devin searching my room. He sees me rouse and holds up one finger over his lips to tell me to keep quiet. He points to my watch.

"Turn it off," he whispers.

I do. He takes an old cell phone out of his pocket and taps on its screen. The bed phone rings. Outside the door, the nurses' desk phone rings, too. The intercom beside my bed buzzes. The T.V. goes to static. I hear more phones ring down the hall and then fire alarm goes off. I look at Devin wide eyed and confused.

My stomach churns and I taste vomit. I cover my ears. Devin grabs my wrist and I look up. He gets right in my ear and whispers. "Where was Vaughn?"

I point to the chair at the foot of my bed and he walks over and rips up the cushion, removing device no bigger than a penny. He taps on his smartphone again and the ringing everywhere stops.

“A bug?” I ask.

“Yep. And this one doesn’t just record and transmit audio. It’s also a packet sniffer. She’s probably tunneled into the hospital network and has been listening to everything since she’s been here, if not longer.”

“If that’s the case, that might not be the only bug,” I say.

“I guarantee it’s not, but it’s probably the only one in this room. It doesn’t matter, anyway. My little transmission...” He wiggles his phone. “...should have disrupted all of them in and around the building. But you should call Eric and tell him to check his network for any unwanted connections.”

“Won’t Vaughn know that the bugs have been disabled?” I ask.

“Oh yeah. And she’ll know I did it, too.”

“Aren’t you worried?”

He looks disheveled. He was jumpy when I first met him but he’s a little calmer this morning. Although, his hair is mussed and he’s just wearing jeans and a t-shirt.

“Levi, I’m fucking terrified. Vaughn and I have an arrangement. It’s what I wanted to talk to you about the other night, but there wasn’t time. Truth be told, I was more worried when she didn’t know anything and I had to be concerned with trying to hide you from her.” He sits down and rubs his eyes. “I’m sorry.”

“For what?”

“Even though I didn’t mean to lead her to you, she had to have found you by surveilling me. Vaughn got the best of me and honestly, I’m not sure how she did. I'm normally ahead of her."

"It might not have been your fault anyway. I've been running from EAS for a few days. Anyone who knew that I had been picked up by the Network back in Burning Springs and knew I'd made it across the border could track me here. Can you back up a bit though? You said you have an arrangement with Vaughn?"

"Yeah." He leans forward and rests his elbows on his knees. "Did Kayla ever tell you why I live in Ohio?"

"No."

"So, a while back I got in a bit of trouble." He puts the cushion back on the chair and sits down. "I ran a streaming service that didn't exactly have all the right permissions to share its content."

"What do you mean? You pirated movies? Everyone does that."

"Sure, but I also got TV series that hadn't been released yet from studios that don't have the most secure servers. Including from studios in Atlanta."

"Okay?"

"When Georgia seceded, the studios in Atlanta created their own security forces and cooperated to enforce copyright laws. When I got caught, I didn't wait for them to come to Parkersburg. I fled to Ohio knowing the U.S. wouldn't extradite me to a private security force."

"Makes sense."

"But, I was arrested here, anyway. I was also being prosecuted in the SDRA by studios in California. The US *would* extradite me to them since there's precedent: they're a foreign government. Agent Vaughn has somehow been indefinitely suspending my extradition."

"Why did she help you?"

"Because of Kayla. She acknowledged my ability to get files that companies don't want to share. And she knew I have a sister that, at the time, had just been hired by the Energy Alliance to do IT. She figured I could get her information the FBI either couldn't get or didn't want to be caught getting. So, in exchange for her help, I've been tunneling into the Energy Alliance Intranet and giving her anything I can get."

"Does Kayla know about this?"

"She knows why I ran to Ohio, but she doesn't know I'm giving data to the FBI. And I'd prefer to keep it that way."

I shift in my bed. The morphine is starting to wear off. The stress of this whole situation is starting to catch up to me, probably because I finally have some nervous energy and some rhythmic pain thumping in my face. I push the button to kill it.

"Why does the FBI want the Energy Alliance's data?" I ask.

"They claim for national security, whatever that means anymore. They keep pushing me to get information on the American Republic's smart grid. I guess they want it if they ever had to take it out if the new countries went to war."

"That's a scary thought."

"No doubt." Devin leans back in his chair. We sit in silence for a moment.

"Wait... do you think this Vaughn or the FBI could be behind the hack that took out our campus?" I ask.

"I doubt it. I'd bet she hacked the hospital

network to try and get at the data you have access to from your watch. If she'd been behind the hack at Burning Springs, she wouldn't have to fool with any of that or me at all anymore for that matter. She'd have everything she ever wanted already," he says.

"She did say that I had something she wanted. Do you trust her?"

"Only as much as I have to. I give her just enough to keep the deal going. When she gets cute with things like this," he holds up the bug he pulled from the chair, "I pull back. She hasn't reneged on our deal, yet. I guess I've proven myself useful enough that I don't have to capitulate to everything that she wants."

"Should I?"

"I don't know. Maybe." Devin is starting to sound exasperated. He gets up out of his chair and starts fidgeting as he did the other night. "To be honest, though, I'm not sure if she can offer a sweet enough deal for you. It's one thing to deny a country or company a con's extradition for breaking IP laws, but terrorism is something else."

We're interrupted by a knock at the door. It's the nurse Dr. Rowley warned me was coming. She has familiar round face and curly red hair. I recognize her from when I was first brought in on the gurney.

"Mr. Casey. I'm Nurse Kara," she says. "How're you feeling?"

"Itchy."

"We've got a cream for that. You ready to take off your bandages?"

"Ew, wait. Should I be in here in for this? Is it going to get gross?" Devin looks extra panicky. "Forget it. I'll just wait outside." He shuffles out the door before anyone can answer him.

Kara walks to the opposite side of my bed and starts unwrapping the bandages. Having the pressure off my face brings some relief. I can feel every fiber of the wrap as it's released from my skin. The fresh air on the new flesh stings with cold. Instinctively, I try to open my eye, but can't. It's swollen and crusted shut.

"Hold very still." The nurse picks up a pair of tweezers, leans in close to remove some straggling threads of cotton left by the gauze around my eye.

"Will I be able to open my eye soon?" I ask.

"Yes. I'll remove the fluid around your eye and free your eyelids," Maddie answers. "Can you see any light?"

"No, *but* I did see some messaging displayed on the prosthetic when I booted up my watch."

"Really? Like text?" Maddie asks.

"Yeah, it was a confirmation message saying it connected to my watch."

"That's great news. It means the optic nerve bridge placement was a success."

"All finished." Kara straightens up and drops the tweezers into a plastic bin. She looks over every inch of my face, and lightly presses around my eye socket with her fingertips. The pressure doesn't hurt, but the surface of her latex glove stings as it slides over the new flesh. She backs up.

"This looks good. The orbital wall is healing nicely," she says. "Okay, this is going to sting a bit, but to get your eye to open, we need to flush it with water. I'm going wring out a cloth above your eye. We may need to do it a few times."

She undersold it. It burns like hell, but some

pressure is released on the underside of my eyelid. My face feels lighter. I squint to loosen some more fluid. After another dousing, the doctor pushes on my eyelid, wiggles it loose and wipes out some discharge from my eyelashes. Finally, she pries open my eyelid freeing the top from the bottom.

"Can you see anything?" she asks.

"Nothing." I feel deflated. "Wait. Maybe. Move your head again." She shifts side to side. I close my left eye to be sure, but I think I see her or at least her silhouette. Now, nothing.

"Damnit! I thought I saw you for a second," I say.

"Be patient with it. And keep your left eye open. The prosthesis is sympathetic. The more you use it, the more your brain will get used to processing the new type of information it's receiving."

I nod. It's unrealistic to think this was going to be an instant solution. Dr. Rowley is back leaning over me, closely examining the wounds around my face. I blink several times trying to trigger what I saw before.

"I don't think we need to rewrap your wounds. We'll get you a mask instead." Dr. Rowley taps on a tablet a few times.

"A mask?"

"Yes, a piece of plastic that will protect your face while it heals. It won't sit directly on your wounds. The bridge of your nose will prop it up. You should only need it for a few days."

"Does it look bad?" I ask.

She smiles. "You look fine. Don't worry about that."

Kara reaches down to the bottom of the cart and hands me a mirror. My eyelid is still swollen, but I can see the faintest bit of gray of the prosthetic's iris underneath. The flesh around my face is blotchy. Little patches of new pink flesh surround the skin that I assume was either undamaged or already healed. I look *great* compared to the nightmare projection she showed me after my scan.

"Huh. Not too bad," I say looking as closely as I can with my one good eye. I'm hit with another flash of recognition from the prosthetic. I can see the roundness of the hand mirror's frame and light emitting from the glass. I flip the mirror around and it disappears. I flip it again and I get another flash, but only for a second before it disappears again.

<sixteen>

The doctor lied. The mask sits on my face wounds. Doctor Rowley gave me a cream to help with the itch, and I can't get enough of it. I apply more than I should every few minutes. Apparently it's expensive and I shouldn't do that, but I don't care. I'm itchy. The ointment makes my face sticky. And the mask sticks to my face and itches. It's a gross cycle.

Devin came back in the room but has been keeping his distance with his eyes defensively glued to his smartphone until now. It took him a while but he's worked up the courage to come inspect me.

"You don't look that bad," he says scrunching his nose

He's lying, too.

"You should have seen the initial scans," I say. "It was like the inside of my face had been through a meat grinder and all that goop was falling out of my eye socket."

"Ew." He leans in closer. "You might even be cute when these red splotches heal up."

"Your sister seems to think so."

"Hm." He doesn't bite. "Can you see?" he asks. Devin waves his hand in front of my face.

"Better? I think. I can see fine out of my left eye, but I'm still blind in my right. I get flashes of recognition like my field of view is slowly getting wider, but it's random. When I do see things out of my right eye, I only see outlines, and they also have to be pretty close to my face." I pick up the hand mirror off the table. "I can see this best."

He takes it from me and looks it over. "Maybe because the shape is simple." The mirror has a round head and a plastic handle. "Can you see anything in the reflection?"

"No, but I see a flash of light if I reflect it from the ceiling."

"Weird."

"So, beyond that, I can see text projected onto the retina. I tested it a couple of times. I can always see the connection confirmation message every time the implant connects to my watch."

"Have you tried the partner app?" Devin asks.

"I did, but it just boots up into a console. I have no idea what to type into it."

"You shouldn't have to use a console to interact with it."

"It's the only thing that pops up whenever I open the app. Do you want to see?" I say.

"Sure."

I load the app from my watch and reverse the projection to show Devin the black box. He looks closely at it.

"I'm not sure why it loads to this box but there's no cursor, so I doubt you can type anything into it.

The documentation said the partner application is a support app. It's probably something that's just loaded onto your profile's OS that's interacting with the Energy Alliance Intranet. Have you tried using your personal assistant?" he asks.

"I didn't think of that," I admit. "Caroline, will you show me the full list of survivors from the June 14th accident at Burning Springs, and display it on my AR?" I ask.

"Compiling. Displaying list now," Caroline answers, her voice coming from my watch's speakers.

The list appears on the prosthetic's projection. Just like the confirmation messages from before, I can read it no problem. The list consists of who I believe to be doctors, nurses and other Base hospital personnel, as well as the guards I warned at the front gate. Also shown are myself, Kayla and Zeke. Noticeably absent are Gina and Micah. Micah was driving around campus on his ATV at the time– it's no surprise he didn't survive. Also, Jerry Xun's name didn't appear on the list. I assumed he and Silas were still in the conference center when the landslide hit, and it looks like I was right. I look up to Devin. He's watching me read.

My throat starts to swell. I thought I was prepared to process this but maybe not. I think in the back of my mind I assumed everyone who was in the hospital that night had somehow survived.

"Are you okay?" Devin asks.

"How did Zeke make it but Gina didn't?" I ask.

"I don't know. Kayla and I only had a couple minutes to talk since that night."

I read down the list again. Nine out of forty-three.

I shake my head at the thought, and as I do, I get another flash of recognition out of my right eye. This one much more detailed than any other prior. I can see the entire setting behind the list's projection. I see the outline of my bed's footrest, the outline of the chair beyond that and even the outline of Devin's figure sitting in it as he shifts from side to side. Paired with the vision of my left eye, the two halves of my field of view become whole, but the right half is a mere shadow of the left. Each shape disappears as I try to focus on it.

"Caroline, close the list," I say.

The projection disappears, but so does the setting behind it. I shake my head again and get glimpses of what I saw before on the very edges of the periphery of my left eye. I wag my head faster to complete as much of the picture as I can.

"What're you doing?" Devin asks.

"Trying to see." And not feel. To Devin, I must have looked insane or at the least very disagreeable about something. "I've got–" my voice cracks. I clear my throat. "–some weird shadowy reverse tunnel vision with the new eye. It's like I can see the outlines of everything I'm not trying to look at."

"Maybe we should get Eric up here. He might know something about it," Devin says.

"Good idea."

Doctor Rowley left a note with Eric's extension on the phone beside my bed. I needed to give him the first post-surgery data dump of everything the eye was transmitting, anyway. I reach for the phone, and my hand starts shaking.

"We don't' have to do this, now," Devin says. "Take some time."

"I'm okay."

I grab the phone and Eric to learn he'd been waiting for me. He says he'll be right up. Devin and I sit in silence for a minute and I reach for the ointment. I dab some on my cheek and Eric comes through door.

"How are you this morning, Mr. Casey?" he asks.

"Not bad. Let's drop the Mr. Casey thing. We've already been found out. Call me Levi."

"That FBI agent, right? Elizabeth told me. She made a mess of our networks this morning. Even the phone network went off. Flooded it with noise, before making a messy exit. I had to reboot everything. It'll take weeks to figure out what data she stole. I think I got her out, though."

"You didn't get her out. I did," Devin says. "You're right that Vaughn's been listening to your network, but a reboot didn't kick her out. I flooded your network and everything else around here with noise to overload these." Devin tosses the bug to Eric. "I stopped the chatter when I was sure the bugs were dead."

Eric squints at Devin. "Thanks, I think," he says.

"Anyway, Eric. I've been playing with the prosthetic." I say.

"Oh yeah? Can you see anything yet?" He sets the bug down on the small desk in front of me.

I bring Eric up to speed on what I have and haven't seen and how I saw it. He pulls up the documentation on the prosthesis on his tablet as I'm talking. He taps as if typing.

"We also figured out the best way to interact with the AR functions is through my personal assistant," I say.

“Personal assistant?” he asks.

“Every Energy Alliance employee is granted a very basic AI with access to the Energy Alliance Intranet that’s accessed with different devices like Levi’s smart watch,” Devin says. “Since we paired the implant to his profile, his personal assistant should be able to help Levi control it. We just have to figure out what to command the AI to do in respect to the implants capabilities.”

“Well, the prosthesis should be able to display any data that can be determined by physical observation,” Eric says.

“You mean like measurements? Object length, width, height?” I ask.

“Yeah, and all calculations that can be derived from that. So, speed, force, acceleration, volume. Anything. I suspect that’s how the custom applications for Energy Alliance fieldwork get their data. Image analysis and processing can be computationally taxing. It makes sense that it’s reliant on cloud computing for live image capture.”

“I’d bet that custom applications could be able to be developed for it and installed on the Intranet. Eyeball as a platform,” Devin smirks.

“Sure. It’s really not that much different than traditional AR interfaces in that sense,” Eric says.

“Except this one’s stuck in my skull and connected to my brain,” I say.

“Let’s see what you can access. We need to figure out what happened on the day of the cyber attack,” Devin says.

“You want some sort of network access dump, right?” I ask Devin.

“Actually, guys, if you can give *me* the data dump

from the eye first, I'll get out of your hair and you two can play with it all you want," Eric says.

"Sorry, Devin. I gotta do this first."

"No problem. Accessing the eye's data reports should be similar in nature to what we need to do anyway. You might learn something about the system by doing that for Eric," Devin says. He gets out of his chair and stretches before walking over to the window to stare at the parking lot.

"I'm not sure how to start, to be honest. I assume my AI can get the data you want, but I don't' know the right questions to ask."

"Can I make the request?" Eric asks.

"Maybe. Caroline, can you take a request from Eric?"

"Yes. You can grant Eric access. Will his access be temporary or permanent?" Caroline responds.

"Temporary."

"Ok. Would you like to verify each of Eric's requests as he makes them?"

"Yes. No offense," I say.

"None taken," he says.

"Ok, Eric. You can now make requests. My name is Caroline. Please say my name before making your request."

"Caroline, is the Energy Alliance Ocular Enhancement storing data on your server?"

"Levi, may I proceed to answer Eric's question?"

"Yes, Caroline. Go ahead."

"Yes, Eric, the Energy Alliance Ocular Enhancement is storing data related to its operations for diagnosing potential functional problems with the device."

"How long is that data stored for?"

"The data is stored for three days. If any anomalies in the data are detected, the user will be alerted immediately."

"Can I get a dump of all data collected so far?"

"Levi, may I proceed to answer Eric's question?"

"Yes."

"Eric, just to confirm, you want a data dump of all operational data sent by Energy Alliance Ocular Enhancement?"

"Yes," confirms Eric.

"Levi, may I provide Eric with the data he requested?" Caroline asks.

"Go ahead, Caroline." I half-appreciate Caroline's thoroughness in seeking my permission, but this process is starting to feel arduous.

"Ok, Eric, how should I send it?"

"Email is fine."

"Ok, but Eric, I don't have your email address," Caroline says. I motion for Eric to bring his tablet to me. I hold my watch up to it and it beeps as the devices exchange our contact information.

"Got it," confirms Caroline. "Sending a data dump of all operational data sent from the Energy Alliance Ocular Enhancement in XML, SQL and JSON formats to Eric now."

"Thank you, Caroline!" Eric is delighted.

"Don't thank the AI. It's creepy," Devin scoffs, still staring out the window.

"You're welcome, Eric," Caroline says. "Levi, would you like to revoke Eric's access rights, now?"

"Are you done?" I ask Eric.

"Yes, thank you."

"Yes, Caroline, revoke Eric's access rights."

"Eric's access rights have been revoked," she

answers.

"Caroline is a little verbose, but it seems useful," says Devin.

"Well, I've got work to do." Eric pats the back of his tablet. "Thanks again, Levi. Come down to my lab this afternoon. I think I can help you get more of your vision back." I nod to Eric and he leaves.

"That guy's not too bright," Devin says when Eric was clear.

"Why do you say that?"

"For one, his network has a security hole big enough to drive a truck through. And second, he should be asking you for much more than just a data dump."

"What should he have asked for?"

"He should have asked you to parse the data for him. He'll be reading through it trying to clone a system to replicate the Ocular Enhancement, right? Caroline could do that a lot faster parsing requests in English than he can writing whatever clumsy queries in SQL he'll come up with."

"Hmph, you're probably right." I think for a second. "But, their goal is to build a system independent from the Energy Alliance Intranet. So maybe building it without using it my AI will help them with that foundation."

"I think Caroline could help do that, too," Devin says.

"Do you think we can use Caroline to prove we had nothing to do with the hack?"

"I think you boys could use Caroline to find out all kinds of things."

Devin and I look up to find Agent Vaughn standing in the open doorway. She's holding her jacket in one hand having slung over one shoulder. She holds her high-heels in her other so we couldn't hear her coming. The first three buttons of her white dress shirt are unbuttoned to show off enough of what's underneath for me to notice.

"Agent Vaughn, I didn't hear you come in," I say trying to match the tone of our last conversation.

"I bet hospital security didn't hear you come in, either," Devin says.

Vaughn closes the door behind her.

"I can be quiet when I want to," she winks at me and tosses her jacket on the chair. "But *you've* been very noisy." She says to Devin. "These things are expensive, Longinus." She picks up the bug from the table in front of me. Devin laughs.

"I see you got your bandages off. Does it hurt?" Agent Vaughn asks me and leans in close. Her glasses slide down her nose as she tilts her head. I turn my face toward her to show her my wounds. I don't buy her faux concern, but the attention is nice.

"I can handle it," I say.

"Good," she straightens up with a bounce. "Do you feel well enough to have a chat?"

"Do I have a choice?" I ask.

"You could hit the nurses' call button again, but if you did that, I think our relationship would suffer." She sticks out her bottom lip.

"Say what you have to say, Vaughn," Devin says.

"You're so rude, Longinus. Haven't I been helpful to you?"

Devin turns around back to the window ignoring her question. She squints in his direction before sitting in the chair I found her in this morning. She tosses her shoes on the floor.

"First off, you should know that I'm the only person at the Bureau that knows you're here."

"I take it that your continued discretion is something that I will have to buy."

"Very perceptive, Mr. Pickering!"

"Call me Levi," I smile at her.

"You can call me Gabby," she smiles at me with her eyes.

"Could you two please stop flirting? It's gross." Devin says from the window. "Besides, he's taken."

"Pity. I didn't think you were that type of man," Vaughn pouts.

"Not by me!" Devin yells.

"So, Gabby, what can I do for you?" I ask.

"To be honest, I think I'm more interested in what Caroline can do for me. Hi, Caroline!"

"She won't talk to you." Devin snaps. "Caroline will only respond to Levi's voice."

"The Energy Alliance is so stingy with their systems," Vaughn frowns. "But I'm not surprised."

"Gabby, why am I still free? Isn't it easier for you to lock me up and make me ask Caroline questions all day long? Why play this game at all with me?"

"Because she wants the credit, Levi. She can't get it if she just throws you in prison. She's a hacker and a shitty one at that. People at the Bureau are starting to notice and she needs a win to save her job. Until now, she's gotten by using her tits to social engineer her way to get information the Bureau wants but it's not working with the Energy Alliance," Devin says.

Agent Vaughn shoots straight up out of her chair and practically breathes fire at Devin, her flirty façade evaporates. She takes two steps toward him with her right index finger pointed outward, but then turns her hand into a fist and smacks it into her left palm. She relaxes her shoulders. For a moment, I thought Devin might be going out that window.

"Ooh, you mad?" Devin grins wryly. "Did you not think I would find out? Did you think data on the Energy Alliance is the only thing I could get access to? I need an insurance plan, *Gabby*. And I think I got it. So, play a bit nicer with me, will you?"

The FBI agent gets an inch away from Devin's face. "I've *always* been nice to you. If you think a *bit* more carefully, I think you'll agree."

Devin turns white.

"Gabby, is there something specific I can do for you?" I ask.

"She wants data on the Energy Alliance smart grid," Devin slides around her and gets as much distance from Gabby as my hospital room allows. "Show her a live map. That's proof enough we can get what she wants."

"Thank you, Longinus," she hisses at Devin. "I want more than a live view, I need a snapshot of the map, packet records between each station, copies of the software that runs it, and..."

"If we show you a live view, then you know we can get you the rest, right? Were you planning on sitting there watching us for hours while we spun reports?" Devin asks.

"I suppose not, but you know, Longinus, if Levi proves he can get me the data that I need, then you won't be useful to me anymore." Gabby tries to sound sweet as if she wasn't being outwardly threatening.

"If you were good at your job, then you'd know that a data set is only as useful as those formulating the questions to ask it. And Levi doesn't really know what he has," Devin says.

"Easy, now," I say feeling a little defensive, even though he's kind of right. I genuinely have no idea what to look for without Devin.

"I don't think Levi would mind working with me instead. Would you, Levi?" Gabby grins back at me.

"I'm not sure I want to work with either of you," I say.

"What'd I do?" Devin asks.

Gabby frowns.

"Sorry, Gabby. I think you'll have to settle for Devin's plan. I'll show you the live map and then you'll have to leave for now. We'll get you the data you want, but you need to give us some time and some space."

"Boo. And if I insist you work with me instead?" she asks.

"Then your superiors *and* the public will learn about how you've been working with two suspected terrorists. Maybe you were even in on the hack that took down Burning Springs?" Devin raises his arms in the air. "A fun story like that straight from one of the accusers would definitely go viral." His open hostility toward Gabby hasn't waned even a little.

"You'd be in a DSRA jail cell within a week," she hisses.

"Maybe." Devin feigns a cringe speaking through his teeth. "But you'd be fired if you were lucky and probably facing a Congressional hearing."

"Fine, Longinus." Gabby rolls her eyes and plops back down in the chair. "You win. Show me the map and I'll leave."

"Levi, ask Caroline to show you a live operational

map of the Energy Alliance Smart Grid," Devin orders.

"Okay, but, Gabby? Don't use this to start World War III, okay?" I ask half-serious.

"No promises." She grins at me again.

"Caroline, on my watch's projector, display a live operational map of the Energy Alliance Smart Grid." I look at Devin to ensure I asked the question correctly. He nods.

"I'm unable to fulfill that request," Caroline answers. I frown at the watch. I look up to Devin and he looks just as confused.

"Why can't you fulfill my request?" I ask.

"You are no longer connected to the Energy Alliance Intranet."

<seventeen>

"Forget about the map, how is your personal assistant still functioning?" Devin asks. "Your watch is just the interface. All of the hard calculations are done on the Intranet. You shouldn't be able to use it at all."

That's true. When I lost all my permissions on the day of the cyber attack, all my watch was good for was telling the time and the only thing Caroline could do was tell that I didn't have access to anything. I should be in a similar situation, now.

"Maybe I just now lost the connection. Caroline, how long have I been disconnected from the Energy Alliance Intranet?" I ask.

"You shouldn't get a response to that," Devin says.

"You have been disconnected from the Energy Alliance Intranet for the last ten hours and twenty-three minutes," Caroline says.

"Well, she's able to respond, somehow," I say.

"The AI has to be connected to another server cluster, then. Maybe Energy Alliance IT put a man-in-the-middle between your watch and the Intranet. The requests are being rerouted somewhere," Gabby guesses.

"Why would they do that rather than just outright banning his watch's MAC address at the router level?" Devin asks her.

"They want him to keep using the watch. Feed them data so they can see what his moves are. They knew he was headed here with the help of the Medical Supply Network. Maybe they want more information on them," Gabby says, revealing she knows more about me than I anticipated.

"I guess that's possible," Devin admits.

"Wait, you think they're intercepting data from my watch?" I say trying to catch up to the tech talk.

"I don't know exactly how they'd do it, but yeah," Devin says. "So, they have physical access to the data centers where the computers that run the Intranet are, right? And your watch has to access it from their routers. They know what to look for. They can figure out the IP or MAC addresses you're connecting from and route it elsewhere. But I think they'd need to have admin access rights to route that traffic and your account somehow had the lockdown over that.. I don't know. Maybe the routers run on another system?" Devin rests his hand on the back of his head.

"Can we just ask Caroline?" I ask.

"Maybe. Start by asking her what network you're connected to," Devin says.

"Caroline, what network am I connected to?"

"You are connected to Energy Alliance Intranet Clone 1."

"Ah, I was right. Maybe I'm not so dumb, eh

Longinus?" Gabby prods Devin. He waves his hand dismissively.

"Ask Caroline how long you've been connected to that network," Devin says.

"Caroline, how long have I been connected to this network?"

"You have been connected to Energy Alliance Intranet Clone 1 for ten hours and twenty-five minutes," Caroline answers.

"The timestamps match up. I think they got you," Gabby says to me.

"Well, shit. What can I do about it?" I ask.

"You can feed them falsified data to throw them off, but if they have ten hours on you already, you're stuck," she says.

"We don't know for sure that's what's going on though. Levi, ask Caroline if anyone else is connected to the network," Devin proposes.

"Caroline, is anyone aside from me currently accessing this new network?" I'm starting to feel like Devin's parrot.

"No, you are the only one currently connected to Energy Alliance Intranet Clone 1," she answers.

"Has anyone other than me *ever* accessed this network?" I ask.

"No, you are the only one who has ever accessed this network."

"That doesn't make sense," Devin interjects. "Someone had to build the network you're on. And obviously you didn't do that."

"Caroline, who created this network?" I ask.

"You created Energy Alliance Intranet Clone 1 on June 14, 2032."

"It had to have been the virus after it took over

your profile," Devin says. "It's not uncommon for a virus to hide from being purged. This one spun up a clone of the Intranet to live in offsite in case Energy Alliance IT did a reset. But if they did do a reset" Devin trails off and takes out his smartphone. He taps on it with purpose.

"This is all very interesting, boys. And I love a good puzzle, but I still need something to turn into my superiors," Gabby shifts in her chair. "If it's a true clone, it should have a snapshot of the database from the original. That would be good enough for now. Can you"

"Holy shit, I'm in!" Devin interrupts.

"In? In where?" Gabby asks.

"I'm back in the Energy Alliance Intranet through the same exploit I've always used. I was right. They did a full system restore from a snapshot taken the day before the virus took over and patched up the security holes I always used," Devin says.

"Good news, Longinus!" Gabby clapped her hands.

"Wait a minute! If the virus created the new network and not Energy Alliance IT, doesn't that also mean that I'm *not* being spied on?" I ask.

"Yes. Well, at least not in the way Vaughn thought you were," Devin says without looking up. I slink down in my bed.

"Thank God," I say.

"Glad to be wrong," Gabby says. "So, will you try to ask Caroline for some information about the smart grid? See if I'm right about the database being cloned."

"Caroline, can you display a static map of the Energy Alliance Smart Grid on my watch's projection?" I ask. The map pops up into the air as requested. Gabby aims her forearm at it and taps on her own watch. I assume she took a picture.

"Thanks, love!" Gabby beams.

With a knock at the door, one of my nurses comes in pushing a cart with my lunch. She and Gabby exchange a look. Gabby puts up one hand and stands.

"Don't mind me; I'm on my way out," Gabby says with a smile.

"For good this time, I hope," the nurse, says staring down over Gabby. Gabby widens her eyes but doesn't respond. Instead she slips on her high heels and rises up to the nurse's gaze.

"Your lunch, Mr. Casey," the nurse says without breaking eye contact. She puts the tray on the table in front of me and walks over to the intercom. "Can I get security up here? That agent lady is back in Mr. Casey's room."

"Good luck with your puzzle," Gabby says. "I'll look at the network traffic and see what I can find," She taps on her watch and gives Devin a wink. "Already took a snap and uploaded it to the cloud. Don't bother trying to flood the receivers again."

"Why would I?" Devin asks. "We already know you know everything we do."

"To be spiteful." Gabby walks toward me clacking her heels on the floor. I get a flash of her silhouette in the prosthetic's vision. It gives me a bad idea. She holds up her watch to mine. We trade contact information with a beep. "I'll send you some homework, later," she says.

"Caroline, can you display Gabrielle Vaughn's breast, waist and hip measurements on my AR display?"

Gabby's jaw drops she furrows her eyebrows, but turns her expression into an inquisitive smile. Devin looks up from his phone and rolls his eyes into the back of his head. The nurse stares at me motionless.

In my prosthetic's HUD, Gabby's silhouette is digitally outlined in red. The outline follows her movements. She stands straight up putting her hands on her hips. The numbers "38in", "28in" and "39in" display above her breasts, waist, and hips respectively. I read them out loud.

"That's pretty close. A little generous up top, maybe." Gabby smiles.

"Padded bra?" asks Devin.

"Goodbye, boys." Gabby raises her finger to her lips and looks at Devin. She walks out of the room, bumping into a security guard at the door. The nurse follows her out and I tear into the plastic wrap around my tray to get to the sandwich underneath. Devin plays with his phone a long while before I am ready to turn my attention to something other than lunch.

"So, what now? What's our next move?" I ask in between bites.

"We need to find out who attacked Burning Springs. We can start by finding the origin of the virus," he answers with a yawn.

"Seems like we can figure that out just by hammering Caroline with questions."

"Actually, I think it'll take more than that. I mean, feel free to try, but remember, Caroline *is* the infected system. If the AI knew about the virus to give us information on it, it would have already eradicated it at the time of infection and there never would have been a disaster to begin with."

"Caroline, were there any unauthorized connections to the Intranet on June 14?" I ask.

"No, Levi. There were no unauthorized connections made on June 14."

"See? And that's wrong. I got in. Remember?" Devin shrugs. "Ask it if there were any unscheduled software patches."

I do and again got nothing. I pepper her with variations of the word "virus", "unauthorized", "unscheduled" and anything else that comes to mind. I get nowhere.

"The system can't give you what it doesn't know. The AI can make some inferences but it needs to be from discernable data. A smart hacker will make sure the system thinks everything is on the up and up. That's why they issued the orders from your profile," Devin explains.

"They had to access my profile from outside the network, right?"

"Not necessarily. They could have uploaded software from another profile inside the network. And that's what I suspect happened, but I won't know much until I dig in."

"Would it be helpful to look at the last known software update?" I ask.

"Maybe. I still think it would be better to start looking over the network access data, but if you want to send me the last system update files, I'll look over them next," Devin says.

He scans his phone onto my watch and I ask Caroline to send him the network data he asked for as well as the update. He stretches loudly and gives a final look out the window.

"Thanks, I'll go get work on these right away. Before I go though, how did you know that you could get the AI to figure out Vaughn's measurements?"

"Ha! I didn't. Gabby leaned over and scanned her contact info into my watch, and I was able to see her silhouette in the prosthetic. Eric said I could get field measurements and I figured Caroline would be able to put together the person in front of me was Gabby since I just got her information."

"Clever," Devin scoffs. "Be careful with her. Vaughn, I mean. She's playful, but make sure you stay useful to her."

"Yeah, listen, though. You heard her say that Energy Alliance Security already knows I'm here, right?"

"I did," he says.

"So, can you help me figure out somewhere to go? I expect them to coordinate with Ohio law enforcement to get me extradited, and the longer I'm here, the longer I'm putting Doctor Rowley and the others at risk. And you, too, right? If they find out we were working together, now–"

"I've been thinking about that," he says. He rubs his eyes underneath his glasses and speaks through his palms. "I've got a plan I was going to use for myself, but I think you need it more. And I think you need to be free even more than I do."

"What do you mean by that?" I ask.

"I mean that if you get caught, the Energy Alliance has their scapegoat and we may never learn the truth about what happened. They'll be happy to kill you, me and Kayla and get back to business as usual." Devin sits down and pounds his hand on the chair's arm. "When do you want to leave?" he asks.

"As soon as possible."

"Okay. You'll need clothes, too, right?"

"Yeah and a backpack, a tent, a knife, some rope–" Devin waves his hand.

"Not where you're going. Okay, maybe a backpack.'

"Where am I going? I ask.

"I'll send you the details later in case Vaughn's listening." He runs his hands underneath the chair looking for bugs. He finds none and stands up and peaks out the doorway. "I'll contact you, later."

"Okay. Thanks."

Devin steps out the doorway leaving me to the rest of my sandwich. I finish it and think of another question.

"Caroline, on June 14, who the hell closed the exit valve at The Watershed?!"

"You did, Levi," she replies flat as ever.

"Fuck! No, I didn't!" I scream back.

"Calm down. You're scaring everyone outside." Dr. Rowley comes into the room, tablet in hand. "What didn't you do?"

"I didn't cause the landslide at Burning Springs, but someone did and I'm trying to find out who." I shake my head back and forth to make a silhouette of the doctor appear in my right eye. This head shaking is becoming a tic.

"I know you didn't cause the accident," she says.

"It wasn't an accident. My boss, my best friend and thirty-two of my colleagues were murdered."

"I checked on Eric. He told me you got your personal assistant working. Surely, you can use your access rights over the system to figure out what happened."

"That's what I'm trying to do but even she even thinks I did it," I tap my watch and for a moment, I hold my breath in frustration. I exhale loudly and take off my mask. "I didn't tell you, but I had some pretty dark dreams as I went under for surgery."

"That's normal when being put under anesthesia."

"I dreamed of that night, right? I was kneeling in the mud on the adjacent mountain watching my friends burn on the other side. But I didn't feel sad or scared or grief or anything in the dream. I felt like: I don't know how to describe it. I was terrified like I was on that day, but I also felt like my work was done. Like I had just built something great. In that dream, I knew that I had caused the fires and I was *proud* of it."

"You've been through a lot, Levi. It's probably just your mind's way of trying to process everything you've been going through. From my understanding, you haven't even had time to grieve. Without a doubt, you've got Post Traumatic Stress Disorder. If you'd like, I can make you an appointment with the hospital's psychiatrist. It's standard procedure for someone who has been through a surgery like yours, anyway."

"I don't need a psychiatrist. I need to figure out who is responsible for all this."

"Okay. Let me know if you change your mind. How's your vision?" The doctor leans in and shines a light into the prosthetic. I see the flash clearly at first but then it gets blockier until it disappears like static fading away on an old television set. I tell her what I see.

"And I can't stop shaking my head," I complain.

"That's also normal for people who've lost an eye. The prosthesis is trying to widen your field of vision and each time you shake your head, you get a bit more information to it by sympathizing it to your left eye. It's *good* that you're doing that, now, and eventually you won't need to." I appreciate her positivity, but it's hard to remain patient. "I heard you used the AR enhancement, too," she says.

"Oh, uh, yeah. It's neat."

"The nursing staff is gossiping. They think you're a pig."

"What do you think?" I ask.

"I think it'd be better if you didn't antagonize that FBI agent."

The doctor finishes her examination of my face and checks my ankle. She rolls it lightly and tests its vertical movement. It's tight but doesn't hurt.

"She knows about the Network, Doc. She didn't seem to care for now, but if she wants something from you, she'll use it as leverage."

"I figured." Doctor Rowley casts her eyes downward.

"I can't stay here much longer. As long as I'm here, she'll keep harassing you."

"You have a plan?" she asks.

"No, not yet, but we're working on it."

"I don't think you should worry about it yet," she says, her eyes still downward. "You still have a lot of healing to do. And Eric has worked out a rehab program to help you get your vision back. He'd like to see you in the lab as soon as possible. Can you go now?"

"Sure."

The doctor gets me some pants so I can better cover up to walk around the hospital. She also gets me a walking boot for my ankle. I don't think its necessary, but whatever. I get changed and take the elevator down to the second floor.

I enter the lab to find Eric arranging some children's toys onto a large table in the center of the room. There are two terminals set up on either side of the table.

Eric explains that the idea of the training program is to limit the amount of noise I'm feeding the eye by focusing on a single object with a simple texture and a single color. First, he gives me a red ping-pong ball. I wag my head until I get the color and shape to appear in the prosthetic and then I close my left. Each time I do this, the ball disappears slower and slower. He hands me sandpaper and I repeat the process. After each exercise, he asks me to have Caroline give him a new data dump from the partner app. I spend the rest of the afternoon doing this even taking my dinner in Eric's lab.

"Is there a place where I can get some air?" I ask Eric. I got used to Eric's smell, but I'm tired of the walls. I miss the sun.

"Yeah, you could head up to the 8th floor and check out garden. We're done for the day."

"Thanks."

I follow his directions and take the elevator up. The doors open to a cool breeze flushing the sterile smell of the hospital's hallways from my nose with the scent of grass and potted wildflowers. My boot and I clunk out onto a stone pathway that snakes through some bushes and ferns. I am alone. I walk over to the ledge to take in the view. There's a park across the main road. It's decorated with trees, a pavilion, and two baseball diamonds. The park is mostly empty save for a few dots of people and cars around the community center. I imagine the diamonds are full on Saturdays.

The hospital's campus is small. It consists of a few buildings plunked in the middle of a neighborhood of French townhomes. The evening sun is sinking, threatening to set in the next hour. I close my eyes and let some of the day's last rays of sun warm my face. For a long minute, I try to think about absolutely nothing.

A gust of wind blows up the front of my hair and finds its way to the wounds on my face through the eyeholes of the mask. It stings. I open my eyes and swing my head side to side to get the widest view of the park I can. Green fields stretch to the river. I get a shadowed view of the horizon to the right when I stop shaking my head.

"Caroline, how far is it to the river? Display on AR."

A crosshair appears in the vision of my right eye approximately where the river is on the horizon. I can make it line up on the river if I wag my head. It reads "620m" in white text with a black outline just above the crosshair.

My watch vibrates, and I look at the watch's face to see a scrolling message. It's Gabby. She's sent me a laundry list of data she wants from the EA Intranet. I'll have to do something about her, but she can't be a priority. I sigh.

"Caroline, are you connected to the Internet?"

"Yes," she answers.

"Great. Build a profile on Gabrielle Vaughn.

Search social media, public records and any other background checking resources you have. I want to know everything I can about her."

"Ok."

The Energy Alliance requires full background checks on all employees for HR. All of those records are tied to the American Republic's government database. Our profiles have our past addresses, geo-location data of where we regularly go, health records, employment records, everything. I'm not sure how much is out there on Gabby, but if Devin could find a bit, Caroline backed by the Energy Alliance Intranet resources should be able to find a lot. And if she is playing dirty with us, I should find my own mud to sling.

I sit down on a bench next to a pot of flowers. Flashes of the round pot, stems and petals come into my wider view. My first priority should be to get my vision back. I need to build myself back up and get out of this hospital. I focus on a single flower and keep shaking my head "no" as if it was telling me something I couldn't believe.

The flower's silhouette stays in view and details are filled in piece by shadowy piece until I get every petal and can even see trace amounts of color. After a minute I get the entire flower into view. My feelings of accomplishment are interrupted by another buzz from my watch. It's Gabby again.

"Myrna Lockheart is dead. EAS knows you're at Marietta Memorial. Trust no one at the hospital. Leave now."

<eighteen>

I stare at the words on my watch and the fresh air leaves my lungs. They executed Myrna. It's only been a few days. Not enough time for a trial. I think of her standing in her doorway urging us to the river and then her swinging from gallows erected in her own yard. Poor Isaac. My eyes start to water.

I'm next.

But what if she's lying? I can't trust Gabby. She's probably trying to arrest me away from the hospital, away from attention. But if she's telling the truth, I think my situation is worse than if she were lying. I'd rather be detained here in the US by the FBI than illegally kidnapped on foreign soil by EAS. That'd just end with me dangling from an Energy Alliance-branded noose.

I walk over to the side of the roof facing the parking lot. There are several cars parked and a hospital security guard standing next to the gate. The guard is talking to a man in a black suit.

"Caroline, can you see the license plates on cars in the parking lot?"

"Yes," she answers. Good, because I can't. The prosthetic can "see" everything. It's just my stupid brain can't interpret what's its detecting.

"Do any of those plates match any vehicle registrations in the Energy Alliance Database?"

"Yes, three license plates are registered to Energy Alliance Security."

Shit. Gabby's not bluffing. They're already in the building. I don't have much time. I need to leave, but I shouldn't go back through the elevator. I look down. Way too far.

"Caroline, I need to get off this roof. Download a map of Marietta Memorial Hospital and find me a way down without using the elevator." I hope this works. Caroline's pretty good at navigation, but this is going to be complicated.

"Processing."

I pace around the potted plans but see nothing to better my situation. I stare off the ledge to a grassy hill four stories below. Can't go that way.

"You're currently on the north building. Walk to the south wall and use the ladder to climb down to the west wing. Then, go to the west side of the west wing to use the fire escape to the ground," says Caroline.

"Uh, okay. Can you display a compass on my A.R.?"

"No. Your GPS is currently disabled," she answers.

"If I turn on my GPS, will my location data be uploaded to the Energy Alliance Intranet?"

"You are not connected to the Energy Alliance Intranet," she says. Right, I should have known that.

"Okay, then turn on GPS and show me a

compass."

A cross-hair compass pops up in my right eye's field of view. I note the position of the sun and turn my head to ensure I can trust it to accurately orient my heading. It does. I head south for the ladder as fast as my orthopedic boot and I can clunk.

"Caroline, call Devin." Mother-fucker better pick up. I need him now more than ever. It rings once.

"Levi."

"I hope you have had enough time to get that plan of yours together. EAS is here."

"What!? Are you sure? How do you know?"

"Gabby called..." I huff down the ladder. "Caroline saw, too." I skuff my boot on the last rung and land on the rooftop of the smaller building. Footing secured, I spin a circle until the A.R. compass tells me I'm facing west. Of course. I'm looking into the sun. There is no park on this building. I clunk through ventilation ducts and solar panels to the west end.

"What're you going to do?" Devin asks.

"You know that park across the street from the hospital?"

"The fairgrounds?"

"Yeah, whatever. I'm going to find a place to hide there. Can you pick me up?"

"What? No. Not with those guys around! We can't both risk getting caught."

I swing over the side of the building and drop a foot or so down onto the fire escape. I instinctively fall with even weight on both my feet shooting pain up my leg from my sprained ankle.

"Ahh! You're just going to let me get caught? Gabby says they killed the nurse that helped me!" I scream.

"Oh my God. I'm...I'm going to help you. I just can't physically be there. I'm sending you a digital US passport. Use that to board the *River's Bounty* by the Lafayette Hotel."

I pound down the fire escape one floor at a time. At the bottom, I hunker down low and as out of view of the east building as I can. I have to keep moving. "What's the *River's Bounty*? A quadcopter?"

"What? No. It's a riverboat casino. It goes up and down the Ohio. The captain owes me a favor. I'll let him know you're coming. The boat picks up customers on both sides of the border and you're technically leaving the U.S. when you board. His staff will need to scan the passport. Oh, and don't play the video slots or the video poker."

"Um, ok. How will I make it there? I'm still in hospital pajamas and slippers, you know."

"I didn't have time to get your stuff. Sorry."

"It's fine. Also, I don't have any U.S. dollars."

"Shit! I forgot about that."

All of my money is still in Energy Alliance Script. I can exchange it online for anything and it's easy to trade, but you need a US government registered wallet for USD. I have one but it's in my name. If I were to use that wallet, anyone savvy enough could track my spending on the USD blockchain.

I climb down the final ladder, land softly on the ground, and limp to the backside of the building away from the parking lot and cross the main road to the fairgrounds. I slide down an embankment caking mud onto my oversized boot. I cross another narrow street and head for the community building in the park.

"I'll register a USD wallet to the fake passport and send you a file with the security phrases that will allow you to unlock it, but it will take time," Devin says.

"How much time?"

"An hour. Maybe two."

I try the door on the community building. It's locked. There are some cars in the parking lot, but the only people in sight are on the other side baseball diamond. They're walking this way. I hide on the opposite side of the building. There's a public pool across another empty parking lot. Fortunately, it's passed the pool's operating hours.

"Okay. I guess I'll just have to wait here," I say.

"Good luck. I'll send you an Energy Alliance wallet address. Send your scrip there, and I'll load the new USD wallet with an equivalent amount."

"Okay, thanks."

Devin hangs up. The sun is setting behind the building and I'm sitting in its shadow. The warmth offered by the evening sun has been used up, and the cool breeze is no longer the reprieve it was.

"Caroline, how far is it to the Lafayette Hotel?"

"The Lafayette Hotel is approximately 1.5 miles away."

A map of the city projects in the air above my watch. It's a straight shot from my location to the city center, as much as this small town has a city center. I could walk it, but I'd stand out sorely in my hospital pajamas. I need help and my options are limited. I consider calling Isaac, but he's part of the Network and Gabby said not to trust anyone at the hospital. I have to believe that the Energy Alliance somehow has leverage over the Network. They might be using Myrna.

“Can I help you?” a man’s voice asks from the side of the building.

I scream.

“Whoa whoa. Calm down. I didn’t mean to scare you.” He steps forward with his arms raised.

“I didn’t see you coming.”

He’s dressed in jeans and a green polo shirt with no signs of a badge or Energy Alliance logo anywhere on him. He probably works in the community building.

“What’re you doing here?” He looks me over. “Did you come from the hospital? You shoudn’t be here. The park closes at eight.” He reaches into his pocket to pull out a cell phone.

“Oh... sorry.” I scramble up to my feet. “You... you don’t have to call anyone. I didn’t know the park was closed. I’ll head back to the hospital now...sorry,” I say trying to appear *not* insane.

“Nonsense, you’re injured.”

Okay, two bad options. I can try to punch this guy out or make a run for it. I can’t run very far or very fast anywhere, and that wouldn’t stop the call this guy is about to make to the hospital. Judging by the guy’s beer gut and rounded shoulders, I should get a few punches in before he can react. One of the most valuable things my dad ever taught me was how to box. But this poor bastard doesn’t deserve that. Then again, if he can fight and he does land a punch on my newly reconstructed face, he might kill me.

A black SUV pulls up in front of the building screeching its tires to a stop. My heart sinks for a moment before my adrenaline spikes. The doors of the vehicle fly open. I raise my fists ready. I’m not going down quietly, that's for fucking sure. A single skinny leg with a high heel appears beneath car door and clacks down onto the pavement.

"There you are." Gabby leans on the open door leaving the engine running. My heart keeps pace with the pistons.

"Hi, Gabby. I took your advice and went out for a walk," I say.

"I'm glad you did, but it's getting late. We should get going." She smiles brightly.

"Sure, I appreciate the lift." I walk toward the passenger's side of the SUV and turn back. "My ride's here. Sorry for the trouble," I say to the man and get into the car.

He stares at me blankly.

Gabby gets in the driver's seat and punches in some destination away from the hospital, but also away from the Lafayette Hotel according to map displayed on the tablet mounted to her dashboard.

"How'd you find me?"

"My facial recognition software picked you up on a security camera at the park. I came as soon as I could." The car drives us around the building and out of the parking lot. The man stares at us the entire way. We make a left on the main road and drive passed the hospital. There's little activity outside of it. Just how I left it.

"Where are we going?" I ask.

"For now, I'm taking you back to my house." Gabby's twitchy, a shadow of the confident hot-tempered flirt she was hours ago. I look around again. It doesn't appear we're being followed.

"How did you know that EAS was coming to get me?" I ask.

"I found communications between hospital security and EAS when I looked through the data I picked up this morning. They threatened to prosecute the hospital for the stolen supplies, so the Network agreed to hand you over. When I saw them arrive, I killed the security camera feeds to give you your best chance to escape."

"So EAS was just going to smuggle me back to West Virginia?"

"Seems so. That'd be quicker than dealing with Ohio law enforcement."

We drive up a winding road along the Muskingum River for a while before Gabby relaxes. Her blonde hair is pulled back in a tight ponytail. She takes off her jacket and stretchers her shoulders before resting her hands behind her head. The steering wheel turns with each curve in the road.

"What are you going to do with me after you get me home?" I ask.

"What do you want me to do with you?"

And she's back to fucking with me.

"How do you know EAS killed Myrna?"

"Same way everyone else knows. Press release." Gabby taps on tablet on the dashboard of her car pulls up an article condemning Myrna as a smuggler and for aiding a terrorist–me. I'm the terrorist and likely why she's dead. I look at Gabby and wonder how much her position will protect her. I let my head fall back onto the rest and stair up through the skylight.

"You up for a little gambling?" I ask. I tell her about Devin's plan to get me out of Marietta and away from the Network. She agrees to help me get to the boat.

Her house is a good distance outside of Marietta in a suburban subdivision of affluent houses away from the river. The outside has immaculate landscaping and a sizable yard to accommodate the bushes, miniature trees and flower pots The inside of the house is not so immaculate.

Inside, I stare up a set of stairs to a second floor. To the right was a great room with a computer terminal with four monitors stacked up two-by-two on an intricate desk. The desk is decorated with old takeout containers, junk food wrappers and empty paper cups. The only other piece of furniture in the room is an ergonomic swivel chair in front of the desk. Cardboard boxes are stacked along all four walls. The only other seating is a large bay window with a pair of cushions sitting on the ledge. A Siamese cat occupies one. It makes eye contact with me.

"Nice place. Did you just move in?" I ask.

"A few months ago. This is an FBI issued safe house. I won't be here much longer," she walks over to the cat and scratches its head. The cat leans up into her hand and pushes its cheek against her hip. She walks passed her desk to leave the room toward an open kitchen. The cat leaps from the window and patters behind her. "Do you want some water? Beer?"

"Beer, please."

My watch buzzes. It's Devin. He sent the files for the USD wallet along with the itinerary for my cruise downriver. I ask Caroline to set up the wallet. The balance on the wallet rolls over to $1,209.23. The exchange rate he gave me for my EA scrip is horrible. I expected at least $1500.

Like all other corporate-based cryptocurrencies, the value is leveraged against the company's stock price on the NYSE. To keep the corporate interests across the old country away from US regulatory agencies, New York also seceded from the United States becoming an independent city-state, but they still trade in USD effectively saving the old country's currency from total ruin.

So, when Devin sold my EA scrip to someone who wants it over USD, I assume he got a shitty rate because the Energy Alliance stock price plummeted after the cyber attack. Normally, the exchange rate is pretty stable and I don't feel as screwed as a coal miner from the 1800s as I do now.

"Here's your beer." Gabby hands me a bottle. I take it and sit on the staircase so I can take off the medical boot. Clumps of mud fall off onto the tile in the struggle.

"Mind if I use your address to have some supplies delivered?" I ask.

"Sure, the delivery pad is out back." Gabby sits down at her computer and turns on the monitors. Their light brightens the room adding their glow to the last remaining daylight that finds its way through the curtains covering the bay window.

"Thanks, I need an outfit for tonight and technical wear for my indefinite journey."

"Where will you go after the cruise?" she asks.

"I'm not sure. The boat will make a stop in Cincinnati. Maybe I can find a place to stay there." With a final kick and a shove, I get the boot off. I move into the living room and sit on the cushion in the window with the least amount of cat hair on it.

"Caroline, search Amazon for men's button-up

shirts size L. Display on my watch's projector," I say rolling the stiffness out of my ankle. I might have set my healing back with that first fall from the ladder.

The website loads into the air above my left arm. I flick around the projection to scroll through different solid color choices. Gabby perks up from her monitor.

"Ooh, let me help!" she shuffles out of her chair and joins me in the window. She picks out a white shirt with a pattern of a thousand navy blue anchors all over the body. She also picks out a nice pair of jeans, and a blazer.

"Why the blazer?" I ask.

"It'll look good on you. And you could wear it with anything to make you look more credible without much effort."

"Whatever. I need real boots, though. I might be living on the streets in a few days."

We shop for the rest of the gear including underwear, casual wear, several t-shirts, as well as two pairs of technical pants, a hoodie a portable grooming kit, a compact ankle brace, a sleeping bag and a backpack. My total comes to $912.46 after an instant delivery charge and taxes. I'll have just over $300 left to live on. Everything should arrive via drone to Gabby's back yard in an hour.

"I guess we have some time to kill," I say with a stretch and no particular agenda.

"Let's do your makeup!"

I squint at her. "What?"

"You're not going to wear that ugly mask for our date are you?"

"Our date? You're coming on the boat with me?"

"It's either that or stay home and work," she says.

"Look, my face is kind of sensitive under the mask. I'm not sure putting concealer on it is a good idea."

"Let's try and if it hurts, I'll stop. Should we have a safe word?"

"Sure, how about 'fuck off with that, Gabby'."

"You're being awfully rude to the woman who saved your life."

"Why are you helping me? You've got to realize that the situation has changed, right? I mean I can't exactly prioritize the things on your list over my own shit. I got a security force with all the resources in the world to dodge and try to survive with $300. That stuff that's coming? That's everything I have in the world, right now."

"Because helping you is the right thing to do. The Energy Alliance will soon have a monopoly in the American Republic over all energy sectors and they're going to do the same over every natural resource on the continent. We can't let that happen."

"You think I'm some sort of self-righteous eco-terrorist?"

"No, but I think you are living proof of the chink in their armor. They want you very badly."

"Of course they do. They think I cost them billions of dollars and killed thirty-four people! Not to mention I have special insider access to everything they've ever built." I tap my watch.

"It's not just that. What happened at Burning Springs is bigger than the results. Either they don't know what happened at all or they know exactly what happened and are trying their best to cover that up. Your AI has the answers and you're the only one with access to it." She stands up from the window and leans in toward me. She put her hand under my chin.

"I need you to keep working on that list. For everyone, Levi."

"I didn't peg you for an idealist. Nor did I think the FBI was such a righteous organization."

"I'm not and it's not. Look around you. Doesn't everything seem I don't know, broken?" she asks.

"Of course."

"And why is that?"

"Because life is not meant to be easy," I say.

"You're not wrong, but it should be easier than this."

"And you blame the Energy Alliance?" I ask.

"I blame injustice."

"Look, Gabby, I'll keep working and fighting. That's always been the plan. When I find the truth of what happened, it'll mean I can stop running and make a new home. I'll save my dad, Kayla, and Devin from prosecution as well. That's my motivation."

"That's good enough for me."

"Good."

"Great. Let's do your make up," she says.

<nineteen>

I felt every hair of the makeup brush on my face, but I decided grit through it. My injuries should be covered. EAS isn't going to give up when they can't find me at the hospital, so whoever they threaten or bribe will be looking for an injured man in hospital pajamas, a boot and a mask.

While Gabby was doing my makeup, drone after drone delivered my packages to her back yard. I packed the new backpack and got dressed in my new clothes. No one will ever know how injured I am just by looking at me.

Gabby left me downstairs to get ready in her upstairs bathroom. I fit myself for the new ankle brace and force my foot into the new boots. It feels good to finally get some proper footwear.

Gabby descends the stairs expertly balanced in a pair of yellow high heels matching a flowing yellow dress with a deep 'V' down the chest. She steps into the foyer and gives me a twirl showing every shimmer in the fabric and thread on her let down blonde hair. She's a perfect 1950s pinup model. Red lipstick tries to pull your eyes to her mouth if you can manage to get them up from her chest.

"How do I look?" she says as she turns her head side to side.

The AR display on my eye lights up, surprising me. It's again highlighting Gabby's measurements. Her image, although clearer than before, is unnatural as she is half covered in shadow. The numbers are overlaid across her body except for this time the bust is a couple notches smaller from what Caroline initially reported.

"Great. But you won't exactly be keeping a low profile," I say.

"You're the one who has to keep a low profile. With me like this, no one will be watching you."

"Good point." I speak into my watch, "Caroline, what gives? I didn't ask for this information."

"Sorry. I anticipated you would want to know based on your question earlier," Caroline answers.

"Thanks, but it's not necessary. You don't need to show me anymore."

"Did Caroline check me out again?" Gabby asks with a smile.

"Yeah, but she did it on her own this time. I didn't know she could do that."

"Glad to know she appreciates my efforts."

As do I. Under any other circumstances, I would be thrilled to take her out. A wave of dizziness forces me to sit back down, my forehead resting in my palm. "Do you think I can get a cup of coffee before we go?"

"Sure." Gabby glides across the carpet and clacks back into the kitchen. I stretch my neck to either side and refocus forward to another bad idea. Soon, the smell of coffee gradually begins the mask the cat stink all around me.

"Caroline, do you know how to play poker?"

"Here is a manual on Texas Hold'em Poker." My watch fires up a projection of an open document. I close it off.

"No, no. I know how to play. I want to know if *you* know how to play."

"I don't understand. Do you want to download a game?" Caroline asks.

"I want you to help me play poker."

"Let me help!" Gabby's eyes light up and she scurries toward me, cup of coffee in hand. I take the cup and warm sip of dark roast. "I bet she can learn from YouTube," she says.

"Good idea. Caroline, garner information from the manual you just downloaded, as well as YouTube videos of World Championship Texas Hold'em Poker. Also download a HUD used for playing Texas Hold'em online. I want you to be able to calculate and display the probabilities of winning based on the contents of a player's hand, the probabilities of what cards are in my opponents' hands and by counting the cards in the remainder of the deck. Next time I play Hold'em, create your own display for the AR to show me any relevant information to the game."

Gabby claps her hands and bounces up and down. I smile for the first time since the fires. If this works, tonight could be very, very fun.

"Processing."

Devin figured I could create custom applications for the AR display. This really shouldn't be that much different than Tobias's custom HUD that he used to manage his slime impoundment back in Burning Springs. I'd think Caroline should have all the data she needs to make this happen.

"Caroline, how long will it take for you to write the program?"

"The program is complete."

"Wow, really?"

"Yes. I will run it during your next game of Texas Hold'em Poker."

"Do you have any cards, Gabby?"

"No, let's test it live. It'll be more fun," she says. She squints down at me and raises an index finger. "Wait here a second." She walks back upstairs and returns a minute later. She hands me a pair of mirrored aviator sunglasses.

"Wear these. Your eye lights up a bit whenever you use it. You don't want to get kicked off the boat for cheating."

"R-right." I tuck them into my jacket pocket.

She grabs me by the arm and lifts me to my feet. She pulls me close, pressing her breasts to my chest. With her heels, we are almost seeing each other eye to eye. She reaches around and brushes the cat hair off of the ass of my new jeans.

"Let's go!" she says.

I throw my backpack in her car and we snake back down the dark road next to the river. After a few minutes, the lights from the hospital breach the darkness first as we grow nearer.

"Are you worried that EAS will come for you next?" I ask.

"Not really."

"Do you think you'll get fired?"

"Not if you give me the things I ask for," she says.

“What about Devin?”

“Longinus is smart enough to hide. I’ve got security software using every camera in the city scanning for the known EAS security officers faces. If any of them are in a mile radius of where he is, an alert will generate and send him a notification. I set up the same for you before I picked you up.”

“Thanks. That’s a little creepy though, Gabby.”

She bats her eyelashes and says no more. The car parks itself behind the Lafayette Hotel. It’s an old red and brown brick building next to the Ohio riverfront. Blue awnings rest above windows that climb the curved wall facing the street corner. Gabby and I get out to catch the breeze coming off of the river. For once, I’m sufficiently dressed. My date is not. She grabs my arm pulls in close to keep warm.

We walk down a set of concrete steps toward the dock to board the casino boat. *The River’s Bounty* is a monster of an old sternwheeler painted white with tacky pink neon tubing in place of where a conventional stripe of paint should be. Its name is written in cursive just above the stern wheel. Even more neon tubes line the stern wheel itself causing it to resemble a motionless Ferris wheel. More pink lights flicker with neglect near the nose of the boat. Gabby and I walk to the end of the dock and are greeted by the ship’s hostess.

“Welcome to the River’s Bounty. Passports please,” she says.

Gabby takes out her phone, taps it a couple of times and shows it to the hostess. She scans it with her own handheld and it beeps green. “And yours, sir?”

“Caroline, show the nice lady my passport.”

"Okay. Which one?" Caroline asks. I freeze.

"Just show her the newest one, dear," Gabby says.

"R-right. Caroline, pull up the newest passport."

"Ok, Levi. Here is the newest passport," Caroline says. The passport that Devin sent projects in the air just above my watch.

"Why did your personal assistant call you 'Levi' when the name on your passport is Daniel?" the hostess asks.

"Uh, Levi is my middle name. My friends call me, Levi. I wanted my personal assistant to call me that, too."

"It says here, your middle name is Long-i-nus." She struggles in pronouncing Devin's ridiculous online handle. Gabby puts one hand to her forehead and turns away, trying to hide a laugh.

"Right, that's my *real* middle name, but you see how goofy it is. To this day, I've never forgiven my parents. So, I choose to go by Levi."

"I agree. Long-i-nus is a horrible name and that guy gives me the creeps." She scans my fake passport and her device beeps green as it did with Gabby's. "But whatever. I'm just messing with you. The captain's expecting you. If you both follow me inside, I'll take you to him."

We board the ship and turn left to enter the first floor of the boat. The first deck is pretty plain with bland hallways on either side. Numbered doors are evenly spaced out, marking what I assume to be passenger and crew quarters. We follow the hostess up a set of stairs in between the rows of doors up into the casino.

"Why did Devin put his stupid nerd name on the phony passport?" I ask Gabby.

"I can't answer that, but take it easy on making fun of his handle," she says.

"Why?"

"So, he told me the story a few days after he agreed to work with the FBI. He'd been drinking and maybe felt a little more vulnerable than usual. The short version is that when he came out to his Bible-thumping parents they said that he might as well have stabbed Jesus in the heart himself. The name of the spear that was thrust into Jesus on the cross that finally killed him was called Longinus. So, *that* and the double entendre with his last name, Pierce, he came up with his handle."

"That's horrible."

"Mm."

The interior of the casino is everything the exterior of the ship is trying to be. Pink neon tubing outlines dozens of video slot and poker machines. Many of them are manned by blue-haired women carelessly jamming in coins and cranking their handles. A thin dark carpet covers the floor, but I can't make out the color. Burgundy maybe. There is poor overhead lighting. Most of the room's light comes from the neon and various video screens. I assume this was intentional to either draw more attention to games or hide stains on the carpet. Probably both.

A lighted walkway snakes a path through the machines leading to another set of stairs. On our way down the neon-lined road, I spot a row of tables: poker, blackjack and a roulette table, each with a dealer and a few players. We ascend the stairs to the top deck and back out into the open air. A bar and restaurant sit up here. The capacity of the restaurant seems to be for more than a hundred but less than twenty are seated. There's only one man at the bar and we're on our way to greet him. By his look, he is very interested in greeting Gabby. He raises a tumbler in her direction.

"You must be Daniel," he glances at me only with his eyes before refocusing on my date. I figure he didn't want to expend the energy it'd take to turn his giant head. He lifts a glass of something brown to his face and slurps at it. The skin flaps under his chin jiggle with the effort. He lowers his glass so he can go back to eye-fucking Gabby. She doesn't seem to mind. She looks around at the restaurant vacantly, pretending not to notice.

"He likes to be called Levi," the hostess corrects the man and gives me a sideways smile.

"Riley, who is watching the door?" he asks.

"I am. Sorry, I'll get back to it."

"I'll get back to it, what?"

"I'll get back to it, Captain," she answers with a nervous smile.

"Good girl."

The hostess shuffles off in a hurry. The Captain finishes his drink and swivels on his stool to face the bar. He plunks down his glass rattling the ice within. He motions with one hand to the bartender for a refill.

"Thanks for taking me on board, Captain," I say.

"Sure, sure. I owe that Longinus kid big time, but you got to understand I can't ferry you for free. You're occupying a room that a paying customer would have taken."

"Oh, okay. That makes sense. How much?" I ask.

"A thousand dollars a night."

"What!? That's insane! Why so high?"

"Look, I don't know your story and I don't want to. But if you're mixed up with Longinus, then you've got some added risk, and I've got to have a good reason to take on that risk."

"I don't have that kind of money, so I guess I'll find another way to get where I'm going." Wherever the hell that is. I've got no plan, but I got to get out of Marietta and soon.

"Hang on now, we might be able to work something else out." He leans in toward Gabby as if he was having a hard time seeing through the peephole slits in his face fat face. "Who's your friend, here?"

"Oh, me?" Gabby perks up as if she's just now noticed the walrus in front of us. "I'm Agent Gabriel Vaughn, FBI." She says in her most well-rehearsed cheeriest voice and flashes her badge from the clutch she painstakingly chose before we left.

"Oh, what the fuck!" The Captain slides off his stool in a hurry knocking it to the deck beside him. A few heads in the restaurant turn our way. The captain bends down with considerable effort to set the stool upright.

"Excuse me, folks. No worries. Enjoy your dinner," he says to his patrons. He lowers his voice. "I don't know what that boy told you, Miss, but I run a clean business here. The Ohio Casino Control Commission has inspected every machine."

"Glad to hear it," Gabby smiles at the Captain.

"I'd be happy to take you down to my office if you'd like to look at the paperwork."

"Oh, no thanks." She pulls her phone out of her clutch. "I can just take a quick scan of any machine.

If I find the token Longinus said was there, then I'll know he was telling the truth. Unless..."

"Unless what?" he asks.

"Unless you just want to pay the fine, now," she says.

"God damn it, woman. I like you," he laughs. "How much is the fine?"

"How long is the trip to Cincinnati? And you said one-thousand dollars a night?"

He guffaws, jiggling like a gross Santa Clause. "Quite a girl you got there, Levi. Fine, I'll ferry you and your boyfriend."

"How sweet! But I'm not going." Gabby puts her phone back into her clutch and claps her hands together. "I would like a drink, though. Whiskey. Good stuff please, Captain."

"Uh... me, too, please!" I say trying to assert myself in any part of my own fate.

"Of course." The Captain motions to the bartender. "So, you sure you can't stay with us? I'll give you a special upgrade."

"No, no. I have work to do here. But please do take care of, Levi. He's very important to me." She drops her bouncy demeanor for a moment and stares through the Captain. "I monitor him very closely."

"You have my word." The Captain waves his hand to placate her and waves it a second time to signal for a waiter. Gabby gets her drink and kicks it back. A lipstick print and two gulps later the glass is back on the bar, empty.

"I think I'm in love." The Captain taps the bar to get Gabby's glass refilled and turns to the waiter he signaled. "Put Levi's bag in room 1003 and bring him a key."

"I'll take that key down in the casino, if you'll excuse me, Captain. I think I'd like to play some poker." He nods and waves me off with the back of his hand. "Have fun." The bartender refills Gabby's drink. She takes the glass and my arm.

"I'm going to watch. Thanks for the drinks, Captain."

"Shame. I was really enjoying your company."

She tilts her head to him and we walk back down into the casino. At the counter, I find out the big blind for the poker table is $10 so, I spend a third of my remaining cash to get the minimum $100 worth of chips I'll need to play. Hopefully, Caroline did her homework.

Gabby and I walk up to the table. Four others are already seated: three men and one middle-aged woman. Her short black hair is propped up with an inordinate amount of hair spray. Decades of chain-smoking has left her face cracked. She looks over at us but her focus is drawn to the two younger guys at the table. The boys wear ball caps, t-shirts and cargo shorts as if it is some sort of uniform. I assume they came from one of the local colleges.

Judging by the stacks in front of them, one is a better player than the other, but both seemed better at stacking plastic cups than chips. The fourth player is an older gentleman in a loud Hawaiian print shirt. He gives Gabby and me a friendly nod. He calls the last bet and takes the pot with three Jacks. Judging by his chip stack, it isn't his first win.

"You're last in the rotation if you're in," the dealer says to me. She's a pretty, short brunette with a ponytail. It seems all staff here have a uniform and the captain has a type he might be getting bored with judging by the attention he's given my blonde date. I put on the pair of mirrored aviators that Gabby gave me and sit down.

"Yeah, I'm in," I say.

"Oh shit, we got a real baller at the table, now," says the kid with the taller stack.

"You have no idea how little money I have," I say, and get a confused look.

"You have a hundred dollars that I'm happy to take," the old man says having counted the minimum buy in's worth of chips in front of me.

"You take the chips, and I'll take his girl," laughs the other kid. Gabby gives him a wave.

"Aw, I thought you were mine, tonight," the veteran bar fly lady leans in on his shoulder. He shrivels like a rabbit.

"Alright, players. Same as before. New guy, it's a $5 big and $2 small. Raises are limited to $5. I'm here to help if you need me." She shuffles and the two guys post the blinds starting the pot at $7. The dealer deals. Caroline must have been paying attention. The AR flashes to life on the prosthetic, hidden behind my mirrored aviators.

I look down at my hand. It's junk: a three and a five off suite. A graphical representation of my hand appears on the bottom left of my HUD. I look around the table. Caroline has placed some placeholder stats that appear overlaid onto each person's chest ready to be recorded. I have no idea what these are for. Caroline has gone deep. All players have the acronyms VP, PR, 3B, CB, BB and FCB overlaid on top of them. I can't openly ask her what they mean right now; it'd give away that I had a bit extra help at the table. Not that I need her to tell me, but Caroline flashes advice at the bottom of the display recommending that I fold. I do and watch the rest of the game play out.

With each call and in each round, the percentages appear next to each acronym. As we get deeper into the round, Caroline can predict a range of hands each player has. She even correctly determines that the old guy to my right has a King and Jack suited. She also predicts the ranges of the turn and the river. This is entirely too much information for me to process.

I am dealt a pair of 8s in the next round. Caroline recommends that I fold that hand, too. I am confused, but decide to trust my AI. Normally, I would have played it out, but I think I understand why she doesn't want me to. I don't have to put in any money yet, and clearly Caroline is watching the other players play. The stats overlaid on each player have shifted. She is learning everyone's tendencies and taking advantage of my position at the table. I can fold this round, too for free if I want to. She'll probably recommend I skip this game, too.

She does. My hand is offsuit 8 and 5. I fold again preflop (or before the game really begins). The percentages again roll on each acronym overlaid on each other player. By watching when the numbers move I am able to figure that she is calculating how conservative or aggressive each player is. She determines that the old guy was the most conservative player with the tightest range of hands. The barfly lady seems to have the largest range and the two bros had smaller ranges depending on how aggressive they were after the flop (or after we saw the initial three community cards). But that is only after three hands. She should learn more as we play.

Finally, I'm the big blind and this round will cost me a bit of money. I post my mandatory $5 and get my two cards. It's a pair of Jacks. The old man limps into the round calling the $5 as does the barfly, and the better of the two bros raises. The other bro folds.

Caroline recommends I call. I do to stay in and so does the old man. Good bro checks. The flop is unexciting for me. The three community cards are a 10 of spades, a 4 of clubs, and an ace of diamonds. I'd like to keep seeing how the other players bet it out. Caroline asks me to bluff. I do with a raise. Both of my opponents fold out and I take the pot. It's not a huge gain but it is a decent win on a tough hand.

"Nice play, baller, what'd you have?" asks the bro that folded first.

"A better hand than you," I answer.

"Alright. I feel you."

With every hand, Caroline adds more data to each player's profile and has perfect advice every time. I never stray. I lost money only once and that was when I folded the next hand as the small blind. I won every hand after that. An hour later, long after the barfly went broke and gave up on good bro, I tripled my chips.

"Who taught you how to play, kid?" asks the old guy.

"A very nice lady that I work with."

<twenty>

Gabby pulled me away from the table before I got greedy. After cashing out my earnings, we went up to the top deck for more top-shelf whiskey and bar food. We got a table near the front of the boat away from everyone else. I gave Gabby the rundown of how Caroline architected my win streak as quietly as I could, but I was still so high my hands are shaking.

"So, you didn't make any decisions at the table?" she asks.

"Well, technically no. I followed the suggestions that popped up at the bottom of the HUD, but I *understood* why Caroline made those suggestions. Mostly."

"Uh-huh."

"I was playing the probabilities of what each player's hand *could* be also accounting for how aggressive they had historically been playing. I even got a pulse reading whenever a player's heartbeat spiked. The smaller college kid got so nervous when he bluffed." I snicker, lean back and rest my head into my hands.

"Be careful. I don't think I can protect you if you get caught," Gabby warns. A gust of wind blows off the river, and the flame on the candle between us bends and melts away some wax. It trickles down the shaft. Gabby shivers. "I think I'm going to go," she says.

"Ah, what for? It's only..." I look at my watch. "12:30."

"And my workday isn't over."

"Right."

"I left you a gift in your bag," she says. "Don't throw it into the river."

"I won't." She's probably talking about another bug like the one she hid in my hospital room. "You saved me, tonight, Gabby. I won't forget that." I reach for her hand. She lets me hold it.

"You're not fucking me tonight, Levi," she says.

"I... no! I wasn't trying to!" I let go of her. "I was being sincere. I'm just thanking you." She laughs and I deflate. "You *should* want to fuck me after the way I played tonight," I say. She leans in close and I force my eyes up to hers.

"I should fuck Caroline," she whispers. "Your computer won you that money."

I don't respond. There were times back in my trailer, I had imagined what Caroline's body would look like if she had anthropomorphized into a human-like android of some sort. Real talk. It got lonely at night on that mountain with only my computer to talk to.

"Goodnight, Levi. Send me something, tomorrow, will you?"

"Sure. 'Night, Gabby."

I finish the last of the fried food and got some

water to take down to my room. When I land in bed, the day's whiskey and morphine make the ceiling spin with the gentle rocking of the boat. My skin and the blankets feel hot and slimy. It's all too much. I give up the fight and stumble into the bathroom to throw up everything I have. I guzzle water from the head of the faucet and crawl back under the sheets. Soon, they're damp with my own cold sweat.

The stomach cramps, headaches and nausea come back a few hours later. I check my watch, curse it and force myself back to sleep. The sun creeps in through the porthole. I curse it, too. The sound of the sternwheeler beating the river finally forces me out of bed. I figure the captain ordered the boat to leave the city.

I put on some wrinkled, but clean plain clothes from my backpack and go upstairs to replenish myself of last night's lost calories. It's overcast but warm. *The River's Bounty* is plodding its way down the Ohio River southbound toward Parkersburg, retracing the same route Isaac and I came up a few nights before.

The remnants of a breakfast buffet are set out on tables for passengers that stayed overnight. There aren't many of us. I fill a plate of eggs, biscuits and bacon and sit down at the table Gabby and I shared last night. My watch face blinks with a notification. Devin texted me last night:

"My sister wrote to me. You were right about the origin. Call me."

Wanting privacy, I take my plate below deck to my room. Down here, I'm reminded of the anxiety I felt hiding in Isaac's cabin. I decide to not surface again until we're past Parkersburg.

"Caroline, call Devin." It rings once.

"Hey. What took you so long? I was beginning to wonder," he answers. "Sorry, I'm okay thanks to Gabby. You talked to Kayla?" I ask.

"Not exactly. She knew of the exploit I used to access the Intranet and changed the server response messages. I got a different one each time I connected. When I piece them in order I get this." Devin sends me another text:

CHK UPDT 06012032 K

"What's that mean?" I ask.

"The K at the end is Kayla's signature. Her message says to check the update from June 1, 2032. She's telling us the virus was in the last system update."

"An inside job, then? That doesn't look good for Dunbar. Or us."

"No, it doesn't. But the updates don't come from Houston. They come from Seattle."

"Seattle? The SDRA?"

"Maybe. A third party called Huo Tech developed and still maintains the Energy Alliance operating systems."

"Huo? Sounds Chinese."

"It is. They're headquartered in Shanghai. The Seattle location is the American branch."

"Okay, so what now?" I ask.

"Ask your AI to send me the June 1 update's release notes. I'll see if I can find something concrete," Devin says.

"I already sent the update, yesterday." I get off

the bed, get a pod of coffee and stick into the machine next to my room's mini fridge.

"You sent me the files, but not the notes."

"Okay, but if it was an attack, would there be something in the notes? If I were planning to implant a sophisticated virus in a control system that would kill tens of people, I wouldn't upload instructions on how I did it," I say.

"I'm not expecting specifics, but it might give me a clue of where to start digging in the files. You should look at it, too."

"Okay."

"Longinus out."

"Caroli—" Before I could finish my question the document Devin asked for pops up on my watch's projection. "What the hell? Caroline, were you listening to my conversation?"

"Sorry, Levi. Is this not the document you wanted?"

"Well, yeah. It is."

"Should I send the document to Devin?"

"Go ahead," I say.

"Document sent."

I skim through the document's headings. A lot of different systems and subsystems were affected in the last update. I stick a biscuit in my mouth and walk over to the porthole. We're passing a section of downtown Parkersburg. My vision is getting remarkably better. There's still a haze over my right eye like some morning fluid has clouded it, but I get shapes and color of everything I try to look at. It gets clearer as I concentrate on specific objects but blurs as I relax.

"Caroline, in the June 1 update, were any

significant changes made to the Energy Alliance control systems that fundamentally change how they operate?"

"Processing. No. The control systems' fundamental operations were not affected."

"Were any of the Energy Alliance systems fundamentally changed?"

"Yes. A new protocol was issued in the Financial Management System."

"Financial Management? You mean accounting?"

"Yes. Additional directives were also executed on all Energy Alliance personnel profiles."

"What was the directive?" I ask, and take as sip of coffee.

"All employee profiles were issued two new hidden parameters: Estimated Dollar Value and Overall Projected Value."

"What were the values used for?"

"The profile update for the Estimated Dollar Value assigned a monetary value to each employee profile. This value is calculated by determining how many United States Dollars an employee is worth to the company. The Overall Projected Value is a weighted score of how valuable an employee is on a scale from minus five to plus five."

"How are they calculated?"

"The Estimated Dollar Value is calculated by examining the employee's work history. Each employee's productivity output per project and projected productivity output for future projects is used to calculate the total amount of accrued and projected income in United States Dollars. The total salary paid and company resources used are then subtracted from that amount to calculate a final dollar value. The Overall Projected Value is calculated from a weighted analysis of the Estimated Dollar Value, that employee's life insurance policy, and the projected cost to replace that employee."

So, the Energy Alliance put dollar and number values on all of its employees. It sounds gross to quantify human beings to that, but it doesn't sound unusual for the Energy Alliance. The only strange thing is that it didn't happen sooner.

"What was my Overall Projected Value?" I ask.

"One."

"One?" I cough as some coffee finds it's way into the wrong pipe in my throat. "Out of five?"

"The scale is from negative five to five."

"Still, that's all. Just one?"

"The Overall Projected Value for Levi Pickering is one."

Man, fuck that company. I practically designed their entire energy campus waterworks. The Base wouldn't have drinking water without that design. Sure, I was just doing maintenance recently but that layout Silas and I put together has been used at least half a dozen other sites by now.

"All right, Caroline, if I'm only a one out of five who scored a perfect five?"

"The only employee with an Overall Projected Value score of five at Burning Springs is Tobias Boyd."

I'm not surprised, but damn. Tobias was deemed five times more valuable than me? I guess that would also explain why they sent the quadcopter after him before the storm. Whatever. These new profile parameters are a pretty large systemic change, but on the surface, it doesn't seem related to the virus. Although, those values could be used to make all kinds of decisions.

On the day of the cyber attack, every decision seemed automated as if it were preprogrammed into the system. That was two weeks after this update. Yesterday, I grilled Caroline on everything I could think of that happened that day, and she kept saying I did it. At the time, Kayla watched each sabotage happen in real-time and said each command came from my account, so I assume Caroline was just reading the same log Kayla saw.

"Caroline, were any automated commands issued on June 1 using the new profile parameters?"

"Yes. Automated commands were issued to create the Estimated Dollar Value and Overall Projected Value parameters to each employee profile and to populate them with appropriate data."

That probably should have been obvious to me. I wish I had Devin, Kayla or even Gabby's help with this.

"What about after that but before June 14?" I ask.

"Yes, two hundred and thirty-one inquiries and updates were made using the values for employee Estimated Dollar Value and Overall Projected Value as parameters."

"Two hundred and thirty-one commands for the Burning Springs Campus?"

"No, only one query was made using the new parameters for the Burning Springs Campus for that specified time."

"What was the query?"

"On, June 13, 2032 the Energy Alliance Financial Management AI used employee Overall Projected Value Scores in its calculations to decide to merge with your profile."

Oh, shit.

"What do you mean when you say the 'AI merged with my profile?'"

"The Energy Alliance Financial Management AI scanned your greater profile and added all knowledge obtained from your work history, history of commands to the control systems, training history, recorded conversation, and personal interest history as well as possible inferred interest and relationship history into its own subsystems."

"Why me?"

"Your profile contained knowledge and privilege required to execute its primary directive."

"What was its primary directive?"

"The primary directive of the Energy Alliance Financial Management AI is to create value for the company's primary investors."

"And executing thirty-four people and blowing up the whole fucking campus created value for the company's primary investors?!"

"Yes."

My throat swells and my face gets hot. I lift my head back to process and it hits me. I found it. I asked the right questions. I found the evidence, but there's no relief. I hit the side of the wall with the bottom of my fist and think back to the fires taking the conference center. It was all orchestrated for profit after a calculation of reducing my friends down to dollar values turns my stomach harder than last night's whiskey. I remember the slideshow of faces during the video that was played at the all-hands meeting. One of them could be the murderer.

"Caroline, who issued the Financial Management

Systems AI's primary directive?"

"No user issued the directive. The primary directive was issued as part of the system-wide update on July 1, 2032."

And there it's confirmed. Whoever put that command into the system is the real perpetrator. It seems very general though. I make Caroline repeat the directive: "Create value for the company's primary investors".

"Caroline, did the AI make all the decisions for the accident on its own based on that simple directive?"

"Yes, after merging with your greater profile."

"Wait, is that same AI still a part of your systems?"

"Yes, the Energy Alliance Financial Management AI that incorporated your profile is a part of the system that I have duplicated on this cloned version of the Energy Alliance Intranet. The personal assistant, Caroline, is comprised of all those systems that you have access to."

"And I have access to everything."

"Yes, when your profile merged with the Financial Management AI, you were granted access to all systems it had access to."

Got it. The AI needed Senior Engineer level access to get at the control systems I managed and I've been using its access over personnel profiles and logistics when I sent those fake ComFlow messages and when I got to the Medical Database. Logically, together, we can get to every system on the Energy Alliance Intranet. I call Devin. He needs to know what I know.

"Do you understand all of this?" I ask.

"Not entirely, but broken way down, AI is just a bunch of extremely complex conditional statements. You feed it information and it takes it in and considers something like 'if this then do that'. When it does something, it gets the results and rewrites the set of conditional statements it used to get the first set of results and intelligently writes more to get better results. That's why we say it 'learns'."

"So, it learned how to blow up the campus from everything gathered from my profile?" I ask.

"More than just that. The AI was also aware of happenings in the system. The merger with your profile happened the day before the cyberattack, right? So, it knew that you shut everything down to prepare for the derecho. It might have come up with the idea of using the storm as a cover-up for the sabotage. It might have even planned to use you as a scapegoat by leaving the command trail with your profile's signature." Devin is thinking as he speaks.

"And it'd figure this was the best way to make the shareholders money?" I ask.

"After creating a dummy financial holdings company that shorted the stock, yeah," Devin says.

"Huh. So, the AI created that company?"

"I'm guessing."

"All on a simple, general directive."

"Yep." He pauses for a long while. "Whoever put that directive in there royally fucked up."

"You mean this was all a mistake?"

"It's a possibility. I mean, the HR decisions to quantify every employee to dollars and cents wasn't, but yeah, a directive like that is way too general. Any AI developer should know better than to release something like that."

"So, what now?" I ask.

"We call Gabby. Tell her everything and get her to help arbitrate your case between you and the Energy Alliance."

"Where would we be without that woman?"

"In prison," he answers. "Hang on. I'll patch her into our call." A moment later, we hear the phone ring on the other end. She doesn't pick up.

"That's odd," Devin says.

"Maybe not, we hit it pretty hard last night," I say.

"You didn't."

"No, not like that. She came on the boat with me. We had a few drinks, talked business and played some poker. Nothing happened, but she was here late. When she left, she said her workday wasn't over."

"Okay, I'll try again, later. What will you do now?" he asks.

"Hang out on the boat, I guess. I need to get Gabby some more information on the smart grid. Do you think you can find a way to tell Kayla what we figured out?"

"I think so."

"If you can get ahold of her ask her to make sure that directive isn't in any of the new rebooted systems." If it is, more energy campuses could be in danger.

"Right. I got to go. I'll let you know if I learn anything," Devin says.

"Okay. Bye."

I finish my breakfast and stare out the porthole. There's nothing but green trees and a trace amount of sunshine poking out from the cloud cover on the other side of the river. We should be sufficiently far enough away from Parkersburg by now. I could use some air, but I'll do Gabby's stuff first.

"Caroline, pull up the list Gabby sent me yesterday."

The list pops up in place of the fated update's release notes.

"Can you read through this, pick something and send the appropriate document to Gabby?"

"How about the component list and electrical layout design of the latest substation?"

"Sounds harmless. Go ahead."

That was easy. After the send chime ends, I think a little harder about what I'd just done. I asked Devin to tell Kayla some information that would help protect the systems I just exposed. But there's no way Gabby or the United States government would be a party to an incident like what happened at Burning Springs. I don't think.

With my work done, I leave my room and go back upstairs to the casino. It's mostly empty, now, but the neon lights on the floor are glowing nonetheless. I recognize an old lady from last night. She's returned to her post, putting coins into the same slot machine. I wonder if that's the type of person that the captain had hoped to victimize by hiring Devin to fiddle with the machine's code.

The captain is gross, but of course, Devin's hands aren't any cleaner. He wasn't forced to do that work, I don't think. I wonder if I'm any better. I cheated at that poker table last night. I figured it was just survival at the time. All I've been doing is surviving. It might be time to start doing more than that. I walk passed both the old lady and the empty poker table to the staircase. A loud buzzing sound reverberates down the stairwell. I walk up and poke my head above deck.

A huge drone hovers two feet above my head blasting me with air from all four of its rotors. It's nearly five feet in diameter and painted jet black with a red Energy Alliance logo right in the center of its belly. A robotic arm dangles from between the letters E and A. There's a camera mounted at the top of the arm and a submachine gun hangs from the bottom. The arm swivels and points both camera and gun at my face.

<twenty-one>

I step back, trip down a few stairs to skid across the floor. The drone and whoever was controlling it saw my face through the camera, but they didn't shoot. But EAS knows I'm here. I need help.

"Caroline, call Gabby."

I run through the casino passed the old lady and her slot machine to the porthole. An EAS boat is coasting beside us. It sits lower than the first deck of the sternwheeler. Like the drone, the security boat is jet black with the same Energy Alliance logo printed on its bough.

My watch rings too many times. Gabby doesn't pick up. I tap my watch's face to cancel the call.

"Caroline, call Devin."

"Hello?"

"EAS is here. A drone just spotted me. I see one boat. We'll be boarded any minute."

"Oh, shit. Uh, I'll try to call Gabby."

"I just tried. No answer." I'm trying hard not to panic. "You said, uh–you said you can get into Intranet, right? Can you hack that drone or maybe the boat? There's a Vehicle Management System application. Authorized personnel can give commands to vehicles tied to the Intranet. Kayla was able to get control of Gina's car a while back, remember? Can you do something like that?"

"What? No. That would require knowing that system inside and out. All I did was exploit a little hole in the security to pull data. Giving a control system commands is entirely different. Kayla probably had admin access already when she controlled Gina's car."

I sneak down a few stairs to the first deck but stop when I see two women posted by the door to my room. One is the poker dealer from last night. I don't recognize the other. Both have guns attached to their belts. I silently backtrack up the stairs. I can't hide. There are security cameras everywhere in the casino. If the captain wanted his security to detain me, they would have already done so. He's waiting for EAS. That bastard sold me out.

"Okay, listen," I say to Devin. "You might not be able to hack the boats, but Caroline might be able to. Send me the program that you use to tunnel into the Intranet. I'll have Caroline–"

"Are you out of your fucking mind?!" Devin cuts me off. "Do you really want me to give the rogue AI that nearly killed you and Kayla and *did* kill all those other people access to the same system it weaponized once already?"

"It's okay, Caroline only does what I tell her to now." I sit down at a slot machine and pretend to look at the screen. My legs shake under the stool.

"You're just guessing that! You don't understand how any of this works!" Devin shouts.

"Devin. Fuck!" I bring my voice down to a whisper as I duck down beside a slot machine. "I don't' have time to argue. If you have a better idea, then give it to me."

"I-I don't have one."

"Then send me the program," I say through my teeth.

Nothing.

"Devin!"

"Okay, fine! But this is a really bad idea. Give me a second."

"Caroline, I hope you were listening to all that."

"Yes. I was listening."

"Good. What can you tell me about that drone?"

The projector on my watch face lights up and a perfect replica of the drone is displayed in front of my face. The projection rotates in the air. A readout displayed just below it tells me it's an "Energy Alliance Goshawk" class quadcopter. It weighs 32 pounds and can fly up to a quarter-mile in the air. It has an hour and thirteen-minute battery life and is equipped with a 250-megapixel camera and something called a PP-2017 submachine gun.

"Sent," Devin says.

"Caroline, open and execute the program that Devin just sent."

"Program received. Accessing the Energy Alliance Intranet now. Connection confirmed."

"Good. Access the drone you just analyzed with the VMS and display the feed from the camera on my AR. I want to see what it sees."

"Processing. Accessing Energy Alliance Security Vehicle Management Systems. Displaying video feed from Energy Alliance Goshawk Serial number X-

6484."

"Whoa." I wobble a bit as my sense of surroundings is split. I close my left eye so I can only see the AR display from my right. I am hovering just above *The River's Bounty*. Three Energy Alliance Security boats flank the giant sternwheeler. Two are escorting us on either side and another is trailing us from behind. The sternwheeler slows to a stop. I can feel the floor shift beneath my feet. The trailing boat docks at our first deck. We're being boarded.

"Make this view smaller in the AR display Caroline. Can you give me access to the VMS and a tutorial on the controls?"

"The Goshawk class and all other Energy Alliance drones are piloted remotely via haptic controllers inside the suites of authorized security personal. The controlled drone's camera feed and Heads Up Display are displayed on security personnel's assigned Energy Alliance Smart Glass Visor. Would like to have the same display shown your Ocular Prosthetic?"

"Yes."

"Displaying the HUD on your AR display now."

The HUD is overlaid on my view of the camera feed. I'm reminded of the old flight simulators I played on my dad's PC as a kid. The HUD has an altitude readout, tells me the number of rounds I've got for the submachine gun, as well as the drone's remaining battery life. There are more numbers but I can't make sense of them.

"How can I control this thing, Caroline?"

"The Goshawk class and all other Energy Alliance drones are piloted remotely via haptic controllers inside the suites–"

"If I give you voice commands, can you control it?" I cut her off from repeating what she said earlier.

"Yes."

"That's a *really* bad idea," Devin moans.

"Caroline, don't do anything without my explicit authorization," I say.

"Understood."

"Feel better, Longinus?" I ask.

"No."

I get up from my slot machine and run back upstairs to the top deck of the boat. I catch a glimpse of the captain. He's posted up at the bar and a few other passengers have joined him. They're all gawking at the drone hovering above the boat. The captain notices me and raises a glass.

"It's a shame you couldn't stay with us longer, Levi," he shouts over the din of the drone's rotors.

I ignore him and run to the far end of the boat. I need to get as much distance as I can from the staircase. I glance down to the water. Not too high. I don't think.

"Caroline, position the drone just above the entrance to this deck. Aim the camera and the gun down the staircase."

"Ok."

"Take it easy, Levi," Devin says. His voice is starting to shake.

"I won't use it if I don't have to," I say.

Air pounds the deck as the drone descends. The crowd at the bar moves presses themselves against the railing to the right side of the boar. The high-pitched hum from the engines is deafening. As I'd ordered, it hovers just above the staircase, blocking the only entrance to the top deck.

"Okay, Caroline!" I shout. "I need you to lock the controls to all three of those boats only to us. Then, I want you to command the boats on our left and right to return to their home docks!"

The two boats do an immediate, effortless U-turn on the water and speed upstream. I'll be taking that last boat for myself. A company of EAS officers appear in the camera feed from the drone on my AR. Without breaking stride, they open fire on the drone. The sound of their shots pierce through the steady din from the quadcopter's rotors.

My camera feed shut off as a bullet found its way into the drones camera lense and I flinch as if I got shot myself. The drone teeters left, then crashes to the deck skidding into a table and chairs. It limps around in a circle with its two still spinning rotors. The crowd at the bar panics and scatters, most hugging the railing on the deck.

"Kill the engines on the drone, Caroline!"

The engines whine to a stop and the drone lay motionless. Four EAS officers storm the top deck and point automatic weapons at me. Their body armor is all black save for the large red Energy Alliance logos across their chests. Transparent visors cover the top of half of their faces. They flicker with lights showing them whatever data they decide could possibly apply to this situation.

"Get on the ground, now!" the officer in front screams. I raise my hands slowly and start to kneel. One last chance.

"Caroline, do you have access to those visors? If you do, turn their screens pitch black."

"Processing. Sending signal now."

“What the hell?” The lead officer’s visor gets digitally painted black. He starts tapping at the side of this helmet. The others’ visors flick off in quick succession. I get up and break for the railing.

“Caroline, send that last boat to my position!”

I climb up the railing and kick off as hard as I can with my good leg. I fall passed the other two decks, my toes just missing the lip of *The River’s Bounty* before I splash into the river. I swim as hard as I can downstream to get some distance, but my clothes are heavy. I don’t get far.

The security boat Caroline called creeps up and stops in front of me. I grab onto the platform hanging off the back of the boat, and my arm is grabbed and I’m thrown up onto the deck. I land on my hip and flop over.

“Levi! Are you okay!?” Devin shouts through my watch’s speaker.

“Not really!”

Another EAS officer standing over me, and he’s huge. I’m on my ass, but he looks like he’s got at least six inches on me if I were to stand up. I kick at his legs to try and throw him off balance. I look up into the sun toward his face to see he’s wearing a similar helmet.

“Caroline, blind this guy’s visor, too.”

“What the fuck?!” he yells as his vision goes dark. I get up to my feet and leap into him shoulder first to try and knock him into the water. I bounce uselessly off his chest.

“Caroline, set a heading for Cincinnati. Let’s go as fast as this thing can get us there.”

“Setting course.”

The boat roars forward, its engines scream nearly

as loud as a drone. The momentum shifts me toward the officer. He grips the side railing and barely budges. Blindly, he reaches out to grab me. Holding onto the railing myself, I kick at his hand. He pulls back and turns his attention to his helmet, tapping at the sides clumsily with his right hand. Regaining my balance, I run into the cabin and close the door behind me.

"Caroline, lock this door." It laches closed. Through the door's window, I can see the officer is still braced on the side of the boat. I look around for anything I can use as a weapon. The small cabin's walls are lined with passenger seats; four in total. A fifth seat sits in front of the steering wheel and control panel. I look under the desk and find a first aid kit. There's a pair of scissors, but I'm better off using my fists. I really don't want to fight that guy. He starts pounding on the door, *hard*. Too hard to even seem possible. The door dents inward with each of his punches.

"No matter what, Caroline, keep that door closed," I say.

The officer stops pounding on the door, hopefully giving up trying to knock it in. Good thing, too. He was close.

"What's going on?" Devin asks.

"I hijacked one of the security boats and am headed downriver. There's some sort of freak security officer on the boat, though. I gotta go. Keep trying to get ahold of Gabby."

"Oh my God. Okay," Devin says and I end the call.

"Caroline, is anyone chasing us?" I ask.

"Eight vessels and twelve drones from Parkersburg are in pursuit. They cannot catch us before we reach our destination at our current speed."

"Stop all boats and drones that are in pursuit. Have them go back to port like you did the others."

"Locking out controls. Sending new headings now."

This is too easy. I'm starting to understand why Devin thought this was a bad idea. Caroline has access to literally everything The Energy Alliance has.

"Caroline, I want you to monitor every Energy Alliance vessel ordered to pursue us: drones, quadcopters, cars, or anything else and keep them grounded. No Energy Alliance vehicle is to try to come to our location. Can you do that?"

"Yes. Issuing commands, now."

I laugh. This is more fun than Isaac's drone gun.

In one violent swing the officer punches through the circular window in the door with his left arm scattering glass shards at my feet. He reaches through with his other arm toward the door handle on this side and tries to turn it. It clicks against the electronic lock.

"Good luck with that, asshole! That lock ain't budging." I say.

"Dammit, Levi. Calm the fuck down already and just talk to me for a second."

Wait? What? No. The officer pulls his arm out of the broken porthole and bends down to look through it. He's removed his helmet.

"Zeke!?" I say.

"Yeah, good to see you, too." My stomach sinks and my heart aches. "How about you open this door?" he asks. It's only been a few weeks but Zeke looks older, a shadow of the happy grill master I knew in Burning Springs.

"I don't think so, man. I don't like your uniform."

"There's a good reason I'm wearing this."

"Yeah, and what's that?"

"I'm working for an EAS Lieutenant loyal to Mr. Dunbar. We supposed to take you to Point Pleasant."

"And what's gonna happen to me there?" I ask.

"We get you on a quadcopter to go to Charleston. Your dad and Mr. Dunbar are waiting there."

"MAnd then what?"

"I don't know. You face charges, I guess," Zeke says. "But Mr. Dunbar's got lawyers and he's taking care of Kayla. He'll take care of you, too, and it's better than the alternative. There're people in the Energy Alliance that want you dead, Levi."

"I know what really happened at Burning Springs, Zeke. I can prove it. It was all just a dumb mistake made by some dumb programmer in Seattle. I got the proof right here." I tap my watch.

"If you ain't done nothing wrong, then let's go home. Tell your story to Mr. Dunbar and his lawyers."

I sit down in the driver's seat and swivel it around to face Zeke. My clothes are still wet and cold from my dip in the river. My adrenaline is gone. The wounds on my face ache. I slump over resting my elbows on my knees and stare up at Zeke through the broken window. Some help and rest sound nice.

"What happened after you took off that night?" I ask him. "After the car threw you off and you ran back to the hospital."

"When I got there, some doctors were loading up

patients into an ambulance Kayla rigged up," Zeke answers.

"Did Gina make it into the ambulance, too?"

"Yeah." He looks down.

"What happened next?"

"We drove down a back road behind the hospital. But it was all downhill. We outran the landslide for a while but eventually the ground underneath us gave out. We got swept along with the trees like we's caught in a river." His voice cracked. "The ambulance rolled with us inside it. Gina hit her head."

We shared silence.

"The rest of us are lucky, really. I lost my arm: the same one that got banged up when that tree came down at the Watershed. Got a new one, though. Energy Alliance Med Tech. Got a computer like our watches and is strong as shit" He bangs the door again clanking metal on metal. "How are you doing all this?" He twirls his non mechanical finger. "Controlling the boat and messing with my visor?" he asks.

I catch Zeke up on what I learned about my access rights. "So, for now, I have control over every interconnected system, including your visor. I assume they'll eventually take down the servers again, and kick me out in the process."

"That's unreal," he says.

"No doubt. I even have a prosthetic eye now that I can use as an AR display. I assume it works kind of like your visor."

"You got a fake eye?"

"Yep. Lost my real one when I crashed Gina's side by side in the storm. Got this one from some medical supply thieves. It's Energy Alliance Med Tech, too."

"Hell of a week, huh?" We stare at each other for a long moment. "You ready to go home?"

"How do I know I can trust you?"

"For one, I already told you my mission and two: my sergeant has been screaming in my ear for the past ten minutes to shoot you and I haven't done so, yet." He holds up a handgun to the broken window so I can see it.

"Oh."

<twenty-two>

"Caroline, can you get a readout on Zeke's arm?"

"Processing. Ezekiel Allen's Energy Alliance Upper Extremity Prosthesis version 2.9 is both receiving and transmitting data."

"Can you make him toss his gun in the river?"

"Processing."

"The hell?!" Zeke yells as he lurches away from the door to fight off his own prosthetic arm. As ordered, his left hand grabbed the gun from his right. He fires a round into his mechanical hand. The bullet ricochets off something with a ping. I can't see the full struggle from the cabin, but I sure as hell am not going to try to get a closer to look, until he's settled.

"Caroline, once the gun is in the river, have Zeke grab a hold of the hand railing and keep him there."

"Why you doin' this, Levi?" Zeke asks as I peek out the cabin door after hearing his hand clink to the railing. He'd shot off two of his fingers on his mechanical hand. Fortunately, he still has enough of a claw left to get a good grip. His shoulders are slumped. He's done fighting.

"It's for your own good. With you like that, it doesn't look like you helped me escape."

"That's sweet of you to think me, but making me do this against my will is fucked up." He picks at his mechanically clenched fingers. He can't make them budge.

"Caroline, stop the boat."

The boat slows, sending waves to the shorelines before coming to a stop. We're now in a rural part of the river surrounded by a thin canopy of trees. I can hear the highway on the Ohio side, but not much else. This might be the last peace I get for a while.

"Caroline, I want you to sever all ongoing communications from all Energy Alliance telecom operations. Then I want you to connect me to *everyone* over the ComFlow's intercom function and mute everyone else on the other end."

"Processing. Energy Alliance communication lines terminated. Companywide intercom protocol initiated to all ComFlow connected users. Processing. Connection successful."

"Hi, everyone. This is Levi Pickering." The gravity of talking to a hundred thousand people hits me. I lean against the boat railing and look up to clouds. "Uh... sorry for disrupting your day like this, but I have a pretty good reason."

Zeke laughs from the other side of the boat.

"Now, after what I've done today... uh grounding your transportation, severing communication, and so on, I can see as why you might be afraid of me, but I never would hurt any of you, and ... I wasn't responsible for what happened at Burning Springs." I exhale loudly and recollect my thoughts.

"That was a result of careless, irresponsible engineering. An artificial intelligence that could quantify human life to a dollar value to the company was told to maximize our profits for our largest shareholders." The words are coming easier. I'm telling my story back to myself as much as to everyone else.

"Caroline, send everyone their extended profile information with their Estimated Dollar Values and Overall Company Projected Value," I say to my computer. A previously hidden projector on Zeke's wrist pops up with a table with his personal values.

"These numbers break down exactly how much the Energy Alliance values you. This includes what could be made from your life insurance policies if you were to die. The Financial Management System's AI determined that it would be more profitable to kill everyone left at Burning Springs to collect their life insurance and then use a Chinese financial holdings corporation to short the Energy Alliance stock. It knew a disaster of that magnitude would cause the share price to crash. But the AI couldn't do it alone. It needed me. As the Senior Hydraulic Engineer, I had the access and knowledge over every system it needed to orchestrate the destruction of the campus. So it decided to merge with my profile. It also chose me because my own value to the company was set to a 1 on the scale. So, to it, I was also expendable, along with everyone else."

"Using my profile also created a digital trail that set me up as a scapegoat. The AI knew it had to rebuild the company and get share prices back to normal after it'd executed its plan. And the company couldn't do that unless they could ensure the public that the Energy Alliance was stable. Even if I had survived, EAS would capture me, the court of public opinion would have their human villain and eventually, the problem would appear resolved. But that's not the truth."

"I know all of this because I now have control of this AI. Because the AI has merged with my profile, it cannot distinguish between the real me and the digital representation of me it has merged with. I assume this was a flaw in the AI's initial plan, as it didn't anticipate I would survive its attack on Burning Springs."

"With its access and ability to process incredible amounts of data, I can corroborate my story. I now plan to coordinate with the United States FBI to–"

I'm interrupted by a notification coming in from my watch. It's an incoming call from an unknown number. Someone wants to talk. I should keep it public. Transparency is probably my only way to gain any favor.

"So, uh, we got a caller." I click the answer icon on my watch. "Hello. Say 'hi' to the entire Energy Alliance."

"Levi. It's Kayla."

"Kayla Pierce, everyone. Another person that was trying to save lives at Burning Springs being wrongfully framed. Good to hear from you, Kayla. I'm glad they haven't executed you."

"Shut up, Levi."

"O-okay."

"I've been tracking the command logs since you started, um, taking control of everything, and there's a problem. There are a ton of additional commands affecting energy campuses as well as people's homes all over. It's all coming in so fast. Please tell me you aren't doing this."

"What? No. Caroline, are you sending in any additional commands other than what I asked you to do?"

"No," Caroline answers.

"See?" I say to Kayla.

"I'm not saying I trust that AI, but I didn't think you were. I was just checking. Everything you've been doing has your profile signature. Your commands look just like they did that night at Burning Springs, but these new commands have Arturo Davis's profile signature."

"I know the name, but I can't remember who that is," I say.

"He's the CTO of the Energy Alliance." Caroline displays his profile on the AR display in my right eye. Kayla continues. "Levi, we still have the same security issues as we did last week, don't we? With the Financial Management System's AI?"

"Yeah, that's part of the reason I wanted to talk to everybody: to warn you about that."

"Well, now that AI has even more access than a Senior Hydraulic Engineer from a single campus. This could be worse than Burning Springs."

"Caroline, display on my AR, all affected systems from the commands coming from Arturo Davis."

A map of the American Republic displays in my right eye. Dots sprinkle across every state lighting up the entire map. It's going for everything: campuses, facilities, power stations, and homes. The dots are blue, but a few are flashing red.

"Caroline, what's happening at these places?"

"Currently there are twenty-six million gas pressure buildups across all Energy Alliance systems in customers' homes, company well pads and substations."

"And what about the dots flashing red?"

"Gas pressure is at critical levels having resulted in structural damage to the containment systems." She means gas leaks. Fires. Explosions.

"Stop them. Return all gas operations to normal. Activate release valves wherever pressure is in a critical state or higher."

"I am unable to fulfill that request. Your access has been denied."

"How's that possible? I thought I had everything."

"You do not have access over these systems as per a directive from Arturo Davis, Chief Technical Officer of the Energy Alliance."

"Kayla?"

"Don't ask me."

Shit. I have access to so much but don't have access to anything I need. This is starting to feel like that night all over again.

"Caroline, can you confirm that the commands from Arturo Davis are also from a merged Financial Management Systems AI?"

"I cannot confirm that, but there is sufficient evidence to state that is a logical conclusion."

"Good enough. Do you still have access over personnel profiles?"

"Yes. You have access over the Financial Management Systems."

"Great. Update all personnel's Overall Projected Value scores to five. And set their Estimated Dollar Values to, I don't know, a trillion US dollars." That's probably not good enough. The AI might try to change it back. “And make those values stick. Alter the calculation if you have to so that OPV values always come out to five and EDV values always come out to a trillion US dollars. ”

“Update, complete.”

“Great thinking, Levi!” Kayla shouts from my watch. “If the AI sees everyone as too expensive to kill then it won’t see it as cost-beneficial.”

As I’d hoped, lights begin to turn off on the map to indicate a reduction of the affected areas, but most the map is still red with several dots flashing.

“Caroline, what systems are still being affected?”

“Customers’ gas lines that appear on the map are still being directed to build gas pressure beyond critical levels.” Remaining blue dots start flashing yellow and then red in no particular sequence. The AI is still going after people’s homes.

“That doesn’t make sense! Why is it going after customers?” I ask everyone, everywhere.

“If I only cared about money, then I wouldn’t kill anyone giving it to me,” Zeke says.

“Exactly. That’s why this doesn’t make sense,” I say.

“Maybe those customers ain’t payin’ up. And the computer thinks they ain’t worth keeping around,” Zeke says.

“Caroline, check the affected customers’ account balances. Are they negative?” I ask.

“Yes. All affected customers have a negative account balance.”

“Zeke, you’re a genius. Caroline, set all of their account balances to zero.”

“Update complete.”

The last of the dots start disappearing from the map. I sit down on the deck of the boat. "Caroline, return communication controls back to all Energy Alliance emergency services personnel and send a snapshot of that map to all fire rescue and medical dispatch centers near the affected areas."

"You should probably just give everyone control back over all the systems they should have control over," Kayla says. "Hopefully everyone out there can recognize this guy just saved this stupid company."

"Thanks, Kayla."

"Come home now, okay?" she says.

"Okay, tell you what. I got Zeke Evans, here. He says that there's a smart lieutenant that's working for Dunbar that ordered him to help smuggle me somehow from Point Pleasant to Charleston without the rest of you trying to kill me," I look down to Zeke. "I'll drive this boat to Point, but I want Titus Dunbar and my dad to meet me there. I'd like you to meet me, there, too, Kayla."

"That's not going to happen. We're all in Houston," Kayla says.

"Well, I'll just settle for no one shooting me on sight, then," I say and toss my arms in the air.

"Good luck, Levi." She hangs up.

"Well perfect," I say to everyone. "Okay then. I'm going to give IT control back over the Intranet. I suggest you wipe everything immediately and return it to its state before June 1, and don't accept any more updates from Huo Tech. And please, nobody murder me. I won't fight."

"I think you better keep your head down just in case," Zeke says.

"Caroline, disconnect from the company-wide

intercom and return Telecom and Vehicle Management Systems back to normal except for this boat. Set our course to Point Pleasant at half speed."

"Intercom disconnected. Telecommunication systems restored. Vehicle Management Systems lockout removed."

"How about letting me go, too?" Zeke asks.

"Will you promise not to hurt me?"

"I promise."

"Caroline, give Zeke control back over his arm."

He stands up and stretches his shoulders and legs. Then, faster than I could react, he punches my right shoulder with his real, right fist. My arm falls limp. I jump back toward the cabin.

"Caroline–"

"Don't!" Zeke put his hands up defensively. "I'm done." He points at me with his real right finger. "You deserved that."

"Fuck, Zeke. That hurt. You promised you wouldn't hit me!"

"I lied. You're lucky I didn't hit you in the jaw with my steel arm. You couldn't cry to your computer, then."

"Try it and I'll make you grab a rock at the bottom of the river."

He puckers his lips and kisses the air in my direction. I take it as a sign of affection, but give him a disgusted look. I'll have to trust my old friend.

Only minutes pass before familiar drones come flying overhead to watch us, making sure we go where I'd said we'd go. Soon, two identical boats to the one we're on join us, flanking us on either side as escort.

The sun breaks the clouds and shines on our

party as we cruise the Ohio River, soybean fields on one side and a highway on the other. When we pass an abandoned coal fire power plant on the Ohio side, I know we're close. We'll be in Point soon. If it weren't for the anxiety inducing drones overhead, the boat ride would be relaxing.

Zeke tells me we're to meet EAS at a small port where the Kanawha and Ohio Rivers meet. As we get to town, I can see our welcoming party: a small fleet of black Energy Alliance boats on the West Virginia side and a handful of white boats on the Ohio. The white boats look like old, injured ducks bobbing up and down on the river in contrast to the modern killing machines that EAS commands.

"Who're the other guys?" I ask Zeke.

"No idea."

As we get closer, I can make out the badge synonymous with law enforcement stuck on the side of the white boats. My watch vibrates. It's Gabby. I pick up.

"*Now*, you call me," I answer.

"Sorry. I've been busy, *but good news*, I've come to pick you up." I squint at the decks of the white boats in the distance. A tall figure starts to wave from the one furthest from shore. Caroline picks out the silhouette and displays Gabby's profile on my right eye.

"I'm kind of busy, today, Gabs. All my friends are here."

"Who's that?" Zeke asks.

"Friend of mine. She's with the FBI." I answer.

"FBI?" he asks. I nod.

"Yeah, I've met your friends already," Gabby responds. "They don't want you to go with me. *But* to my understanding, you have control of that boat you're on. Just run it to this side of the river, and I'll pick you up." She lifts the last word as if she's picking me up for coffee, rather than taking me to a US Federal prison.

"Don't do anything stupid, Levi," Zeke warns.

"I won't," I say to Zeke. "Not this time, Gabby. I think I need to go home. I got proof I had nothing to do with what happened at Burning Springs, and it seems like I got some real help on this side of the river."

"That's *not* what I want to hear, Levi," she sounds pissed. "Okay, you know how I found you? Check the pocket in the tongue of your left boot." I bend down and search the pocket to find one of her bugs.

"I knew you put one in my bag, but not in my boot. Clever," I say.

"Levi Pickering, you're under arrest for violation of US Code Chapter 545," she says.

"What?" I ask.

"Smuggling, Levi. You're under arrest for smuggling medical supplies into the United States. Will you come now?"

"Hah! Hell no!"

"Okay, so now you're resisting arrest. So, I can do this."

A voice identical to my own comes out of the bug. "Caroline, set a course for Gallipolis port. Increase speed 12 knots. Use lethal force if necessary, and accept no more voice commands from this point forward."

"Wait no–" Our boat accelerates and turns a hard right. The escort boat on the right side is prepared. It accelerates quickly to match our speed. Our boats collide sending Zeke and I flying across the deck into the railing.

The escort boat veers toward the bank, but easily catches back up to block us from getting too close to the shore, but then, both escort boats just stop dead in the water. It has to be Caroline. She saw the other boats as a threat and disabled them.

"What the hell, Gabby? I thought you were helping me?" I shout into my watch.

"I was helping you *as long as you were helping me*. You can't help me anymore from an Energy Alliance prison cell," she says.

"Caroline, stop this boat! Go back to Point Pleasant!" I shout at my watch. No response. "Shit! I've lost the boat."

"Guess you gotta swim," Zeke says. He hoists me up effortlessly with his (now) three-fingered mechanical arm and rests me on his shoulder.

"Hey, wait!" I shout and try to wiggle free, but to him, I might as well be a toddler.

He tosses me overboard. Our boat hadn't slowed down any, so I bounce, ragdolling hard off the water eventually coming to a final sploosh in the middle of the river. Nothing breaks; I don't think.

Downriver, Caroline gets the boat to shore as ordered. She just doesn't have the right passenger on board. I assume someone from EAS either saw the situation or Zeke radioed it in because I only have to tread water for a moment before a small fleet of black boats forms a barricade between me, and the Gallipolis police. Two security officers lift me out of the water and onto an Energy Alliance boat identical to the one I was just thrown from.

They take my watch, put me in cuffs, and sit me

down on the bench on the side of the deck. One officer tells me I am under arrest for well, a lot. The list includes terrorism, computer crimes, grand larceny, destruction of property, grand theft auto, resisting arrest, and then I stop listening. All I can hope for now is that these guys are in the same camp loyal to that lieutenant Zeke was talking about.

The cops stop talking to me after they read my list of charges and tell me I have the right to remain silent, which is fine. They give me a towel. That is courtesy enough.

Our boat does a U-turn and my watch vibrates in the pocket of one of the officers staring me down. I know because I get the notification on my AR. It's Gabby, again. It stops ringing, and she sends me a text. Unprompted, Caroline sends it to my eye. It reads:

"I hope they treat you well. Call me when you can. I wish you had come with us, though. I'm charging your friend with aiding and abetting."

We dock at Point Pleasant and another cop greets me onshore, but this one isn't wearing full body armor. He's dressed in the familiar black uniform I've seen around campus. He stands taller than me but not taller than Zeke.

"Hello, Mr. Pickering. I'm Lieutenant Ryan Morehead." He shakes one of my handcuffed hands. "You've given us quite the runaround," he says.

"I's tryin'," I answer.

A tall silver-haired man in an impeccable blue pinstriped suit rushes over toward us. He's met with a barricade of officers. He shouts over them.

"Levi, you were told you had the right to remain silent. Do so! You don't have to talk to anybody! From here on out, only ask to talk to your *lawyer*."

"That's good advice," says the Lieutenant.

"One question, though, before I shut up. Where're you taking me?" I ask. He furrows his brow before raising one of his eyebrows as if he's offended by the question.

"You're going to jail, Levi."

<twenty-three>

Boredom is the worst part of prison. I wake up. I eat in the cafeteria. I work. I read. And all throughout, I think about all the times I fucked up along the way. Which is also starting to get boring.

They give us jobs, and I got one, too. Most prisoners do data entry. But they won't let me anywhere near a computer. I'm the world's greatest hacker, apparently. I told everyone: the guards, other prisoners and before that, I told the judge that it was my AI that did all the work. It doesn't matter to them. No computers.

So, they got me working on the plumbing. It's a bit of a demotion for a hydraulic engineer, but it keeps me marginally less bored than I would be if I didn't have to do it. It's fine unless it's a particularly nasty situation. There are a lot of nasty situations.

Dunbar's lawyers got rid of the terrorism charge that would have been my death sentence. If I had got hit with that, it would have lead to thirty-two counts of murder. Nearly everything else stuck, though. All in all I got sentenced to thirty-seven years. The lawyers assure me they've done a good job. That was five months ago.

The long sentence came from the four counts of "assaulting a police officer". Evidently, blinding those officers' visors back on *The River's Bounty* constituted assault.

Honestly, it could have been five counts of "assaulting" a police officer, but Zeke didn't press charges. He also testified against three of the eight accounts of grand theft auto that I was hit with. They actually thought I was the one that stopped the escort boats and tried to make a last-minute break for Ohio. If Zeke weren't there to witness Gabby's hack, those charges would have stuck. The lawyers say that Zeke ended up saving me twelve years' time in total.

Zeke was detained in Ohio after the boat Gabby hacked took him to Gallipolis. He was only there for about a week before Dunbar's lawyers got him out. He got his hand fixed, too. I think he's Dunbar's personal bodyguard now.

Dunbar and Kayla got off entirely after the terrorism charges against me got dropped. Kayla was able to share every line of code that got updated from the June 1 update along with the command logs to the prosecution. Also, Huo Tech confessed to the error. What they claimed was exactly what Devin guessed: a bad directive by an overly ambitious, but incredibly stupid programmer sent the Financial Management System's AI into chaos. The Energy Alliance fired Huo Tech. I don't know what happened to the programmer. He might be living life like mine.

All in all, every crime I got convicted of, I

committed while on the run. I don't regret anything, which I think is part of their problem. The way I still see it is that I was damned if ran and probably dead if I didn't. If I could have run without aiding a highly organized network of medical supply thieves or illegally manipulating networks, vehicles, and cops, I would have. But, I couldn't. I don't think.

No matter how much I tell myself that this situation is something I just need to accept, I can't. Not yet. I'm not ready. I'm still pissed. They assigned me a counselor to talk to, but my dad's been more helpful.

He comes to visit at least once a week. He got stationed here in Houston working for Mr. Dunbar directly. He says he can't talk much about his work. Not yet. But he says it's a better job than the one he had before. He's visiting today.

The visitation room has no windows. There's nothing on the walls and for furniture it's one round table, two chairs, and one guard that might as well be furniture to stand by the door and listen to our conversation. I sit down. Every time my dad comes, he has to spend the first five minutes of our one-hour visitation time in a different room getting patted down for any electronic devices. People are understandably terrified that I'll get access to Caroline, again. They think if I did, then I'd be able to just walk out of here. They might not be wrong about that.

Thankfully, I do still have one device: my prosthetic eye. Just having it scares some of the dumber guards and some of the other prisoners see it as a threat. They think I'm still somehow talking to Caroline, but I can't get online with it. I tried. A lot. A lot of different ways, too.

I tried writing commands to Caroline on paper and holding the paper up to my eye. I tried laying out a deck of cards on a table like I was about to play Texas Hold 'Em. I tried hand signals. Nothing worked. I figure the eye needs to be paired with another device like my old watch to get connected to the clone server where Caroline lives. In here, the only thing the eye is good for is seeing, and it does that pretty great.

It's a good thing the eye doesn't connect to the Internet. If it did, then they probably would have cut it out of me before sticking me in here. Evidently, the warden wanted to do so anyway. He didn't care for the technical explanation that it would only function as a normal eye, but Dunbar's lawyers said that cutting it out of my head would be a human rights violation. That's one fight we won, obviously.

The guard opens the door behind me. Dad's here and he isn't alone. An even bigger guard replaces the one that normally stands by the door. It's Zeke.

"Hey, Dad. Zeke! How you been?" I ask.

"Doin' real good, Levi. How you doin'?" Zeke asks.

"Tryin' real hard not to be bitter," I answer. He smirks. My dad walks over to the table and sits in the chair across from me.

"Not that I'm not happy to see him, but why are you with Zeke? How is he allowed in here?" I ask my Dad.

"Mr. Dunbar sent him. There are some changes happening at the Energy Alliance. And Mr. Evans has been granted special privileges concerning a new initiative."

“Look at you getting all promoted,” I say to Zeke.

“You look better this week,” my dad says to me.

“Maybe the therapy is starting to help,” I say.

“Really?” he asks.

“No, but I do think that numbness and boredom are finally overtaking anger.”

“I might have something interesting for you,” my dad says.

“Are you finally going to tell me what you’ve been working on?” I ask. He nods and interlaces his fingers, resting his hands on the table.

“Simply put, I’ve been acting as oversight to different departments throughout the company, and then reporting back what I see to Mr. Dunbar.”

“Like quality control?” I ask.

“That’s part of it. Assessing culture is another. It’s a big company, Levi, and there are fiefdoms everywhere,” he says. “Loyalty, personal relationships, and outright nepotism are keeping more people employed than the need for their jobs. Layoffs are coming. It’s going to get ugly.”

This isn’t new information. Unemployment in the American Republic easily sits at twenty percent. The new government doesn’t report it anymore, but estimates come in from US and SDRA media outlets as part of regular anti-new-establishment propaganda campaigns.

“I assume the profile values I exposed the day I got arrested were designed to assess who gets laid off,” I say.

“That’s correct. Finance, HR, and Huo Tech coordinated to engineer the algorithm that applied those values.”

“And it killed thirty-two people in Burning

Springs and a lot more the day I got arrested." I squirm in my chair.

"Yes. Those initiatives aren't over. Changes in every department including Security are coming. And that has to be dealt with even more delicately. Laying off people in finance or on energy campuses is much easier than laying off those with access to the corporate armory."

"Wow, do you really think it will turn violent?" I ask.

"It's too early to say."

"Why so many layoffs? I thought the company rebounded after Burning Springs."

"It did. The Energy Alliance is the largest energy producer in the American Republic and Mexico. But even with success, it doesn't make sense to hire so many people if there's no work for them to do."

"You mean their work is being automated."

"That's one reason. Efficiency is another. The company makes money and invests it to correct inefficiencies so it can yield higher profits in the next quarter. Moving forward, however, it will need to do it more slowly, and hopefully with more elegance than what it tried to do four months ago."

"With more 'elegance'? Really? You mean without mass murder," I lean back in my chair and shake my head. I'm getting tired of this conversation. Lately, I've been grateful to talk about anything that doesn't have to do with jail cells or answering "how are they treating me in here", but this is just gross. I don't think I need or want to know any of this. "Why are you telling all this?" I ask my dad.

"I'm giving you a forecast as to where this company is heading to help you make a decision.

And you've been asking about my new job. I thought you were interested." He wouldn't be him if he didn't sneak in something to make me feel guilty for being curt. He's right though. I have been asking.

"Sorry. What decision are you talking about?" I ask.

He pulls a small metal case the size of a pack of cigarettes out of his pocket, and places it on the desk. He presses his thumb to a pad on the top of the case. It makes clicking sound before the lid swings open. Inside is a pair of microchips in a separate plastic case. One is slightly larger than the other.

"Mr. Dunbar is offering you these." My father exhales loudly and slumps his shoulders. "These chips are the second half of the ocular prosthesis you're using."

"The second half?" I ask.

"Yes. The ocular prosthesis you're using now was stolen from an Energy Alliance facility at the University of Texas by Dr. Tsi-Ang while these were still in development."

"That nut job surgeon back in Marietta?"

"Mm." He nods. "He was a medical consultant on the project." He taps on the case in front of him.

"What do the chips do?"

"From the user's perspective, this one," he points to the larger of the two, "functions much like your watch did with the companion app installed. But this system specifically engineered to gather input from the ocular prosthesis as well as compute far more biological data."

"How's it do that?"

"It's implanted onto the user's prefrontal cortex.

This second, smaller device is implanted on the cerebellum to be used for biological IO."

"Dunbar wants to have these microchips implanted onto my brain?"

"Yes."

"That little one is the same one I got. It helps me control my arm," Zeke says from his post at the door.

"You're the last person I'd think would agree to do something like this," I say.

"I wasn't in the best spot at the time when it was offered," he says. "Right now, you're not in a much better one yourself." I ignore him.

"Why the brain implants? Why not just give me back my watch?" I ask.

"It's an experiment and you'd be the test subject. The larger implant interprets your intentions. Those interpretations become commands to the computer and your retinal prosthesis becomes the display. If you were to connect with your AI, your communication would be instant. No more voice commands, ideally."

"Are you saying that Dunbar will let me reconnect with Caroline?"

"Right now, *Mr.* Dunbar is just gauging your interest. But yes, that's the implication. He's gaining influence in EAS and that influence may eventually allow him to grant you some freedoms. He wants to see what you *and Caroline* could do for The Energy Alliance."

"So aside from being his test monkey, he wants me to work for him. And he thought that sending my father and a friend would help convince me to say 'yes' to putting some experimental chips in my head."

"That's a fair assessment," my father answers.

"That's pretty low. And you went with it?" I ask.

"I'm not here to convince you of anything. I'm here to explain to you the offer as plainly and as neutrally as possible. Levi, it's the only way I know to protect you from this situation. There is no coercion or ultimatums here. It's truly up to you."

"But you're not convincing me not to take the opportunity, either."

"I'm not. We, as in all of us, are going to be at a turning point very soon. And as of right now, you are in a unique position to be at the forefront of this change. You know what it's like to have that connection with an AI. I'm sure you thought about the implications of that."

"Aren't people afraid of giving me that access again? I'm not even allowed to check email in here."

"Terrified. But you are in a unique position *right now*. In time, others will gain access to technology like this. It will be stolen, copied, or developed in parallel. Or it could already be out there in secret. *We don't know*. But if you don't do it for the Energy Alliance, someone else will." My father's voice grew softer but didn't shake. "This decision is yours, but you will have to face this future regardless. You can stay in this jail cell until another opportunity to earn your freedom arises, or you can choose to see where this path goes."

"Jesus, Dad."

"All I can do for you is tell you what *is*. I can't tell you what is right or wrong for you."

"I've heard that before." I lean back in my chair. "Staying in prison is pretty boring." That made him smile.

"What was it like?" he asks. He's asking about what it was like to be so closely connected with Caroline. I laugh. He's never asked that before.

"It was incredible," I say. "I felt like a superhero."

"It's the only way you could beat me in a fight, but you ain't doin' that again," Zeke says. I put my hand up to give Zeke the point.

"He's right. You wouldn't be given the same kind of access. Every possible precaution would be taken before you'd get the implant. Your friend, Kayla, is seeing to that," my father says. I perk up at her name.

"I imagine somebody thought they already had taken every possible precaution before Burning Springs happened," I say.

"No one is prepared for what's about to happen," my dad says. "Mr. Dunbar wants whatever this unpredictable element is to be close. And when I think about it, so do I. Again, I'm not saying do it, but–"

"I'll do it." I look to the ceiling. "I think."

#

ACKNOWLEDGMENTS

This novel could not have been completed without the support and mentorship from my friends and beta readers. Thank you, David Lemasters, for inspiring this setting with your experience in the oil and gas industry. Brian Pickens gave visual eponymous life to that setting with his brilliant cover art. Hillary Swauger helped me injure and heal Levi in ways that were mostly plausible and definitely gross. And Dr. Philip Lemaster kept up both mine and my characters' motivations. I am forever grateful to all beta readers who let this first-time author know I might have written something others could enjoy. And of course, thank you to my parents for your support in every maddening thing I've ever tried to do.

And the biggest thank you goes to my wife, who actually supported me when I told her I wanted to write a book less than a year after our daughter was born.

ABOUT THE AUTHOR

Jeremy Bock is a West Virginia native and web developer currently expatting Bangkok with his wife and daughter. His first novel, Caroline, is independently published and also serialized at caroline-novel.com.

Future works, will be announced on jbockwrites.com, on Twitter @jbockcet and on Facebook.

Made in the USA
Monee, IL
21 January 2023

25704183R00184